PRAISE FOR

# a Million Miles away

"*A Million Miles Away* completely wrecked me.
Romantic and heartbreaking. **A MUST-READ** for
anybody with a sister—and anybody without one, too."
—Katie Cotugno, author of *How to Love* and *99 Days*

"Love, loss, sisterhood, deceit—the stakes are high in this
**CAPTIVATING ROMANCE.** Kelsey's story is beautifully
told, equal parts gut-wrenching and heartwarming."
—April Lindner, author of *Jane* and *Love, Lucy*

"This is definitely several steps above the standard romance;
Avery is **A VOICE TO WATCH** in this genre."
—*Booklist*

"Those who are looking for something similar to
**NICHOLAS SPARKS** will appreciate this light romance."
—*SLJ*

# a million miles away

## LARA AVERY

**POPPY**

LITTLE, BROWN AND COMPANY

NEW YORK   BOSTON

Copyright © 2015 by Alloy Entertainment
Excerpt from *The Memory Book* copyright © 2016 by Alloy Entertainment

Lines from "And The Wind Sings Boo" from *The Wish Book* by Alex Lemon (Minneapolis: Milkweed Editions, 2014). Copyright © 2014 by Alex Lemon. Reprinted with permission from Milkweed Editions. milkweed.org

Poppy

Hachette Book Group
1290 Avenue of the Americas, New York, NY 10104
Visit us at lb-teens.com

Poppy is an imprint of Little, Brown and Company.
The Poppy name and logo are trademarks of Hachette Book Group, Inc.

The publisher is not responsible for websites (or their content) that are not owned by the publisher.

First Paperback Edition: May 2016
First published in hardcover in July 2015 by Little, Brown and Company

**alloyentertainment**

Produced by Alloy Entertainment
1325 Avenue of the Americas
New York, NY 10019
alloyentertainment.com

Book design by Liz Dresner

Library of Congress Cataloging-in-Publication Data

Avery, Lara.
  A million miles away / Lara Avery. — First edition.
      pages cm
  "Poppy."
  Summary: Shortly after her boyfriend, Peter, is deployed to Afghanistan, high school senior Michelle dies in a car crash and when her bereft twin, Kelsey, connects with Peter she is unable to tell him the truth as, through their separate woes, they support each other and begin to fall in love.
  ISBN 978-0-316-28368-7 (hc) — ISBN 978-0-316-28372-4 (pb) — ISBN 978-0-316-28369-4 (ebook)
  [1. Death—Fiction. 2. Twins—Fiction. 3. Sisters—Fiction. 4. Love—Fiction. 5. Soldiers—Fiction. 6. Afghan War, 2001—Fiction.] I. Title.
  PZ7.A9515Mil 2015
  [Fic]—dc23
                                    2014032552

10 9 8 7 6 5 4 3 2

LSC-C

Printed in the United States of America

*To my brother, Dylan*

You know you're in
The choicest of spots,
When, staring out the window,
You feel a gaping void wheeze
Inside you. Bang, bang, bang,
Flounders a bluebird against
The plate glass. Slap, slap,
Thump, drops the sad truth
Through your bones. So there
It all is.

—Alex Lemon, from "And the Wind Sings Boo,"
*The Wish Book* (Milkweed Editions, 2014)

# CHAPTER ONE

"Cops?"

"Where are my shoes?"

"Turn the Beyoncé back up."

Just a few blocks from Massachusetts Street, under the branches of century-old oaks, across a yard full of dozing sunflowers, silence fell over a peach-colored house with a wide porch. This was the Maxfield house. It had been the Maxfield house ever since Rob and Melody Maxfield returned from their honeymoon thirty-odd years ago, and filled the rooms with two daughters.

It was Friday night, and their Subaru was absent from the redbrick driveway. Inside, a hush had fallen over the room, punctuated by the static of girls laughing behind the shoulders of their friends, while plastic cups of Bud Light were emptied and tossed aside.

Kelsey Maxfield moved through the crowd, holding the

sweaty hand of a younger girl not so different from herself when she was that age—no hips, no boobs, body-glittered and hair-sprayed. Kelsey had been the one to turn down the music, and with a reassuring glance back at the nervous girl, who was still wearing her Lycra dance team uniform, she cleared a space around a silver beer keg resting in a bucket of ice.

"Y'all," Kelsey yelled. She gave them a Crest-commercial smile.

Kelsey's husky voice carried through the house. Her dark eyes changed color in the light from the kitchen. Her hair— not quite blonde, not quite brown—was pulled into a high, tight bun, left over from their halftime performance at the final football game of the season. The younger girl beside her adopted Kelsey's hand-on-hip pose, following her captain's lead.

"Hannah T. here has a proposition."

A few catcalls from the male voices.

"Shut up," Kelsey said, flipping the bird with a blood-orange nail. "As I was saying, Hannah thinks she can break my keg-stand record. Twenty-four seconds. You know it's twenty-four, right, Hannah T.?"

Hannah whooped, and a chant began, building volume.

"Hannah, Hannah, Hannah . . ."

Hannah gripped either side of the keg, while Gillian and Ingrid took her legs.

"You ready, Hannah?"

"Ready," Hannah's small voice called.

"Go!"

Kelsey could picture the beer, flowing steady from the keg into the spout, into Hannah's mouth, into her stomach, probably full of lasagna and Gatorade from the pregame dinner.

"Three . . . four . . . five . . ." the onlookers chanted.

Funny, Kelsey had always been the one to do the first keg stand. She felt kind of nostalgic. They used to count for her.

But she was a senior now. She was cocaptain of the dance team. She had to be responsible, or, you know, as responsible as possible. She had put the jade Buddha statues from the living room under her bed, pulled down the wooden Venetian blinds, and then called her mom and dad to make sure they wouldn't be coming home early after another pointless argument with their friends over sauvignon pairings. (All had seemed well, or well enough, on the only vineyard in Central Kansas. They wouldn't be home until tomorrow afternoon.)

Kelsey had also promised her sister she would lock her bedroom door. Michelle didn't want anyone spilling beer on her paintings. *But wouldn't that give them more character?* Kelsey always joked. Michelle didn't find it funny.

"Ten . . . eleven . . . twelve . . ."

Oh, shit. She'd forgotten to lock Michelle's door.

"Thirteen . . . fourteen . . . fifteen . . ."

Hannah was really getting up there. Close to Kelsey's record. Too close. Kelsey looked at Hannah's concentrated, upside-down face. "You had enough, Hannah T.?"

Hannah responded by continuing to swallow beer.

Kelsey knew how to deal with Michelle. She imagined her sister's fist forming when she saw her sticky stereo equipment. They were a couple of punchers, the two of them. What did their parents expect, making twins share a room most of their lives? No head shots, no kidney shots, but the rest was fair game. The fights usually ended in split lips. *It's how they show affection*, their parents had told suspicious teachers when they were younger. It's healthy.

"Eighteen . . . nineteen . . . twenty . . ." Shoulder to shoulder, red-faced partygoers crowded the keg, getting louder.

Kelsey forced herself to chant with them. She started to plan her concession speech. And so the time has come. I must pass the keg-stand mantle. . . .

But right at twenty-three seconds, the younger girl lifted a finger, the universal Lawrence High keg-stand symbol for defeat. Guiding Hannah's skinny legs back down to the floor, Kelsey allowed herself a celebratory swig and a couple of fist pumps.

"Don't worry, Hannah," Kelsey's cocaptain, Gillian, said. "Kel's keg-stand record is higher than her ACT score."

"Shut up," Kelsey said. "Nice job, Hannah T."

Hannah made an elaborate, tipsy bow, and accepted a glass of water Gillian had gotten her from the sink.

Ingrid draped a long arm around Kelsey's neck and spoke in the terrible British accent she always adopted when she had been drinking. "My deah, I see an extremely attractive college fellow in the corner. I believe he belongs to you."

Kelsey searched the dim room. Davis's parted sweep of dark hair was towering above a couple of baseball players and the yearbook editor.

She could hear snatches of his baritone. "And I was, like, gimme the hammer. You've obviously never held a hammer in your life. . . ."

Kelsey maneuvered toward him. Michelle's security emergency could wait.

Everyone was down here, anyway; even Michelle's friends, who were standing in the corner, looking like anthropologists studying a youth species from under their asymmetrical haircuts.

But no Michelle, nor her boyfriend. Not boyfriend. More like object-of-temporary-and-obsessive-lust. Kelsey had even offered to pick Michelle and what's-his-abs up after the game, but she never answered. Because of him, Michelle didn't even respond to the Facebook invite for a party at her own house.

Davis caught Kelsey's eye, flashed a smile. "And then I walked out of there with a free shelf. Hello."

He bent to Kelsey, all other conversations now over.

"Hello, handsome," she replied. She took his face in her hands and kissed him. His skin smelled like he'd been partying. "When did you get here?"

Davis lifted her up and pulled her into a piggyback. "Just now. All the frat row parties were, like, if you don't have a girl, you can't come in. So."

"Lucky for me!"

"Lucky for you." Davis advanced, causing her to accidentally kick a cheerleader or two.

"Where are you taking me?"

"To Beer Land!" Davis called.

Hannah T. stood swaying near the keg, sipping water. She looked at Kelsey on Davis's back, to her arms around his solid chest, and back to Kelsey. "Who is that?"

Kelsey laughed and took on a late-night radio DJ voice. "My lover."

Hannah T. shrugged, half of her mouth lifting in a lazy, incredulous smile. "Why do you have, like, the best life in the world?"

"She bought it on sale at Sears," Davis said.

"Please don't tell people I shop at Sears." Kelsey slid down to the floor, winked at Hannah, and gave Davis her Solo cup. "Refill me, please? I have to go do damage control."

The sisters' rooms were a recent addition to the Maxfield house, after Michelle had given Kelsey a bruised rib, fighting over the remote when they were fourteen. As soon as their parents were sure Melody was tenured and Rob's second restaurant was going to survive, they had knocked off the back upstairs wall and built the girls adjacent dwellings, complete with locks on the doors and a back porch. Kelsey used her side of the deck to tan; Michelle, for drying the hyperreal paintings she did of their neighborhood, perfect replicas except for the colors: Everything was neon or reversed or slightly out of focus. Kelsey didn't get it, and she liked it that way.

Once at Michelle's room, she would have to lock her sister's door from the inside, exit through her balcony door, and climb through a barrier of small trees that acted as a "fence" between the two sides.

But when she got to Michelle's door, it was already locked.

"Yo!" Kelsey called, banging on the still-unfinished wood.

No answer. Movement. Laughter. It sounded as though someone was using Michelle's room as a temporary brothel.

Kelsey banged on the door again. "Hello! It's Kelsey."

More laughter. Still, the door remained shut.

"Hey!" Kelsey called. She jiggled the handle.

Lost cause. This would have to be a rescue mission. She stepped through her own dark room, over piles of discarded leggings and sports bras, and opened the screen door to her side of the deck.

Light poured onto the wood on Michelle's side of the

porch. Slipping between the trees, Kelsey looked through the glass to see her sister stretched out on the bed. A sandy-haired dude in jeans sat in her desk chair, bent over a book. He was reading aloud.

Kelsey yanked open the screen. "Oh," she said loudly. "Interesting."

Michelle turned her head, brushing the same lumber-colored hair out of her eyes. "Oh," she said, echoing Kelsey. "Hey."

Michelle's new boyfriend closed the book and smiled at her. "Wow, you guys really are identical."

"Yeah," Kelsey said, still looking at Michelle. It was probably better she didn't see his face up close, as she was going to have to forget it anyway. "Come out in the hall for a sec, please."

"Okay." Michelle was doing that thing where she talked and moved slower than necessary just to piss Kelsey off.

When Michelle emerged, Kelsey closed her sister's bedroom door with a bang.

"Is he sleeping over?"

"Yeah, he has to. He's on his way to ship out from Fort Riley. Can you believe it?"

"I don't know! Why didn't you respond to my texts?"

"I was busy."

"You could have at least come down and said hi. Some of your townie friends are here—"

"Hi!" Michelle said, giving Kelsey a double wave. Her dark eyes lit up with fake enthusiasm. Something was different about her sister. She was wearing mascara. Kelsey's mascara. "Can I go now?"

"Don't be a bitch."

"I'm not. Thank you. I'm sorry. Whatever you want to hear. I haven't seen Peter for two months, and he's about to be halfway across the world."

"So? You'll just find another, like, film school student or something."

*Or a Brazilian on KU's soccer team*, Kelsey thought. *Or a theater major who looked exactly like a brunette version of Woody Allen, or a record-store employee who had to wear prescription yellow-tinted glasses.*

Kelsey was there for all of them. She knew how to listen politely to Michelle over the dinners their father cooked, as she went on about how each one was "love at first sight," and to watch her get in their cars after school, sit on their motorcycles, balance on their handlebars. Then, to watch for the silent signals that her sister had stopped caring— the drifting eyes, the legs crossed and recrossed. Last, she would stand on the deck with Michelle, composing the breakup texts for her, because Michelle was terrible at typing anything less than a novel. And then they would walk back to Massachusetts Street, where it would start all over again.

But none of that had happened with this one. Kelsey shot him a quick glance through the door, his toned, pale arms resting on his knees as he flipped the pages of an Andy Warhol coffee-table book.

Michelle sighed. "Peter is different. You haven't been paying attention at all, have you?"

Gillian came up the stairs and yanked at Kelsey's arm. "Time to get back. Who's that?" she said as she glanced through Michelle's cracked door.

"Don't know," Kelsey said, letting out a snort. "It's kind of hard to keep track."

Suddenly, Michelle's fist shot out. Right to the solar plexus. Kelsey seized up in pain as Michelle went back into her room. "A soldier, huh? Don't get syphilis," Kelsey choked out.

Kelsey straightened, rubbed her stomach, and made her way back to the party with Gillian.

"He's cute," Gillian said.

"Whatever."

Michelle hadn't even introduced them.

On the stairs, Kelsey stopped to survey the crowd congregating around the beer, the coupling off, hands in the air bouncing to the music. Ingrid was doing a handstand against the wall. Davis was surrounded by girls in UGGs. He found her gaze and beckoned.

Kelsey took another step down. "Hey!" she yelled. Heads

turned to behold her tanned arms lifted, her legs silhouetted in tight jeans. The world's eyes were on her. Well, her world's eyes, at least.

"Who wants to see me break my own record?"

# CHAPTER TWO

The party had emptied in the wee hours of the morning, leaving a silence that throbbed through the house, the rooms dotted with red cups. Kelsey woke up next to an openmouthed Davis snoring like the revving of a Vespa, with memories of her drinking beer out of a boot. Shifting his weight, Kelsey kicked past their clothes scattered on the floor. Something smelled like bacon.

She made her way to the doorway of the kitchen and rubbed her eyes, about to warn Michelle not to burn it like she always did.

"Bacon" was all she could get out.

"For you," a voice said. "Hope that's okay."

Kelsey lifted her head with a start.

Peter was standing at the stove, eating a bowl of Life cereal. The mysterious Peter. And without a shirt. He was very pale, wasn't he? But not in a bad way. Kelsey found she was running her fingers through her hair. She stopped, opening the fridge for the orange juice.

"Hang on," he said, his voice ringing with tenderness. "I thought you were in the shower."

Kelsey straightened. Oh, God. Not him, too. It still happened in the hallways, at Thanksgiving with relatives, at La Prima Tazza when Michelle's barista friends started making her hot chocolate, as if Kelsey would drink hot chocolate.

When she could feel him behind her, just inches away, she turned, a pasted smile on her face. "Kelsey," she said, putting a hand on her chest.

Peter narrowed his eyes, put a hand to his lips, and sat down at the table. With his mouth full, he looked up at her.

"You're not going to believe me, but I realized that a millisecond before you said your name."

"You're right, I don't believe you."

"Let's pretend it didn't happen, then. Oh, hi," he said, tilting his head. "I didn't see you there. I'm Peter."

"Yeah, well. Michelle used to have creepy mermaid hair down to here so it was easier to tell us apart. Then she stole my haircut."

She looked at him over the orange juice carton. She was finding it very difficult to keep her eyes off his bare torso, which was lined with muscle but not to the point of excess, as if it were carefully drawn and then erased. Like one of Michelle's sketches.

He moved back to the stovetop, glancing at her. "I like your shirt."

Kelsey looked down at her braless chest, inscribed with the words MY MOM WENT TO A SHIRT STORE AND ALL I GOT WAS THIS SHIRT. Michelle had found it at Wild Man Vintage. She crossed her arms. "Thanks."

He picked up a fork and poked at the bacon in the pan. "What do you think?"

She moved next to him, the smell of the grease simultaneously turning her stomach and making her aware of how very empty it was. "They're ready to be flipped."

As he moved, Kelsey noticed Peter's forearm was tattooed with the simple black outline of a dove. The symbol of peace. That was ironic.

"So you're on your way overseas."

"Right." He looked at her, revealing dark blue eyes. "First to Maine, then from there we get on an air force plane to Afghanistan. I am not excited." His eyes were sort of sad. "I'm scared as hell, to tell you the truth."

"Where in Afghanistan?"

"They're not telling us. I'm sure Michelle explained."

"Not really," Kelsey said. "You don't live here, right?"

Peter ripped off a paper towel. "Out west. Near the Colorado border. I had a little time after infantry training to see my family, and I figured . . . Where are the plates?"

"Cupboard above you."

"I figured I would swing by. You don't know any of this?"

"We've been busy." Kelsey decided not to go into Michelle's penchant for attracting lonely souls like pixie flypaper, or the raised eyebrows their parents gave her when she brought another one home. It kind of made sense now, why she didn't talk about Peter.

He told her their story as he laid pieces of bacon on paper towels with the same attention one might give to laying a baby in a crib. They'd met at the Granada at an Avett Brothers concert.

"The one with the banjos?" Kelsey asked.

Peter scoffed. "It's not just banjos."

"Whatever you say."

Peter had come into town to see them, and ended up crashing in Lawrence for a few days after. "I told Michelle I had stuff to do here, but I didn't really. She started catching on when I told her I needed to visit the Natural History Museum. Like I was that interested in dinosaurs. Yeah, right."

Kelsey was suddenly remembering the way Michelle had hung up her phone lately. Holding it in her hands and staring at it with a little smile on her face. Michelle never used to like talking on the phone. Not to Grandma, not to anyone. She must have been talking to him.

"How long have you guys been, you know—"

"Seeing each other? Three months. But not often enough. I work a lot. I was at basic. We talk when we can."

Peter stopped, shaking his head.

"Well," Kelsey said, "she seems crazy about you, so don't forget about her—"

"I couldn't. I love her."

She took a step back. Peter froze, plate in hand. It must have occurred to them at the same time: He meant it. She could tell by the way he was standing, breathing, his eyes steady ahead. Kelsey pictured Davis upstairs, asleep. It had taken him a year to say he loved Kelsey. But Peter meant it right now.

"I'm glad," she said.

He broke, smiling at the plate of bacon.

"I'm, uh—" Kelsey started. "I'm going to go see if the shower's free."

"Nice to meet you," he called to her back.

Kelsey waved, taking the stairs slow.

She could hear Michelle humming to herself through the bathroom door. "If I'm butter, if I'm butter," she sang. "If I'm butter, then he's a hot knife. . . ."

The water stopped. She could never hit the high notes. Kelsey slipped in.

"Mitch."

Michelle's voice came through the curtain. "Just because we took baths together does not mean you can invade my privacy."

"I just talked to Peter."

Michelle's face emerged, spilling steam and the smell of coconut shampoo.

"Now I have your attention." Kelsey handed her a faded beach towel from their trip to Puerto Rico.

"What did you talk about?"

Kelsey thought for a minute. "Nothing," she said. It was usually her job to roll her eyes, but that didn't fit now. "I like him."

"I more than like him. I—" Michelle stepped onto the tile, wrapping the towel around herself. "I don't know, Kels." She was lost, grinning. "He's smart. Smarter than me, even. He's going to use the GI Bill to go to a good school after he gets back. Maybe he'll come to Wesleyan, too."

"I bet he would," Kelsey said.

Michelle had applied early decision, and she'd get in, they were sure of it. Kelsey had always told her sister that she used too much brain space for homework and not enough for avoiding sidewalk musicians on Mass Street. Then again, Kelsey had focused her "academic efforts" on making friends with the weak-willed Geography teacher so she could scrape the 3.0 she needed to audition for the KU dance team.

Michelle raised her eyebrows as she applied moisturizer in the mirror. "Boy, you've changed your tune."

"I don't want to get punched in the stomach again."

"But really," Michelle said, eyes fixed on her sister in that intense way that Kelsey could never duplicate, "what do you think?"

"I think . . ." Kelsey sighed. "I think he's going to be good for you."

Michelle did a little victory dance in her towel.

"So," Kelsey said as Michelle opened the bathroom door. Kelsey looked around before she whispered, "How is he, you know?"

"What?"

Kelsey made a motion she had imitated many times on the dance floor, a motion one might see in a raunchy music video. It was one of Kelsey's favorite moves.

Michelle held up her chin, drifting past to her room. "How presumptive of you."

"Come on!"

"We're waiting."

"Waiting until what? He gets back?"

From below, Peter called, "You ready?"

Michelle gave Kelsey a look, expecting her to get even for the sucker punch. Kelsey had a good one, too, something about Michelle not sending him off to war properly. Then she thought of Peter standing in the kitchen, loving Michelle and meaning it. Kelsey threw up two peace signs. Michelle mouthed, *Thank you.* Last night was forgotten.

"Five minutes!" Michelle called, and disappeared behind her door.

"I'm going to miss my flight!"

Kelsey looked over the railing at Peter, who was now in his camo. "Wow, you're going now, huh? You're off to the airport?"

Peter rubbed his head nervously. "We'll have to take breakfast with us."

Briefly, Kelsey considered going down the stairs to give him a hug. He looked so alone down there. Scared.

She put as much cheer behind her voice as she could. "Good luck, Peter."

He flashed a grateful smile toward her, drifting toward the front door.

Inside her room, Kelsey lay back down beside Davis, bringing him to her, smelling like sleep. She hoped this Peter thing would work out for her sister.

*Michelle should be so lucky*, Kelsey thought. She really should.

# CHAPTER THREE

It was six. The house was spotless, perhaps suspiciously so. Davis had left; Kelsey's parents had come back. Quiet banging sounded as her father set out plates for dinner and her mother cleared space on her desk for stacks of student papers and giant volumes of constitutional law. Kelsey was trying to subtly move the Buddha statues an inch to the left. Then, after looking at them, she moved them back to the right.

"Turkey burgers!" her dad yelled. "Turkey burgers or nothing."

"No bun for me, please," her mother called back, bouncing on the large exercise ball she used for a desk chair.

Kelsey checked her phone.

**Me (12:03): How'd the drop-off go?**

Still no word from Michelle. It took thirty minutes tops to drive to Kansas City International, forty-five if she got stuck in traffic. But it was Saturday. And it had been seven hours since she left.

Me (2:16): ??

Me (2:30): Don't tell me he missed his flight . . .

She's probably being bummed out in a coffee shop somewhere, Kelsey had thought. Then two more hours had passed. Kelsey was checking the driveway every fifteen minutes or so for the 1992 Volvo they shared. The car could have broken down, but she would have called. Even if her phone had died, she would have found a way to call.

Me (3:52): Pls call when you can, mom and dad are on their way.

Michelle might have lost her phone, Kelsey figured, but that didn't explain why she hadn't come home.

Kelsey laid it out again, to try to soothe herself through a weird panic that had set in: If—no, when—Michelle came home without her phone, she would have to make a PowerPoint presentation, stating her case for a new phone. Whenever either girl wanted anything expensive, a computer or a phone or a three-day camping pass to Wakarusa Music Festival, the Maxfields made them prove their need in a cost-benefit PowerPoint on the monitor in their mom's office nook. Kelsey's sophomore year presentation on the desire for a Coach duffel, which had included animated fonts and a conclusion set to John Mayer's "Waiting on the World to Change" had really set the bar high, in her opinion.

**Me (4:17): For real Mitch. Where are you?**

Kelsey had cleaned up Hannah's (or somebody's) vomit from the basement sink, getting stink all over her cardigan and leggings. She and Davis had rolled the keg to the back of his Jeep, and returned it to Jensen's Liquor. And finally, she had put the jade Buddhas back in their prized place. Still no Michelle.

**Me (5:23): Not funny.**

Kelsey took a step back, surveying her handiwork. The Buddhas were a relic from her parents' trip to Cambodia, before they were married, back when trips to Cambodia were rare and cheap and disconnected from modern life, her mother had explained.

"Kelsey? Burger?" her dad shouted.

"I can hear you when you talk normally, Dad."

"Burger?" he repeated. "Burger? Burger?"

Kelsey rolled her eyes. "Yes! But without the chives and crap."

"And one for Mitch, or what?"

"Um . . ." Kelsey hesitated. Michelle should have been back hours ago. She was supposed to come straight home from the airport. She was going to help Kelsey clean. More importantly, she should have been there to tell her own goddamn story. Their parents didn't know about Peter. What was Kelsey supposed to do? Say that Michelle was probably painting lovesick portraits of a member of the US Army somewhere? Kelsey was starting to get nervous again. "I think she's at the library or something. Plus, she's still a vegetarian, Dad."

"When is she going to give that up?" Kelsey heard her father mutter. It had been a few months on and off. The family's interest in meat was a matter of personal pride to Kelsey's dad, whose restaurants were called Burger Stand and Local Burger.

Kelsey flipped back to the texts she had sent her sister.

**Me (6:05): Told em you were studying. You owe me one.**

"Ha-ha!" Kelsey's mom let out a laugh. Michelle always said their mother's laugh sounded like the mating call of a tropical bird. She was reading through one of her students' papers. "Listen to this one: 'In a unitary state, the constitution will vest ultimate authority in one central administration and legislature and judiciary, though there is often a delegation of power or authority to local or municipal authorities.'"

Kelsey glanced at her mother, her dark, graying hair shooting out from her head in thick waves. "Funny, Mom," Kelsey said. "So hilarious to all of us."

"Good one, M," her dad called from the kitchen. "We don't know why that's funny, but as long as you're happy."

Her mom was no longer listening, now making wide strokes with a thick red pen on the essay.

"Order up!" Kelsey's dad yelled. "TB, 86 bun, side of Brussels."

"That's me," her mom said, standing, putting the pen behind her ear. When the girls were younger, and her dad was just starting out, they used to pretend every dinner was at the Burger Stand. Michelle would make menus with crayon, and Kelsey would walk around in her princess dress, taking everyone's order.

Her mom paused next to Kelsey at the mantelpiece, staring.

"Did you move the Buddha statues?"

"Huh?" Kelsey's heart beat a little harder. "Yeah. I was dusting."

"Right." Her mother gave her a pat on the back.

The three of them stood around the counter, chewing.

Her mom stabbed a Brussels sprout with her fork. "Michelle's out studying, you said?"

Kelsey coughed. Instead of answering, she took a sip of water.

"Rob, can you call her?"

Kelsey's dad wiped his hands on his jeans, fishing for the phone in his pocket. Her dad always looked unnatural with the phone up to his bearded face, with his bushy caveman eyebrows. Silence. The sound of muted rings as he listened for an answer.

"You've reached the voice-mail box of Michelle Maxfield."

He hung up. "Hmm."

"Hmm," her mother echoed. "What's she working on?"

Kelsey snapped, "How am I supposed to know?"

Her mother's eyes got wide. "I don't know, hon, I was just asking." Her parents looked at each other. They were beginning to suspect something.

There were two possible scenarios: Michelle would either walk in the door any minute, or she would come home much later, probably with a new dreadlocked friend who smelled like the Kansas River. No, wait. Kelsey held her breath, not looking at her parents.

There was a third option: Michelle wouldn't come home at all. She would call them from Canada or somewhere, where she and Peter had eloped to a cabin or a commune or something.

*Oh, God*, Kelsey thought. Michelle's recent hush-hush. Peter's pensive, smiling good-bye. What if they took the car and ran away together?

While her parents chatted back and forth, recounting their trip to the vineyard, laying out their schedules for the week, Kelsey's stomach started to turn.

No. She could totally shrug this off. She wasn't her sister's babysitter. Michelle would come back soon, right? But Kelsey couldn't shake the feeling that something was wrong. Something was really, really wrong. While her parents were distracted, she tried Michelle's phone again. Nothing.

**Me (6:37): ANSWER ME**

**Me (6:39): PLEASE**

"Kelsey," her mom interrupted. "No texting at the table."

"I'm trying to get ahold of Michelle," Kelsey said, and then she swallowed some spit. Her mouth was starting to get dry.

"I thought she was studying," her mom said, deadpan. She raised her eyebrows at Kelsey. She knew. She always knew.

Kelsey's father drummed the counter with his fingers, which was a bad sign. "Is this another boy thing? It's another boy thing, isn't it?"

"She distracts herself," her mother murmured, shaking her head. "She always has to distract herself."

"I don't know where she is," Kelsey said. Even though it was the truth, she still didn't feel any better. If this was as serious as it felt, maybe she should tell her parents the whole story. She'd been gone eight hours. It was serious, right?

Kelsey's mother took on a lawyer's tone. "What did she say this morning?"

But what if Michelle was just fooling around somewhere?

She would come home to an interrogation about Peter. Everything had been so good before she and Peter had left. Michelle would never trust Kelsey again.

"Well, she said—"

The chime of a doorbell. Kelsey stopped. Her parents turned their heads. No one used the doorbell except for UPS and Jehovah's Witnesses.

When her mother opened the screen, a policeman stood there, his hands crossed in front of him. Sounds from the outside filtered into the house; cars passing over the brick road, insects buzzing.

"Can I help you, Officer?"

"Is this the home of Michelle Maxfield?"

Her mother took a second to answer, the shape of her body so small in the door, next to the policeman. "Yes," she said.

Kelsey's dad reached for his daughter, found her hand.

"You may want to take a seat. There's been an accident."

# CHAPTER FOUR

The day of Michelle's funeral, cars lined the road in front of the Maxfield house. People moved in and out, standing on the front porch staring into space, watching oak leaves fall and collect on the yard. A pile of coats gathered in the front hall.

Inside, Kelsey moved through the crowd, holding the hand of her six-year-old cousin, Tabatha. Kelsey's classmates and friends, Michelle's friends, their relatives—all muted their conversations as she passed.

This funeral field of mutters and quiet music was the most activity her house had seen in a week. She and her mother and father had slept in shifts, three or four hours at a time, giving one another quiet hugs in the hallway if they were to pass, before returning to sleep.

Kelsey hadn't looked any of her friends in the eyes. She hadn't really spoken to anyone that day, either, except to

Tabatha, for some reason. But her parents had asked her to do this.

Tabbie was wearing shiny buckled shoes and a black velvet dress. She didn't quite understand what was going on, just that Michelle was gone, and that she should be sad. Kelsey caught glances of her practicing an exaggerated frown, her little cheeks turning red from the effort.

Kelsey stopped at the fireplace, one jade Buddha on each side of her head, her hair pulled up in its typical, tight bun. She had changed out of her dress into black jeans and a gray sweater.

"Everyone," Kelsey said, still holding her cousin's hand. "I'm supposed to tell you that there are food and drinks ready in the kitchen." Their eyes stayed on her, waiting. "Thanks," she added.

A few people, mostly students that hadn't even known Michelle that well, trickled toward the food.

Kelsey had never been to a funeral before. She had only ever seen them in movies. She thought everyone would be in tears. Instead, only a few people were crying—not counting a couple of babies, who didn't know why. She wasn't one of them. She thought there was going to be a coffin lowered into the ground, and that it would be raining and gray. Instead, they had all stood outside the funeral home on the bright, cold day with Michelle's burnt remains in a gilded tin, like a take-out box.

She thought she would have a moment with the body, bending over Michelle's waxy face looking up at the ceiling forever.

Instead, once they confirmed her identity with the coroner, her parents had decided not to look at her sister again. She had only had a few cuts. After the Volvo had veered off K-10 on her way home from the airport, the bleeding had mostly been internal, the doctors said.

Kelsey thought she would weep and moan and clench her fists, like her mother had done when she first heard the news, like she had been cut open.

But she couldn't do any of that. Even if she wanted to, Kelsey couldn't feel a thing.

She took a seat, putting Tabbie on her lap, wrapping her arms around the little girl's velvety body.

Kelsey heard someone, probably a teacher or an aunt, say, "What a beautiful photo they chose for the memorial."

It was her school photo from last year. Michelle had hated that picture. Her mermaid hair had covered the straps of her tank top, and everyone had made fun of her for looking naked. But there weren't a whole lot of photos to choose from; most of the ones their mom and dad had around the house were of Kelsey and Michelle together.

Facing each other, blowing bubbles in the backyard.

At Christmas, holding up their presents.

Wearing matching hideous dresses for their first middle

school dance, back when they were really into dressing alike.

And the one they took when they were fifteen, Michelle's hair dyed purple and Kelsey's bleached blonde: standing on the newly built porch in the summer, giving "rock on" signs with their hands, their tongues out.

Prints of these photos were scattered on a white tablecloth, with a book and a pen for people to write messages.

*Michelle*, one of the messages read in the loopy handwriting of the art teacher at Lawrence High, *Your spirit and enormous talent will never be replaced.*

*Michele*, said another one, her name misspelled in chicken scratch, *You were my favorite wandering soul.*

Kelsey recognized her grandma's cursive. *You're with the angels now.*

"Bunch of bullshit, right?" Davis sat next to her in pleated pants, filling the air with the smell of mint. Kelsey covered Tabbie's ears.

"I guess," she said.

"You don't have to be here if this is too much," Davis said. He scooted close, putting an arm around her.

"Yes, I do," she replied.

"You can do whatever you want." Whatever she wanted, he said. Like it was her birthday or something. He leaned in close to her to kiss her lips, but Kelsey turned away.

"Hey," a voice said above her. The word went down at the end, as words said to Kelsey did a lot lately. Gillian and Ingrid stood in front of them, mascara streaked under Gillian's almond-shaped eyes, Ingrid's blonde hair looking unwashed.

"I brought your homework," Gillian said. "It's just history and calc. Mr. Schulz said not to worry about Geography."

Ingrid sniffed, her jaw clenched. "Screw that. Screw school, Kels. You come back whenever you want to. We will be waiting for you." Her voice started to shake. "We won't do any new dances until you come back. We won't choreograph anything, because you are our captain, and we're not going to—"

"Ingrid," Kelsey said. "It's okay."

Gillian put her hand on Ingrid's back, and they smiled close-lipped smiles down to her. They told her to call them anytime.

"Well," Davis said jauntily. "What now? You want some inedible food?"

"No, thanks."

For the first time in Kelsey's dad's life, she imagined, he hadn't been up for cooking. Her mother didn't care much, either. One of the aunts had gotten tasteless crackers and cold lunch meat from Dillons.

Kelsey spotted two of Michelle's ex-boyfriends talking to each other, the film student and the Brazilian. She felt like vomiting, but she didn't have the energy for that.

"I have an idea," Davis said, brightening.

*A time machine* was Kelsey's first thought. *A potion. An eraser.* Nothing was making any sense.

"Kansas City." He gave her a knowing smile. "Let's get you away from all this. Let's go to St. Louis. Let's go to Colorado."

Kelsey didn't have the energy to get up from the couch, let alone take a road trip. She got a strange urge to ask Davis to smack her in the face. She wanted him to wake her up, to shake her, to tell her to crack so all of this would come pouring out of her, and then away.

A memory came to her, peaceful, of the morning before everything changed. In it, she saw Peter. Kelsey hadn't thought of Peter once, but she supposed she should have. Did Peter know about Michelle? She couldn't imagine that anyone would have told him the news in Afghanistan. His family probably hadn't even met Michelle yet.

But they loved each other. He should know, and Kelsey would tell him.

Kelsey hugged Tabbie tighter to her, bouncing her on her knee.

"Can I go now?" Tabbie asked, trying to unhook Kelsey's hands with her chubby little fingers.

"No," Kelsey found herself saying. "Please don't go."

But Tabbie squirmed, slipping through her arms, and the warmth of her was suddenly gone, leaving Kelsey alone.

# CHAPTER FIVE

A few weeks later, Kelsey still had not cried. Or talked. Or eaten very much. There was a part of her that had wanted to cry, but it seemed like every time she moved, someone put their hands on her internal organs and squeezed. Why did it hurt to be alive? The Maxfields' counselor had told Kelsey that in lieu of tears, her grief must be manifesting itself physically in other ways.

To throw it in her face, Kelsey imagined, her parents had gone and volunteered their house for a support group. Mourning parents and widows and widowers and lovers sat for hours on folding chairs in their living room, drinking their coffee, nodding at one another with bags under their eyes.

"Are you going to come to grief group tonight?" her mother would ask.

"Not tonight," she would reply. Or ever.

Kelsey could hear strings of their testimonies from

downstairs whenever she emerged from her room.

". . . like there's a hole next to me in the bed, dug into the mattress. And all I want to do is fall into that hole."

"I keep thinking I see him around town. I swear. I'm not supernatural or nothing like that."

". . . and I said, God, I know there's a reason."

Their frail voices made them sound as if they were the dead ones. And what was worse: her parents' voices among them, talking about Michelle as if she were the Patron Saint of Daughters. Like they had forgotten all the fun, stupid things about Michelle that made her herself, like that time she'd spent all of her birthday money on a new, elaborate "elfin maiden" costume for the Kansas Renaissance Fair. But that's not what support groups were about. Thanks to the slogan they all said before every meeting, Kelsey knew exactly what support groups were about.

"LEARNING TO LIVE AND LOVE AGAIN," they chanted before they sat down. Like a bunch of zombies.

Kelsey had to get out of there. But she wasn't going to go back to school. Not yet, at least. She found her shoes and the car keys.

As she snuck past the foyer, she noticed a postcard among the unopened mail.

*At the airport in Maine,* it said. *On the plane out tomorrow. Ate a lobster sandwich. Can't see the fall leaves through the darkness. Love, Peter.*

*  *  *

Kelsey drove the Subaru five miles under the speed limit. Because any amount of light hurt her sleepless eyes, she had taken to wearing sunglasses at all times. She yelled along with the lyrics on the radio, and when she didn't know them, she just yelled. Then she parked and held her breath, waiting for whatever it was she felt to go away.

The sign read KANSAS ARMY AND ARMY RESERVE RECRUITING STATION. It was a tiny storefront in a strip mall at the corner of Louisiana and 23rd, next to a Schlotzsky's Deli, and it was the only trace of military Kelsey could find in Lawrence.

Inside, one chair sat across from a neat, empty desk with a bell on it. An American flag stood in the corner. The walls were pasted with posters of burly men helping each other over walls, Army Strong emblazoned across their determined faces.

Kelsey reached her hand to the bell and rang it.

No one came. There was no noise from the other room.

She rang the bell again.

"What can I do for you, young lady?" A woman with a blonde bob and an official-looking sweater vest materialized behind the desk. Kelsey jumped.

"Hi," Kelsey said. It was strange to hear her own voice.

"Would you mind taking off your sunglasses, please?" Even as the woman sat, she still seemed tall.

Kelsey crossed her arms. "I'd rather not."

The woman's eyebrows knit together. "All right, then."

The woman stared at her, waiting. "My sister died," Kelsey said. Wow, there it was. It had just come out. Over the days since it had happened, Kelsey had never once said it aloud.

The woman pointed at the chair. "Have a seat, honey."

Kelsey found herself sitting immediately. She wanted to lay her head on the desk for a second. Just for a second. But she remained upright.

"Was she deployed?"

"Who?"

"Your sister."

"Oh, no. No."

The woman folded her hands. "I'm confused."

Kelsey hadn't really thought this through, and the lack of sleep was no help. With the woman's eyes on her, unmoving, Kelsey found she missed the feeling of being able to talk. Of knowing what to say. She forced herself to continue.

"Here's the deal. My sister had a boyfriend in the army, Peter, and he doesn't know that she . . . that she's gone. He's in Afghanistan somewhere, and I think someone should tell him."

The woman spoke slowly, emphasizing her words. "So you came to the Army Recruiting Office?"

Kelsey could see the woman searching for her eyes behind her sunglasses.

"How else am I supposed to reach him? I don't know his parents or any of his friends. And I was thinking maybe you could look him up and send him a letter or something. His name is Peter."

A smile twitched on the woman's mouth. "You said that."

Kelsey sighed. "Can you look him up?"

The woman turned to her computer. "If he enlisted around here, I might have a record of his address, but I can't give that to you."

"What about—" Kelsey began.

"Nor can I give you his location in Afghanistan. But I might be able to talk to someone who can reach his parents. What's his last name?"

Kelsey's mouth, which had opened to tell her, closed. She didn't know Peter's last name. The person who knew his last name was now nothing more than disintegrating dust and molecules, sitting in a tin can.

All she could do was shake her head.

"You don't know it," the woman said. She wasn't being mean. It was just the truth.

"Nope," Kelsey said shortly.

The woman took her hands away from the keyboard, and they hovered for a second, not knowing what to do.

Kelsey pictured herself from the woman's view: a morose

teenage girl in Victoria's Secret sweatpants, refusing to take off her sunglasses, asking her to search the entire army database for a boy named Peter.

A laugh escaped the woman, but she wasn't mocking Kelsey. She could tell by the way her eyes wrinkled when she laughed. It was just funny, that's all.

"Pretty ridiculous, right?" Kelsey stood up. "The whole thing is just goddamn ridiculous."

The woman stood with her. "I'd help you if I could."

Kelsey turned. "I'm gonna go now."

"Just a minute," the woman said. Kelsey paused in the door. "Eat something, all right? You look like you need to eat something."

Kelsey nodded. Something was rising in her throat that she had to push down. She sped home with the radio turned all the way up, not really hearing the music. The brown tint of her sunglasses made everything look like an old-fashioned movie.

When she came in the front door, her father was standing in the middle of the circle of sad adults. They were all holding hands like a bunch of preschoolers. Tears were running down her dad's face, through his beard. Though the room was completely silent, no one had noticed she'd come in. Or that she'd left, for that matter.

Kelsey's eyeballs felt on fire.

She ran up the stairs as quickly as possible, but she

couldn't un-hear her father's voice. "This is part of a poem I've memorized. It helps me. If you'd like, you can repeat it after me. Okay. 'As there is muscle in darkness' . . ."

A chorus of voices. "As there is muscle in darkness."

Michelle's room stayed dark, even during the day.

"'There is cowardice to holding on.'"

"There is cowardice to holding on."

He continued, "'A cottonwood flare' . . ."

They echoed, these strangers. "'A cottonwood flare' . . ."

Kelsey kicked open the door to her room. She could still hear their voices. There were cottonwoods lining her street, lining the highway where her sister veered off the road, lining every street in Kansas.

"'A hand to straighten her collar' . . ."

She slid open the screen to her porch. Her and Michelle's porch. She kicked over the potted trees that were meant to be a barrier, cursing them.

"'A bravery in good-bye' . . ."

She collapsed on Michelle's side, putting her cheek to the wooden slats still splattered with the outlines of paintings, her palms pressing where the two of them stood not long ago.

By this time, Kelsey was crying. Her sobs shook every muscle in her body. Every new breath could not come fast enough, and with each exhale, she said her sister's name.

Not out loud, but speaking it with every ounce of her

being. She was putting it into the air, and realizing, then, that each time she said the name was another time Michelle would never hear it. Each time Kelsey said it, a little more of Michelle was gone, and she would never come back.

# CHAPTER SIX

It was basketball season. Kelsey had to make changes in the Lions Dance Team halftime routines in order to accommodate the wooden court. Their newest dance was to a mash-up of a popular indie song and its hip-hop counterpart: a lot of shifts in speed and general tone. Sexy but innovative. Tight formations with subtle movements, all in sync. With ten minutes left in practice, they still hadn't gotten the timing of the final cancan line. Kelsey and Gillian paced in front of their team, chests heaving, their red practice shorts soaked in sweat. Ingrid, who could never seem to get in shape, was practically purple in the face.

"I'm not mad at you guys," Kelsey announced. "Just totally focused. I promise you, if we do it again, it will be perfect for Friday."

"And it has to be perfect," Gillian added, tightening her sleek black ponytail.

"This could be the one we use for competition, ladies. Okay, Ruben?" Kelsey lifted a hand to the scraggly junior who was in charge of sound. "One more time. Cue it to 2:57."

Kelsey stopped in front of Hannah T. "Hannah, try your part a beat faster. Cool?"

"But won't that throw everyone off?"

"Try it."

Kelsey took her place in the center with a bowed head, hands extended. This portion of the routine required total concentration. She would begin by completing a backflip into a split, and move directly from there to the standing line.

The music started and Kelsey was lost in her body, exactly how she liked it.

It had been six weeks since she returned to school. People had finally stopped randomly touching her on the arm, looking for signs of watery eyes or suicidal tendencies.

The backflip was smooth, though it could have used a little more bounce.

It had taken her several weekends home drinking sugar-free Red Bull to catch up on her missed schoolwork, but Davis had helped her fill out useless biology worksheets and copy and paste Spanish essays into Google Translate.

The splits were seamless.

The University of Kansas Rock Chalk Dancers weren't holding tryouts until May, but Kelsey had memorized their requirements: quadruple pirouettes, fouetté turns, leaps (right, left, center), turning discs, kicks, fight song. She would learn the jazz combo online, which would be posted two weeks prior. She would also be taught a short hip-hop combo at tryouts.

Kelsey pulled her legs together into a stand, and when the wave of legs came her way, she kicked straight, high, head up with a smile, like she had always been taught.

Hannah T., toward the end of the line, hit her mark. A full bow by all of them at once, then the finish: arms up and crossed with one another at a perfect diagonal. They had nailed it.

The Lions Dance Team burst into triumphant shrieks and high fives. Friday was the first home game, versus Blue Valley North. They were so ready.

Kelsey gave her girls a thumbs-up, told them what time they should show up at the locker room, and went straight to the bleachers to find her stuff. She didn't like to linger. Lingering meant memories, and she didn't like those. She had to keep moving.

Gillian and Ingrid caught up with her.

"Whatcha doing now, Kels?" Ingrid asked, awkwardly poking her in the bare stomach.

"Oh, my God," Gillian said, staring at her phone. "Check out this guy who friended me on Facebook. He is so cute. Let's go stalk him."

Ingrid grabbed her duffel bag. "Let's go get frozen yogurt and stalk Gillian's boyfriend."

"He's not my boyfriend," Gillian replied.

"FroYo, Kels?"

"I can't," Kelsey said automatically.

"Why not?" Gillian said, furrowing her brow.

"I have to—" But Kelsey didn't really have anything to do. She had hurried through all her homework in free period, and probably wasn't going to study for her finals that much, anyway. "I have shit to do."

Ingrid grabbed Kelsey's wrist. "Can you let us be friends with you? For once? It's been a long time."

Gillian caught Ingrid's eye and shook her head, as if to say, *Let her be.* "Text us if you feel like it, okay?"

Kelsey softened, pushing out a genuine smile. "I definitely will." She zipped up her puffy jacket and waved good-bye to her teammates. Soon. *Just not now,* she thought.

When she arrived home, all the lights in the house were out, except for one lamp in her mother's office.

She kicked off her boots.

"Kelsey?" Her mother's voice had become so thin, like it would snap at any minute.

"Yep, it's me."

"Why are you home so late?"

"Dance practice went long."

"Come here."

She found her mom already in pajamas, her glasses on the tip of her nose, poring over final papers next to a glass of red wine.

"Have you eaten?"

"I'll find something."

Her mother tipped her head back, examining her over the top of her lenses. "You look so unnaturally tan for winter."

Kelsey said nothing. She had been using her allowance to go to the tanning salon since she was sixteen. It was part of who she was, who she liked to be. And all the Rock Chalk Dancers got tans. Or most of them, at least. Her mother knew that.

"If you could, I need you to rummage for a few things."

Rummage. Kelsey's stomach dropped. That was the family's code word for entering Michelle's room. They had "rummaged" for things like her overdue library books. They had "rummaged" for her prized prints and paintings, which Lawrence High wanted to put on display.

Her mother handed her a list: Grandma's necklace, email password, cancel Facebook.

"I would do it myself, but I don't know how to work the Facebook."

Kelsey's jaw clenched. She had done so well at avoiding it this week. She had kept moving. "All right."

Her mother sighed. "I love you, Kels."

"I know. I love you, too."

At the door of Michelle's room, Kelsey flicked on the light. The room had started to lack any sort of smell. It had smelled like coconut and oil paints and even dirty laundry for days and days after, but that was all fading. Cacti in pots at the foot of her bed had gone brown from lack of care. Dust collected on the frame of the print of a Campbell's soup can on the wall. Grandma's necklace was easy to find because Kelsey had borrowed it before: a gold chain with an emerald hanging from it, lying on Michelle's dresser, next to her wooden rings and nail polish.

The email password was more difficult. After booting up Michelle's laptop, Kelsey had searched everywhere for some small piece of paper on Michelle's desk, or maybe a file on her desktop with all of them listed, but no luck.

She tried all combinations of "password" and their birthday. Then "warhol" because that was the artist Michelle was obsessed with. Still nothing.

As for Facebook, Kelsey was glad to discover she didn't have to sign in to cancel the account. Apparently, you could just write an email to the company.

"Dear Mark Zuckerberg," she wrote. "Please delete my sister's Facebook page. People write stupid posts on her wall, pretending to be sad, but they are full of shit. Plus, she will never see them because she is dead. Thank you, Kelsey Maxfield." Then she attached a link to Michelle's obituary in the *Lawrence Journal-World*.

Kelsey had no trouble crying anymore. She cried in her room, mostly. She cried in the girls' bathroom sometimes, ducking in from the halls when she could feel it coming on. And she was crying now as she pressed SEND. She didn't stop herself. It was the one thing she could do that didn't ask her to think, to remember, to pretend that everything was going to be all right.

When she cried, Kelsey didn't have to do anything else.

Suddenly, there was a strange sound. A sort of musical beep, over and over, coming from the computer. A green phone icon appeared. "Peter," the name read.

Peter? Peter. The mysterious Peter. Before she knew what she was doing, Kelsey wiped her nose and pressed ANSWER.

A fuzzy image, cutting in and out, filled the screen. Then it became Peter's face. He was sunburnt, smiling, laughing, leaning back in his chair with what appeared to be relief, then coming forward, touching the screen where he must see her. Kelsey hadn't seen someone so sincerely happy in a long time. He was mouthing words, but no sounds matched them.

"What?" Kelsey said. "I can't hear you!"

The words finally came, as if they were traveling through water to reach her. "I've been trying to get you for two da—!"

There was a green tent behind him, with sunlight filtering through. He was calling from Afghanistan. He was calling for Michelle.

Peter mouthed more words. They came to her as "Can't say where I am, but we've ju— got set— after going through all these little towns. Is the connec—?"

"The connection's pretty bad," Kelsey said loud and clear. "Listen, Peter—"

Peter hadn't heard her yet, because he was still glowing, his movements in choppy poses. His audio broke through. "I missed you— Where have you bee— What have you bee— doing?"

She tried again. "This is Kelsey!"

But all he could do was put a hand to his ear and shake his cropped sandy head.

Kelsey noticed a dark line resting on the bench behind him. A gun. He wore ammo around his chest like a pageant queen wore a ribbon.

Her voice was caught in her throat. Even thousands of miles away, through a screen, Peter sensed something. His forehead clenched in concern. "Are you oka—?"

She shook her head and smiled in a mimed don't-worry gesture, but immediately stopped. Her heart raced. He really had no idea Michelle was dead. He thought Kelsey was Michelle. Here and now, Peter was looking at her dead sister.

The corner of his mouth lifted into a smile, his sad-shaped eyes following suit. "I don't know if you ca— hear me, but this is making my whole mon—. To see you." He looked around him, then back to her. "It's s— bad ou— here.

This—" He took his hands out, as if he were holding her image. "This is goin— to help me sleep toni—."

He put his fingertips to his lips, reached out toward his screen, and then stayed there, frozen.

"Peter?" Kelsey asked, moving the cursor over his face.

But that was the last image that remained before there was a popping sound, like a rock dropping in water. Peter disappeared, and the screen read CALL ENDED.

Kelsey clicked on the aqua-blue Skype icon, opening the contacts window. Peter was Michelle's only contact, and he was now offline.

Kelsey replayed the conversation in her head. Had he not seen the well-wishers on Michelle's wall? Kelsey vaguely recalled Michelle smugly telling her that her new boyfriend didn't have Facebook, didn't care for the waste of time. That must have been Peter.

"Oh my God," Kelsey said to Michelle's quiet room. *What the hell did I just do?*

# CHAPTER SEVEN

By the following Saturday, the Midwest had fallen into a mild winter. The University of Kansas campus was lit up, holiday lights hanging from every lamppost, casting golden circles on the limestone of massive lecture halls. Lawrence was one of the only places in Kansas that wasn't desperately flat. Some of the hills were so steep, cars weren't allowed to park on them. It was a walking city, anyway. It was a college town.

As the four of them plodded toward Allen Fieldhouse, Kelsey noticed Davis and his father had the exact same walk. Long legs with knees weakened by years of soccer, hands in pockets, head up, winking at the world. Dudes in Kansas basketball jerseys jogged past them, holding tall boys in paper bags. Girls in tight "Rock Chalk" hoodies and leggings staggered toward them down the perilously slanted sidewalk.

The stream of people was steady and exuberant, yelling across campus with fist pumps and high fives whether they knew one another or not, like churchgoers under some blind, divine light. It was infectious.

Davis turned to where Kelsey and his mother walked side by side, buttoning up the blazer he always wore when he was with his parents, and pointed to a giant brick fraternity house with white columns.

"There's the smart frat!" He walked backward, like a tour guide.

Kelsey wrapped her coat around her, against the chill, and smiled to herself. Davis was full of it.

"And what does that make Delta Sig?" Anna, Davis's mother, asked, turning up her manicured hands. "The handsome, intelligent, gentlemanly frat?"

Davis rolled his eyes. Fraternities, especially in his parents' eyes, were supposed to turn out lawyers and CEOs and politicians. Once he made pledge, his future was set. Davis's father, George, was one of the most generous alumni to the University of Kansas. Generous enough to have lifetime courtside tickets to KU basketball games, for example.

"Delta Sig is the anti-frat frat," Davis said, turning around. "They did, like, reverse-psychology hazing on us. They just treated us super nice for two weeks. At first it was cool, and then you realize that it is kind of traumatizing to eat cupcakes for breakfast every day."

George looked at Kelsey over his shoulder, and slapped his son on the back. "Such a hard life my boy has."

Kelsey tried to keep herself from giggling. Unbeknownst to his parents, the Delta Sigma house was just a "place to crash" until Davis could find his footing elsewhere. He went to some fraternity events, frequently enough not to get kicked out, but spent most nights in Kansas City, trying out jokes he wrote on notebook paper. Kelsey had always known how much he enjoyed making people laugh. He liked to quote comedians he saw on Comedy Central specials, or reenact ridiculous scenes from the animated shows. But now he was getting serious. He told Kelsey he wanted to go to every open mic in the area, following his true dream: to be a stand-up comedian. Michelle never liked that he was going to be a frat boy. She would have been proud.

Oh, there it was. The inescapable thought. Michelle. A little rip in the wound that she would have to restitch over and over.

"You excited for the game?" Anna put her arm around Kelsey in a quick squeeze as they walked, her bangles clinking together. Since the funeral, Anna had been sending her a card in the mail every week. Not a cheesy Hallmark, just a square piece of thick white card stock. Sometimes they simply said "Thinking of you." Sometimes there was a quote, like the last one. "Death ends a life, not a relationship." It was weird, but Kelsey kind of liked that her support came in small doses, unlike her parents, whose new group slogan was LET US HEAL.

Kelsey took a breath, letting the hole in her stomach fill with air. She glanced up at the two men, now debating the starting five. She kept her voice low. "Is it bad that I'm more excited for halftime?"

Anna threw her silver hair back and laughed. "Not in the slightest. That's going to be your future after all!"

Every time Kelsey went to Allen Fieldhouse, she worried that the pure energy of the people inside would bring the fifty-year-old building down to a pile of bricks. The walls and metal seats and wood of the court—everything literally vibrated. As she joined the sold-out crowd bathed in crimson and blue, Kelsey felt herself lifted. Whether she had wanted it or not, the tradition of this place had soaked into her skin.

By halftime, KU was beating Nebraska by twenty-two points. At any other court in the country, fans would probably be sitting down, smugly checking their phones, making plans for after the game. But not here. A win was a win was a win, whether it was down to the minute or an easy blowout. They would be there to the end, standing.

"And now, please welcome to the court . . . the Rock Chalk Dancers!"

Kelsey turned her head, her blood heating up as the volume increased, the student section whooping and catcalling. The dancers' steps were as matched as their deep blue sequined sports bras. Each girl, regardless of color or height, had loose, shoulder-length curls, intimidating abs, and bright red lipstick.

The routine mirrored the volume of the blaring bass behind it, a lot of bends, body rolls, and beckoning hands. It was also flawless. Like a machine.

Davis watched the dancers, his mouth slightly open. Even Anna couldn't take her eyes off them.

They were hot, sure. But they were even hotter because they loved what they were doing. Kelsey knew exactly how they felt.

The dance ended, the girls standing with their hands on their hips, legs spread apart in a power stance. Through the waves of cheering, Davis put his lips next to Kelsey's ear, his breath tickling her neck.

"I can't wait until my girlfriend does that."

Kelsey felt an electric jolt of pride, watching their perfect walk back to the locker room.

With two minutes left in the game, KU had put in their bench. The fresh-faced boys added layups and three-pointers to their thirty-point lead. The crowd chanted, "Freshmen! Freshmen! Freshmen!"

Then, in the final seconds, the crowd began their haunting, serene battle cry. Kelsey, Davis, Anna, and George filed out. The Rock Chalk Chant sounded more like a Gregorian choir than a fight song.

Michelle had told Kelsey it made everyone sound like they were in a cult.

"Yeah, but it's a fun cult!" Kelsey had said, and they had cracked up.

Kelsey pushed the memory away. The night had gotten colder. Davis huddled next to her as they walked back down the hill to the car.

Anna called up to Kelsey, using George for balance. "Have you gotten your application in yet, Kelsey?"

"Not yet," Kelsey said. "I still have to write my personal essay."

KU applications were due at the end of January. She was putting it off as long as possible. She wished there was Google Translate for personal essays. Like, *here are my experiences, please translate them into what I've learned.*

"I know your parents are busy, so if you'd like, I can take a look at it."

Kelsey's parents never looked at her essays for school. Her mom was too harsh, and her dad was too easy. That was Michelle's job. *Write how you would speak*, she had always said. And it usually worked, too.

Kelsey managed a grateful smile. "Thank you. I would like that."

"Do you know what you want to study?"

Kelsey was suddenly finding it difficult to breathe. Her heart had started beating hard without warning. Walking through campus, the very true part of next year was descending upon her. This place was her future, and she had always thought it would be so happy and easy and exactly like she imagined it. But it would not be. Not only because Michelle was gone—she would have been gone anyway, across the country—but also because Kelsey was different. She wasn't herself. No matter how much she tried, she wasn't sure she would ever be herself again. The next phase in her life seemed impossible. It was impossible.

She stopped, almost causing Davis's father to run into her from behind.

"You okay?" Davis asked.

She nodded, and kept walking forward. Sometimes she knew she was secretly pretending Michelle was just on vacation. Or busy. Or asleep.

Another deep breath, looking into Anna's kind eyes. "I'm not sure what I want to study. I'm not sure about anything, yet."

"Of course," Anna said quickly, touching her arm.

They continued in a moment of silence. Breaking the quiet, Davis clapped his hands. "Well, I'm tired of this talk. It might be time for Kelsey and me to retire."

"Retire, sure," Anna said. "I think you mispronounced 'victory party.'"

"Don't 'retire' too hard," George said, elbowing his son.

When they were down the block, Davis wrapped his

arms around her, kissing her on top of the head. "Parents suck," he whispered.

"Everything sucks," Kelsey replied.

"Don't say that," Davis said, and took her hand, leading her forward.

*Please just let me say that*, Kelsey thought. *Just let me say that*.

The jolt she had received from the game was gone, and now everything was lead again. Time didn't make any sense. She was supposed to be moving ahead, but half of her always circled back to that dark spot, two months ago. Kelsey didn't want any more time to pass.

She let go of Davis's hand and sat on the curb.

She wanted to go back to before. She wanted to go back.

# CHAPTER EIGHT

Kelsey returned home from Davis's room in the early morning, still dark, her thoughts slow and cold. She shed her wedges and coat inside the door and made her way sleepily upstairs, not bothering to mute her footfalls. If her parents weren't completely knocked out, they were some version of half-asleep, at least.

She went straight for the sink in the bathroom, splashing hot water on her face and hands, and with a dollop of remover, she cleared her face of foundation, her eyes of liner and mascara, her lips of gloss.

On her way to her bedroom, she paused in the hall, listening. A cheerful, beeping sound was emanating through a crack in Michelle's door. Kelsey peeked in.

Still open from her last visit, Michelle's laptop had rewoken, the blue light from its screen bathing her desk. Michelle. It was a wild thought, too fast and strange to be real, as if she were a kid again, believing in ghosts.

Without bothering to turn on the light, Kelsey slipped into Michelle's chair, found the green phone icon with the cursor, and clicked ANSWER.

Peter filled her screen clearly this time, no glitches. But he looked tired. Hollow.

"Michelle," he said, breathing in and out as though he was sinking into a hot bath. "Michelle."

"Hi," she replied, and a smile grew on his face.

Kelsey couldn't get the words out just yet. What would she say first? Michelle died. Or she could start with, I'm Kelsey, and go from there. She should ease into it.

"Why weren't you on last night? Did you not get my email?"

Kelsey opened her mouth. I wasn't on because . . . No. Michelle wasn't on because . . . No, that wouldn't work, either. Her thoughts were all mixed up.

"I'm sorry," she said.

"You can't do that to me. I was worried you'd started dating someone else or something." Peter looked around the green tent, and leaned toward his screen. "I hate it here," he said quietly.

Kelsey noticed the dark circles under his eyes. They didn't match the relaxed way he said his words. People from out West, where his hometown was, often spoke lower and with a little bit of a drawl. Funny that he kept that, even as he was panicking. She would just give him a minute. Just another minute or two to relax. "How bad is it?" she asked.

"It's hot. Of course, it's hot." He shook his head, smiling at her apologetically. "We carry our gear around everywhere, too. Fifty or so pounds of extra weight, all the time."

"You're not in immediate danger, though, right?"

Peter rubbed his hand over his hair, looking away. "You never can tell." When he looked back at her, his arms twitched, as if he wanted to hug her. "There have been a few scares, but it's quiet most of the time. More than most of the time."

Peter looked down, and when he looked back up, he was smiling as broad as he could, trying to hide the fear that had risen up in his eyes. Kelsey knew that game. She played that game every day.

"It's boring, really. So boring. I draw every day. I write you letters."

"You write me . . . you write letters?" Kelsey hadn't seen anything for Michelle in the mail for a while. Only college acceptance letters, which her mother had promptly thrown into the trash.

Peter shrugged. "I've only sent one. But I write you every day."

Kelsey started to reply. Peter, there's something you should know. That's it. That's what she would say.

But then he continued, "I write you in my head, too. As

we walk around in the hills, and ride around to villages. I talk to everyone back home in my head. Is that insane?"

"It's not insane," Kelsey said quietly. She did that sometimes with Michelle, too.

Peter's shoulders loosened. A happy, faraway look returned to his eyes. He didn't communicate like any other boys she knew. He wasn't shifty, or distracted. He thought long, and as he thought, his face was an open book.

"I always mean to write down what I say, but I forget," he said. "I remember wanting to tell my dad about how the men sit around in barbershops and yell at the TV when they watch the Pakistani cricket team, just like he does. I think he would like that. I'll have to remember that one."

The mention of his father brought her back to reality. He would learn of Michelle's death somehow, wouldn't he? "Do you Skype with your family?"

"Sure, all the time."

"Do they—" Kelsey paused. "Do they know about me?"

"They know I have a girlfriend but they don't dig too deep into it. Said I shouldn't be distracted." He laughed to himself.

He was quiet then, looking at her. Kelsey was quiet, too. They were both lost.

Finally, he spoke. "I mostly write to you, though. I think about the different things I would tell my dad, what I would tell my mom, my sister. But I tell you everything. A lot of these guys are really . . ." He looked around the tent again, getting quieter. "A lot of these guys are really closemouthed, you know? I don't have to talk all the time, but I've got to say something."

Then Peter's eyebrows knit together. "People are dying. No one I know, but we are going to have to . . ." Kelsey could see Peter's jaw working, trying to hold back. It hung in the air, sinking into both of them. Kelsey speculated the end of his sentence. Kill people.

"Ugh." He let out a sound, shaking his head. "I'm not allowed to talk about it, but, anyway," he said.

She didn't know what to say.

"Tell me what have you been up to. Distract me."

Kelsey felt like the wind had been knocked out of her. "It doesn't really seem important—"

"It's very important," Peter interrupted. Kelsey could tell he was determined to put all he had toward her, to forget. "How did finals go?"

Kelsey's instinct was to answer *terrible*, as usual. But that was her, and Peter wasn't talking to her. He was talking to Michelle. I'll just let him have this. Just a little while longer until the right time comes.

"Great, I think! The, uh, Art History essay questions were fascinating."

"I'm sure you nailed it." Peter lit up. "Did you listen to that song I told you about? The Cicadas?"

Kelsey would say, Uh, no. Kelsey only listened to songs you could choreograph dances to. Including musicals, which Michelle made fun of mercilessly. The Cicadas sounded like an indie band. Michelle would probably say, "Yeah! I loved the . . . guitar."

"And? It's better than Weast, right? But it still has that six-ties sound."

She kept going. "No way. I'll never give up on the sixties."

Peter laughed. "It's so nice not to talk about supply trucks that I'm not going to argue with you this time."

It was that easy. All of this had come out of Michelle's mouth so many times, it was impossible to forget. Kelsey had a strange, brief feeling of relief. As if Michelle were next to her, telling her what to say.

"Can I say something else?" Peter asked.

"Sure," Kelsey said. Slowly, the guilt crept back. She shouldn't have said that. She should have stopped him.

"You look so beautiful. I know you hate it when I say that, but you do."

Kelsey closed her eyes to him. She couldn't look at his face. She didn't want to picture it on the screen, how it would fall when he knew the truth.

"Look at you," she heard him say softly. "I don't know what I would do without you."

Maybe Kelsey could just keep her eyes closed when she told him. Peter, she would say to the darkness, I lied to you. But he seemed sensitive already, showing his fears and doubts to her. She didn't know what to do.

When Kelsey opened her eyes, a figure darted into the tent behind Peter, yelling at him to move. Crackling sounds, like fireworks, rang out from somewhere in the distance.

"Okay," he said, turning back to her. "I have to go."

"What's going on?" Kelsey asked. But she knew. He was under fire.

"I have to go. Write me back."

"Peter, I have to—"

"Tell me you'll write me back."

He was looking at her straight through the screen, his scared eyes digging into her, begging her. She would have to write as Michelle, but then again, she didn't know if he would ever get it. She didn't know if he would even make it through the next half hour.

"I'll write you back," she said.

He swallowed, taking her in for one last second, and smiled. More shouts echoed behind him, and the rumble of an engine. The call ended.

For a moment, Kelsey didn't quite know where she was.

Panic seized her. She rubbed her face with her palms. Her identical face. Michelle's cheeks. Michelle's eyes. Michelle's nose. What would she do? Michelle would protect him, at least until she could find a way to let him down gently. This wasn't a text message breakup situation. Michelle had loved him. Peter had one of those smiles that could transform everything else about his face, his eyes, even the air around him. Kelsey didn't know how, but she wasn't going to take that away from him. Not now.

She was left alone in her sister's room with the sound of absolutely nothing, which was different than silence. It was the sound of being covered with a blanket, of falling with no end, of being very deep inside something, so deep you can't see a way out.

# CHAPTER NINE

Kelsey woke up to a naked ceiling, her covers gone, feeling like she had been kicked by a horse. She struggled to hold what she knew to be true and so very, very false. Peter saw Michelle when he looked at Kelsey. In Peter's mind, he had talked to Michelle. But Michelle was nowhere.

A noise at her door made her jump.

Her father's face poked in, beard first. "City Market day," he said, a little hoarse.

"What?" They hadn't made their monthly road trip to the Kansas City farmers' market since the summertime. They used to buy oddly shaped produce their mother sliced and put in salads, useless trinkets the girls collected and eventually gave away at garage sales, cuts of meat her father used on burger specials.

"City Market day," her father repeated the phrase louder, as he did lately, instead of giving an explanation. He closed the door.

When they were very little, his grizzly-bear body was their playground. He'd stand in the middle of the living room, feet apart, knees bent, hands on hips, and she and Michelle would put their feet on his knees and become mountaineers from either side, racing to get to his shoulders.

They used to pretend to go to bed, but wait until he got off work from the restaurant late at night, and surprise him when he got home by sneaking into the kitchen and leaping up from behind the counter.

"Who are these girls?" he used to say, pretending to be shocked.

"Michelle! Kelsey!" they would scream.

"Who?" His eyes would go wide, trying not to smile.

It was fun to tell him the story of who they were, what they meant to him. "I'm Kelsey and that's Michelle! I'm your daughter, silly! You love me and all that! Remember?"

Then the moment when he remembered, even though they knew it was coming, ended in glorious hugs and kisses, as if he were remembering them after such a long time. As if eight hours away from someone you loved was such a long time.

And it was, when she was a kid.

But every time she and her father tried to comfort each other now, they ended up just forcing words into a thick silence. Because they reminded each other of Michelle, she guessed.

Kelsey, especially, was a reminder to him. She was a reminder to everybody. She had no choice. People in the hallways, people on the sidewalk, people in the grocery store. Their eyes widened and they drew in breath. Their mouths tightened in pity and they looked away, as if it were too hard to look at her. Try looking in the mirror every morning, Kelsey wanted to tell them. She was used to being mistaken for Michelle, but Michelle used to make people smile, not cringe. The only person who still smiled at the thought of Michelle was Peter. Maybe that's why she did what she did.

Kelsey blew out a thin breath at the thought.

She sat up and stood on her mattress, shaking out her arms and legs. She cleared a space on the floor covered in dirty clothes to do a sun salute, then some splits, and some butt-bouncing in the mirror for good measure. She put in her gold studs. She put on a cardigan and tight, dark jeans. She straightened her hair and layered on blush and mascara until she was unmistakable. She pointed and flexed her toes. She was put together.

She was Kelsey. She lifted her arms over her head and let her belly breathe. No need to explain. She let her body do the talking.

When her parents pulled up to the entrance of City Market to let her out and park the car, Kelsey was hit by the sounds of laughter and other languages, the smells of cinnamon and pine. Christmas was close.

Both she and Michelle had always wanted a real tree, and their mother had always refused, giving excuses. "Out of respect for your Jewish grandparents," she would say, or, "The kind of gifts we give you don't fit under a tree." It was true. They had always gone on trips at Christmas, and when they remembered to put one up, it was a tiny artificial tree from Walgreens that sang carols until it was out of batteries.

After getting a cup of hot cider, Kelsey searched for her father's uncut hair towering over the crowd. She shuffled around young couples wearing large glasses and small, stumpy women with carts, wandering toward the butcher's booth.

Michelle's ghost was everywhere, her baggy plaid coat darting in and out of a line of people. Her sister always got sulky on these trips to the market. Kelsey could grin and bear the hours for tradition's sake, for the sake of her mom and dad humming happily to every corner, but her sister would burn out. Now was about the time she would start moaning for money to go to the thrift store or keys to the car.

But Kelsey missed that, too. She was slowly finding out you don't just get to miss the parts you liked about someone who had died. You had to feel the whole weight of them, tugging at you.

She found herself in the middle of a makeshift grove of trees standing crooked in their asphalt pots. When the two of them appealed to their dad for a Christmas tree last year, he took them out to the garage, pointed to an ax, and invited them to go to the river and chop one down themselves.

Kelsey felt a smile come on at the memory of Michelle taking the ax from her father and swinging it with enthusiasm, almost cutting off a limb. She could feel her sister laughing next to her, see her breath in the air, urging her to *Get one! Get one! Mom and Dad will understand.*

She approached the salesman, a gangly kid in a KU pullover, much younger and taller than her. "How much for that one?" She pointed to a sickly pine tree about her height.

"On sale for twenty," he replied.

"If you help me carry it to my parents, they'll pay."

"No way."

Kelsey stared at him for a long moment, inching closer. She mouthed the word *Please*, and gave him a wide smile.

Bridged by the skinny tree, Kelsey and the boy parted the City Market crowd in a trail of needles. She imagined her and her parents sitting around the lit-up tree in the living room, with syrupy, old-timey Christmas music in the background. She could feel her blood getting warmer.

"This will be the first time our family has a real tree," Kelsey called back to the boy, searching for the Maxfields' car.

"Cool," he said, his breath heaving.

"What's your name?"

"Kevin."

"Kevin, this tree is special. It's kind of a tribute. To my sister."

Kevin said nothing. He was too busy lifting his end over the hood of a car. She could barely get a word out to her parents, her friends, but people like Kevin didn't feel the remotest bit of sadness for Michelle to begin with. Unlike her, they could only see Michelle in what she told them: from far away, an outline.

"We used to come here every month. She used to pick up onions and tomatoes from the booth and ask for the price in French, just to practice. No one could understand her. It was embarrassing."

Kevin still didn't care. She kept going.

"When we were eight we snuck into a concert they held in that pavilion," she told Kevin. "It wasn't even fun. It was just a cello. But we were proud."

As they crossed the street, Kelsey called back to him, "Once I caught her reading aloud the steamy parts of my mom's romance novels to her Barbies."

That one got a laugh. Or at least it sounded like a laugh.

After ten minutes of wandering through the neighborhood, Kevin put his end of the tree down and made a noise that was supposed to be exasperation, but sounded more like a malfunctioning blender. No sign of the Subaru.

Kelsey pulled out her phone.

Her mother picked up.

"Mom?" Kelsey put on a smile.

"Where are you?"

"Fifth and Walnut. So, Mom—"

"We're coming to get you."

Silence. Her mother hung up. Kevin blew a bubble with his gum, popping it. As the Subaru rolled up next to them, she took the tree from him, leaning it on her shoulder. Her mother's window rolled down, revealing a stone face, glancing at the tree.

"No, Kelsey."

Something between a laugh and a cough escaped Kelsey. "But—"

Her mother jerked her head toward the backseat. "We're going home."

Kelsey threw up her hands. "We just got here!"

Her mother sighed. Kelsey noticed she had tried to put on lipstick for the first time in several weeks. She wanted to go back to normal, too. "We didn't even make it into the market. Your father isn't feeling well."

Kelsey looked at her dad through the windshield, and rubbed her cold hands together. "I'm sorry," she called to him. "Maybe this will cheer you up."

Her father leaned across the seat toward the window, his voice cracking. "You're a very sweet girl. But it's not that easy. Your old dad isn't quite there, sweetheart."

Kelsey was sputtering, which she hated to do. "This is a nice thing, a nice thing I'm trying to do for everyone. I would really, really like to put up a Christmas tree. It's what people do."

"I'm sorry, Kelsey," her mother said. But she didn't look sorry. She wasn't even looking at her. Kelsey stayed still.

"Please get in the car. We'll come back and get it later."

Disappointment cut, sharpened by the rare hope she had just felt a second ago. And the guilt of it all, of lying to Peter and lying to herself, was weighing on her, pushing her. She caught her mother's eyes.

"Michelle would have wanted a Christmas tree."

She shouldn't have said that. Her mother tightened her grip on the steering wheel. Kevin stood quiet, looking back and forth between them, not knowing what to do.

Kelsey's mom's voice came out shaky. "Put the damn tree down, Kelsey. I love you, but I don't have rope to tie a tree to our car, I don't have a stand to put it in, I don't have a working vacuum to clean up after it, and I'm tired. I don't—please put the damn tree down."

"Just leave it?"

Kevin's gum popped in the silence. A family with a stroller rolled by, staring.

Her dad's voice floated out. "We need to go home."

"I'll take it back," Kevin said quietly.

Instead, Kelsey lowered the tree to the brick street and

gave it a shove with her foot toward the curb. Kevin picked it up and, with a glance at her, carried it away.

She got into the backseat. No one said anything more, and her father put on the radio. "Part of you pours out of me, In these lines from time to time . . ." Kelsey heard a woman's voice sing, but as they got on the highway, her mother turned down the volume so it was barely audible, a whine that got lost in the drone of the wheels on the road.

# CHAPTER TEN

Twenty minutes later they were in the driveway, and Kelsey walked inside fast, ahead of her parents, closing the door behind her.

She turned to go upstairs, but a streak of primary colors on the front table stopped her. Yesterday's mail sat on top of a pile of bills, and on top of that, an envelope with official-looking postage. Then, in careful handwriting, all capitals:

MICHELLE MAXFIELD
1316 VERMONT STREET
LAWRENCE, KS 66044

Peter's letter. Kelsey grabbed it and took the stairs two at a time. In her room, she paused. This was wrong. But it wasn't the same kind of wrong she had felt before. It was the wrong she felt seeing the tree grow smaller in Kevin's arms as he walked away, the wrong that cut Michelle's happy ghost from her. As soon as she had picked up the letter, the guilt had faded.

*Michelle would want to open this, but she can't,* Kelsey thought as she slid her finger under the seal. *So I'll do it for her.*

12/14

Dear Michelle,

I'm writing this sitting against a fir tree. We made it from the desert to the Kunar Province a few days ago, all rugged mountains and green valleys and meadows with cattle. We ride in huge trucks on narrow paths up through the peaks and the rock formations. It's like a slow roller coaster. It's so pretty I have to try not to get distracted. I've never been this high off the ground before. Most of the people in my company have been in these valleys once or twice already. Sam and I go on errands to the village for chewing tobacco and in exchange they show us how to find the best watch spots in the cracks between boulders. They use chewing tobacco to stay awake, and pass the time. Almost every soldier chews while they're here, whether they chewed before the tour or not. Except for me, of course. I am the youngest. They call me Petey.

Sam is from Iowa. They call him Rooster because of his red hair. He's short and raises beagles and loves death metal. We joke about how dumb the cows are and how the interpreter Alex (Alex isn't his actual name, but that's what he calls himself when he speaks English) has seen more American TV than I have.

Sam says I need to shut up about you already. He's looking over my shoulder right now and says if I don't cross out the part about him being short he'll roundhouse me. Tough luck, Sam.

I have to admit that I didn't expect to miss you as much as I do. I miss you next to me, but we didn't have all that much time in the same room, anyway, so I miss talking to you most of all. In that little time, I told you things I've told no one else. Not secrets, just parts of the way I see the world that I didn't know could be said aloud. So what I'm saying is, you hold all these parts of me, these parts I dug up, and you hold them inside your beautiful hands and brain and skin, so far away. And I have your hidden parts, too. I promise I'm keeping them safe. They're still here, under all this body armor. I remember everything.

One guy lost it this week. His name is Joel and he has all these moles on the back of his head and he didn't go to high school and he loves Disney movies. Someone got ahold of a bottle of vodka and we passed it around and it seemed to affect him most. He was laughing a little too hard at nothing and then he wandered off somewhere and no one knew where he went until we heard screaming from the med tent. He was crying and kicking over gurneys and shelves, yelling about wanting to go home. The sergeant didn't let him, of course. Now he doesn't say a word to anybody.

Soldiers sometimes ask each other what their reasons for fighting are, so we don't end up like Joel, you know? Then, once we've got them, we're supposed to let these reasons lie, never draw them out while we clean our guns or go on missions. But sometimes I wake up in the middle of the night—and the nights are so dark here, darker than even country nights in Kansas—and I have to hang on to the bed because I feel like I'm falling. Even if I'm supposed to have reasons for being here, I have no idea where I am or who I am or what the hell I'm doing.

I'm starting to do this in the daytime, too, which is even worse. I wake up while I'm polishing my boots or something and everything feels and looks wrong and sort of spins and aches like I'm sick.

But then I feel the parts of you that you gave me, and I see you on my last night before I left, the lamplight on you while you sat on the bed, and I can feel you keeping me. You may not know it but everywhere you go parts of me go with you. I snap to and know you're happy somewhere, or at least you're something somewhere, not here, and I know there are parts of me that are safe inside you, that will always be safe inside you, and I can breathe and go on without losing it.

Write me back. It doesn't have to be as crazy as what I just said, but I tried to tell you about normal things like the goat meat and the little kids who ask for chocolate and it didn't come. I'm reading *The Unbearable Lightness of Being*. What are you reading? Send me a book if you want. Tell me about the art you're making. Write me back. Even if we move bases, they will forward your letter to me.

Thinking of you,
Peter

By the end of the letter, tears were running down Kelsey's cheeks, catching in her mouth, dampening the collar of her sweater. Michelle's room was still full, but so desperately abandoned. No reading would happen here, no art would be made. There was nothing.

She wondered what happened to the parts of Peter that Michelle was supposed to keep safe. Where did those parts go now that her body was gone? Who would hold him together?

Kelsey realized she had stopped breathing. If there was no letter back, Peter would know something was wrong. He would become like her, and break apart. But Peter wasn't just going to slip his grades or ignore his friends or toss perfectly good trees on the pavement. Peter was in the mountains of Afghanistan. If he felt as weak as she did, he'd wake up one day in the middle of gunfire.

Before she could question herself, she slipped from her door to inside Michelle's room. She prayed her mother hadn't thrown away the stationery the two of them had received for their birthday a few years back—one set with Kelsey's initials, one with Michelle's. If she had already written letters to Peter while they were apart, she would have written them on the crisp cream-colored paper.

In the top drawer, Kelsey found the stack. She sat at her sister's desk, wiped a makeup-smeared face with the back of her hand, and began to compose a response. She spent the rest of the afternoon there. She dug for the parts of Michelle that Kelsey herself had kept. She searched her memories and Michelle's books and stared at her paintings. She imitated the wide loops and unfinished rises and falls of her sister's handwriting.

She sat, and she searched for the words that would bring her back to life.

*MITCH TO PETER (FIRST ATTEMPT)*

12/20

Dear Peter,

I'm sorry I wasn't able to write to you for such a long time. I just received your first letter. As for the email, well, I was grounded from using my computer. I'm still grounded. Don't ask why. My parents are seriously off their rockers. I can't wait to get out of Lawrence and go to college.

Otherwise, life here is quiet. I am trying hard not to eat meat. I take walks to the river to draw it, and then I use high-lighters to fill in the colors. Finals were easy for me. My sister is probably angry with me, because I told her again that she is better than her boyfriend, even though they have been dating for three years.

*I would also like to say—*
*I just want to tell you that—*

I miss you every day. Don't worry, I am not dating anyone else. I am so full of admiration for your courage. It must be difficult to be away from everything and everyone you know. You are a good person for your service and so are your friends. Trust me, I know how it feels to doubt where you are and why you are even there. Not as much as you but I know a little bit and I promise things will—

*I don't know what I'm saying—*
*—use bigger words*
*—find a book that she would read*
*—this is crazy*

# CHAPTER ELEVEN

The narrow streets up Mount Oread filled with carefully coiffed couples who met outside their brick mansions and traveled in packs to the party at the top of the hill. Mount Oread was the area of KU's campus where the fraternities and sororities had settled. Kelsey stood at the picture window of the Delta Sigma house, watching her future counterparts in heels and crimson and blue beads step on the sweeping lawn toward the white columns, holding drinks.

Inside, a pair of ESPN announcers loomed over the dining hall on a flat screen. Girls and guys who had begun the day looking like they walked off the cover of a J. Crew catalog had dissolved into a red-faced gaggle of haphazard warriors, ties around heads, Oxfords unbuttoned, screaming obscenities at a shot of the Missouri student section.

Davis was among them. A T-shirt that he had made

himself read HOW DO YOU GET A MISSOURI GRADUATE OFF YOUR PORCH? PAY FOR THE PIZZA. The guys slapped their arms around him and the girls kissed him on the cheek. His plan to crash at the fraternity seemed to have been sidelined by actually enjoying the fraternity. He couldn't help it, Kelsey knew. The only thing Davis liked better than making people laugh was making people laugh at parties, and there seemed to be a new one every other day.

As a whistle blew and the announcer shouted, the college students jumped together in a line, a soup of crimson and blue T-shirts with Greek letters.

"Lawrence, Kansas, and Columbia, Missouri. Two college towns, sweet and small, nice downtowns, just a few hours' drive from one another across the Kansas River. Peaceful, right? Heck, I've heard this area called Flyover Country. But boy, if you could be here in Kemper Arena tonight, you'd never know it. The energy is practically visible in the hatred between these crowds, folks. Crimson and blue, black and gold, clashing in the air, and it is deafening. The Kansas Jayhawks and the Missouri Tigers meet in the middle for their Border Showdown, and this has gone beyond basketball. This is war."

War. Kelsey was thinking of Peter. This was such a small, silly version of "war." She took a large sip of her rum and Coke.

Kelsey was wearing a Jayhawks jersey she had belted

into a dress. She joined in the fight song, clapping at the right parts.

A girl all in blue, her black hair in a bundle of braids, set her drink next to Kelsey's. At a second glance, Kelsey noticed the words emblazoned on her warm-up jacket.

"Excuse me," Kelsey said, raising her voice above the din.

The girl turned, revealing brown eyes and polished lips.

"Are you a Rock Chalk Dancer?" It made sense a few of them would be partying; not every dancer traveled with the team.

Though she was shorter than Kelsey, she had a way of appearing taller. Perfect posture. "I am."

Kelsey stuck out her hand. "I'm Kelsey. I'll be trying out in the spring."

The girl cocked her head. "Are you? Then what's that in your hand?"

Kelsey looked down at her rum and Coke, feeling her face turn hot. "I'm not drinking—I'm just here to watch the game. My boyfriend is—"

The students joined in with the blare of the Rock Chalk Chant through the TV, gaining volume with each verse.

The girl got closer, yelling into her ear. "Did I ask who your boyfriend is?"

"No, but—" Kelsey's mouth fell slack, unable to form words.

The girl's face broke into a smile, and then a full-on laugh. "I'm messing with you."

"Oh." Kelsey's heart was still beating out of her chest, though she wasn't quite sure why. She allowed herself a smile, and joined in another round of the fight song. Clap, clap, clap, clap-clap-clap. She and the girl paused conversation and dutifully yelled, "Go, Hawks!"

"I'm Nicki." She grabbed Kelsey's hand and shook it. "Hey!" She gestured to another pair of girls in blue warm-up jackets. A redhead and a blonde approached them, holding drinks, filling the surrounding air with different perfumes. Their solid thighs filled their jeans and their lower abs were visible under their cropped shirts. *And I thought I was in shape*, Kelsey mused.

Nicki pointed at them one by one. "This is Missy, sprained ankle, this is Jen, pulled hamstring. Everybody, this is Kelsey. Cheers!"

The girls lifted their red cups. Kelsey felt the stares of surrounding partygoers and gulped the rest of her drink down.

Nicki nodded toward her. "Kelsey's trying out."

The redhead, Missy, gave a whoop. "Good for you! Are you ready?"

Before Kelsey could answer, Jen, the blonde, leaned toward her and touched her hair in its bun. "Whatever you do, make sure you do your hair."

"Totally," Missy said. "I got a blowout last year. Completely ruined by sweat the first routine. It was worth it, though. The girls wearing plain ponytails might as well have not even been there. The captains, like, barely looked up from their clipboards during their dances."

Kelsey found her voice, feeling the hot rum travel to her belly. "What else do I need to know?"

A flood of voices came at once, bouncing back and forth around her.

"Everything's intense."

"You can't just coast by on looks."

"But it's a big part of it."

"We're the distraction, you know? We're the eye candy."

"If you have a decent pair of splits, you'll be fine."

"You look the part."

"You just need to smile a little more."

"Yeah, smile!"

Kelsey smiled.

Nicki cupped Kelsey's chin. "There you go."

Missy and Jen gave her hugs from either side. Their smiles were wide and real, and Kelsey worked hard to match them.

Soon, the girls were joined by more Rock Chalk Dancers, who took it upon themselves to climb on the Delta Sigma pool table and perform pom-pom routines during commercial breaks.

After a while, Kelsey was sweating. She couldn't keep up with all the names they shouted, the places she didn't know, the inside jokes.

When the fight song started up again, she had to move away. She found Davis among a sea of sorority sisters, refilling his drink.

"It's my baby," he sang in a made-up song. "My baby gi-i-i-rl."

She straightened his collar as he swayed in front of her, not sure if he was actually moving back and forth or if her vision was wonky. "Hi," Kelsey replied, her tongue heavy.

He bent close to her ear. "Are you having fun?"

"You are. That's for sure."

"I love these guys." He said it again, shouting at his brothers. "I love these guys!" They shouted and pointed back. "And I love you."

He kissed her, warm and wet, and bundled her in his arms.

"I love you, too," Kelsey said. The sight of him bobbing through all these people, electrified and red-cheeked like a little boy, made her happy. But Kelsey was feeling hot and dizzy. She needed air and silence.

"I'm tired, baby," she found herself saying into the folds of his shirt.

He brought her out, holding her by her shoulders. "But we're winning!"

"I know!" Kelsey used her last bit of party energy to high-five two sorority sisters on either side of Davis. They looked so tiny and perfect, like My Size Barbie dolls.

"And everyone's here!"

"I know," she continued, and finally, Davis paused, looking into her eyes.

He put his arm around her. "Let me drive you home."

"Ha!" Kelsey let out. "No way. You've been drinking."

"I can give you a piggyback ride? Or maybe call a taxicab? Does Lawrence even have cabs?"

Kelsey laughed at his confusion.

After convincing him that the well-lit, friendly streets would be fine to walk, and a long, kiss-filled good-bye, Kelsey zipped up her coat and started down the hill and into town. Streetlights pulsed in her tipsy vision, and the cold wrapped her exposed skin. Soon, she was on Massachusetts Street, weaving between the celebrators, hearing cheers erupt from inside the bars as she passed. She felt a pang of envy. She wondered if she should have stayed. When she realized she couldn't feel her fingers or toes, she slipped into La Prima Tazza. Michelle used to practically live in the coffee shop, especially during finals.

The place was dim and a little busted, with cherry-brown counters and mismatching lamps at every table, empty except for two middle schoolers playing a fantasy card game in a corner and the barista, a skinny college-aged man. When she got closer, Kelsey couldn't help but notice how big and luminous the barista's eyes were compared to his face. He was singing along to an indie song on the radio as he worked.

His T-shirt, which was too small for him, had a Campbell's soup can on it.

"We don't sell beer," he intoned from behind the rows of flavored syrups, cleaning a cup.

Kelsey realized he must be referring to her KU gear. The place was probably mistaken for a bar because it was open late. "Good," she said. "Because I want the opposite of beer."

"Oh." He stopped cleaning and looked up. Then he narrowed his eyes at her. "Stop," she heard him say. Kelsey met his gaze. He was biting his lip in serious thought. "Holy shit."

"What?"

"Just a second."

He glided around the counter and pulled her into a hug.

Kelsey didn't move her arms inside of his skinny ones, wrapping her tight. Then he returned to his position, smacking his hands on the counter. "You look just like Michelle."

"Yeah—" Kelsey started.

He put up a hand, shaking his head in disbelief. "No. It's freaky. There are twins, and there are *twins*."

Kelsey nodded. "We were twins," she said, because that was all she could think to say.

He sighed. "I'm sorry. I'm being dramatic. I've had a long day. Espresso?"

"Lay it on me," Kelsey said, rubbing her numb hands together.

While he pressed the grounds, his eyes kept flickering in her direction, searching for something. He set a tiny cup on the counter with a flourish.

Kelsey shuffled in her purse for her wallet. She put out a five to pay for the drink, but he pushed it away. She looked up at him, his large eyes blinking.

"Honey, please," he said. "Your money's no good here."

"Thank you," she said, and inside, she felt a trace of the first real laugh she'd had all night. She giggled and took a sip of her espresso. "You are dramatic."

"So?" He leaned on the counter, watching her. "What's the point of experiencing life if no one else takes notice?"

"Like, 'if a tree falls in the forest and no one is there to hear it, did it really fall' type of thing?"

"Exactly. I'm Ian, by the way."

"Kelsey. So you knew Mitch?"

"Yes. She came in here to draw late at night. Sometimes we went to parties together."

Kelsey searched her memory, but she couldn't remember him among Michelle's boyfriends. "I wonder why she never brought you home to meet us."

"Not together together." He smiled wryly. "Michelle's not really my type."

It appeared girls in general were not his type. Kelsey clicked her tongue and pointed a finger gun at him. "Got it."

"I should have just told you I was a dancer, like you."

"How did you know I was a dancer?"

He furrowed his brow. "Michelle talked about you all the time. You think I would just hug a stranger because she looks like my friend?"

Kelsey felt a smile come on. "No, but you know who would do that?"

They said it together: "Michelle."

After they laughed, they sat in silence, remembering. Finally, he spoke. "She said that your parents pretended to approve of you both, but secretly they were afraid you would grow up to be starving artists."

Kelsey felt her mouth drop open. "Michelle said that? That's funny, because I'm no artist. Michelle was the artist."

Ian made a *psh* sound and pretended to be offended. "You're saying dancers aren't artists?"

"No, no, I didn't mean it like that. Just that I don't do any modern dance. Nothing that expresses, like, feelings." He was still staring at her with those all-knowing eyes. She threw up her hands. "I'm not a tortured genius! I want to be a Rock Chalk Dancer with the hair and the uniform and the crowd. I just like to shake my ass."

Ian threw his head back, laughing. "Hey, me, too. Me, too. But don't sell yourself short. You don't have to be tortured to be an artist. I'm happy. Michelle was happy."

Kelsey paused, thinking. "I think she wanted to be a genius, though. She wanted to be original. I don't care about any of that. I like being a part of something bigger than myself, something that everyone can understand." She pointed to the Jayhawks logo on her jersey. "Like this."

In response, all Ian did was point to the soup can on his T-shirt.

Kelsey recognized it from the poster in Michelle's room. "Warhol, right? Yeah, he was her favorite."

He turned away from her to the sink, back to his task. "You want to know why Michelle called you an artist? Look up Andy Warhol."

Kelsey didn't know Michelle even talked about her when she wasn't around. She didn't know Michelle was worried their parents disapproved. She hadn't even had a conversation with one of Michelle's friends lasting more than "I'm the other twin," or, "Michelle's upstairs."

Kelsey put her hands around the tiny cup, soaking in the warmth. "God, there was so much I didn't know about her."

Ian shrugged. "Maybe it never occurred to you to ask because you didn't have to."

"Yeah. When someone lives next to you, eats next to you, looks just like you, you think you know them."

*But you don't. You didn't know her, not really*, Kelsey told herself. This made her unexpectedly sad, sadder than the dull ache of absence. And desperate to know more.

She finished her drink and zipped up her coat.

"See you around, Kelsey." Ian reached across for another

hug, whispering into her ear, "And please don't ever wear a basketball jersey as a dress again."

*MITCH TO PETER / USING BIG WORDS THAT MITCH WOULD USE (SECOND ATTEMPT)*

*1/7*

Dearest Peter,

I must apologize for the delay in returning your letter. I was otherwise occupied with my academics, which as you know are of the uttermost importance. Let me paint a picture for you. I enter my home around three thirty and sit down to my studies at a rolltop desk, which I found at a nearby estate sale on Tennessee Street. My sister tells me the desk is not in fact antique but actually finds its origin at Target.

*???*

*—find a book she would read. Jane Eyre?*

*—this is crazy*

*—copy parts of her journal*

# CHAPTER TWELVE

The next time Peter called, Kelsey would be ready. She had received a Skype message from him earlier that week, telling her that he'd call in two days, sometime that evening.

She daydreamed through classes, planning what to say.

She arrived home from dance practice to a house full of random mourners, trying to lose Gillian and Ingrid at her front door. They stood in the entryway with their backpacks, looking over Kelsey's shoulder.

"You don't want to see this," she told them, gesturing to the circle.

"Is this the group you were telling us about?" Gillian asked. Her mouth turned down, and she shrugged. "I guess they gotta do what they gotta do."

"It's nice they have snacks, too," Ingrid offered.

This month's mantra, as they heard thrumming from the living room, was WE MUST EMBRACE PAIN AND USE IT AS

FUEL FOR OUR JOURNEY. This month's group leader was a woman named Patti who had lost her son to cancer. This month's refreshments were ginger ale and banana bread.

The way Patti passed out cups of sodas to the support group reminded Kelsey of a Catholic mass she once saw. All the talk of the soul and the spirit, each person bowing their head in thanks as they received their bread, including her parents.

Finally, as the group started their personal testimonies, her friends left.

She headed upstairs and moved Michelle's laptop to her room.

Now Kelsey was doing a handstand against her bedroom door. She could see herself in the reflection of the deck doors, belly exposed under black leggings, hair touching the floor. She hadn't straightened her hair that day, or put on mascara. Her door was painted a light pink, her walls turquoise, the lamps on either side of her bed funneling light into orange-tinted triangles. It was supposed to be tropical, her room, but from that angle, it looked like a retro vision of a spacecraft.

When the beeping rang out from Michelle's computer, Kelsey went upright, letting the blood rush from her face back down to her body. Peter. Kelsey moved with the laptop to a less conspicuous location, ran her fingers through her wavy hair, and pressed ANSWER. Her hands were shaking.

Peter's cheeks were tinted bronze and his hair was lighter. The dark circles were still visible under his big blue eyes.

"I got your letter," Kelsey said before he could speak.

His eyes opened wider, hopeful. "Did you write me back?"

She nodded in response.

He was smiling, and he looked natural, sitting in his uniform. Well, maybe not natural. As his smile faded, his eyes darted to either side of him, tense.

Kelsey took a closer look at the scene behind his shoulder, trying to determine if he was in the same place. "So, are you still in the—" she began.

"Guess what? My parents sent me a gift," he continued.

"What?"

Kelsey watched him reach down to pull out an acoustic guitar with a black body and a blue patterned strap.

"Nice," she said quietly. She knew nothing about guitars, but anyone could see it was a beautiful instrument. When Peter knocked on it, the sound was full of layers.

"I've been working on some Cicadas covers."

"Oh, yeah?" Kelsey tried to lift her voice with recognition.

He strummed a few chords, looking at her. "'The Sworn Secret,'" he said. "The English version, not the Portuguese."

Kelsey nodded in encouragement.

And then he sang slowly, tripping over the syllables as he found the chords. "Things I never told you / Listen and believe / They said it was never gonna work out / As long as we don't tell them, just you and me."

His voice was shaky but clear, and in tune with the guitar. He wasn't afraid to hold the notes.

When he was done, Kelsey gave an awkward thumbs-up. She found her mouth had gotten stuck in a dumb smile, so she tried to reel it in a little, putting her face in her sleeve.

"Thank you. I've had plenty of time to practice," Peter said. "So, any requests?"

"Uh—" Kelsey's mouth went dry. She was hitting nothing but blanks. Something old. Something classic. "Uh. Elvis?"

Peter looked puzzled, but pleased. "Elvis? Really?"

Kelsey shrugged. "Sure!" Maybe Michelle would have asked for something more sweet and serious, something with a hard-to-pronounce name from a high shelf in the bowels of the record store. There were always people with guitars outside that record shop, at the corner of 9th and Massachusetts. Michelle would make the Maxfields stop on the sidewalk to hear them play, running through songs like a catalog until she found one that the musicians knew, listening to them until the song was all the way through. Then she'd clap no matter how bad it was, like she was at a concert, and ask their parents for a dollar to toss in the case. Kelsey could have listened, too, but she always moved as far away down the sidewalk as she could, never appreciating the effort.

Kelsey tried to tell Michelle that the kids would just go back to their dorm and use the cash for beer money, but she never cared.

Kelsey always thought she just liked the attention. But as Peter played, she was starting to get how electric it was to hear someone play an instrument right in front of you.

Peter played snippets of "Hound Dog" and "Jailhouse Rock." He lowered his voice and drawled from the back of his throat in his best Elvis impression. He had to stop when they were both laughing.

Kelsey thought of Michelle, and remembered to clap.

Once they were quiet, Kelsey heard the rumble of a truck, then yelling. It sounded as if two men were getting into a heated argument.

"How are things over there?" she asked, tentative.

Peter scrunched up his face. "I don't want to take your time with all that. Okay?"

"Of course," Kelsey said.

"Tell me about home. What did you do last night?" He set aside his guitar and leaned close to the screen. "By the way, I told my sister about us. She wants to know why she can't find you on Facebook."

"Because . . ." Kelsey licked her lips, buying time. "Because I deleted it. You inspired me, I guess."

Peter held up his hands. "What can I say? It's just a waste of time."

"Yeah, it really is. And homework," Kelsey said, in answer to his question. "That's what I did last night."

"What about the night before?"

"Homework," she said, smiling. "And we ate at Dad's restaurant."

"Night before?"

"I went to a party." Kelsey swallowed, aware she was answering as herself. She didn't know if this was right or wrong. But Michelle went to parties, too.

"Oh, yeah? Was it fun?"

A loud boom sounded in the distance. Peter twitched slightly and clutched something in his lap. His gun. He turned his head, listening. They waited.

"A muffler," he finally said. "So was it fun?"

Kelsey resisted the urge to cry out. Her hands were shaking again. "I left early."

Peter was taking deep breaths. He nodded, egging her on.

She put on a smile. "I took a walk."

"Then what?" They were both listening for another boom, Kelsey knew it. But they were pushing each other forward, lifting each other up.

She relaxed her voice. "It was freezing. The game was still going on, so the streets were pretty empty. I visited Ian at La Prima Tazza. We talked about Warhol."

Peter flashed a smile, raising his eyebrows. "Your favorite subject."

Kelsey had looked through Michelle's Andy Warhol book, but she still didn't understand why the multicolored prints had anything to do with her. One of them was a still from a film of a girl eating a hamburger. That was it. She shrugged. "What can I say?"

"Speaking of, did you see that sculpture I told you about? The one in the middle of the Flint Hills?"

"Remind me," Kelsey said, and his eyes started to look more alive.

"It's just a steel circle. Painted red. But it acts like a picture frame for the landscape, right? No matter how close to it you are, or how far away, the portion of the Flint Hills that you focus on is determined by the circle."

"What if you decide to look outside the circle?" Kelsey asked.

"Then you're still being influenced by the circle. Get it? Because you're looking away from it on purpose, but whether you rebel against it or accept it, it's still on your mind."

"So that's what modern art is." Kelsey tried to sound sure of herself. "An interruption you can't ignore."

"An interruption!" He was thoughtful. "That's good, Michelle."

Her sister's name aloud seemed to echo from his mouth, the way he looked at her. Goose bumps rose on her skin. It was strange, how easily she fell into this conversation with Peter, a conversation that would have seemed impossible if she wasn't thinking of Michelle. Kelsey adjusted her position on the floor, her eyes locked on his through the screen.

Peter's voice sounded, low and soft, less wired up than before. "We might have to move from the Province."

"When?"

"I'm not sure. It depends. I might not get your letters right away, though." He looked concerned.

"Oh, don't worry about that. Just worry about staying safe."

Peter shook his head. "No, they'll get them to me. They have to. But no matter what, don't stop writing. Because if the first one doesn't come, then at least the second one will. And I never know when I'm going to get access to a computer."

"Okay." Kelsey swallowed, knowing what she was agreeing to, that she would have to imitate her sister's handwriting again. She still hadn't figured out Michelle's email password, either. Of course, none of this would matter if she could just tell him the truth.

"Everything you say to me about home is, like, nourishing. You get it? It's like each memory is a piece of food that I can eat—" He made a scooping motion with his hand. "It makes me stronger."

Kelsey smiled in spite of nerves. "You want me to feed you another one?"

"Feed me another one." He opened his mouth.

She laughed. "What are you in the mood for?"

"How about the Flint Hills? Oh, I know. You could paint them! Paint them."

Kelsey cleared her throat again. "Nah," she finally said. "That will take too long. Let me tell you about them, instead."

This she could do. Her family had made the drive from Lawrence through the hills a million times, to Seneca, to Manhattan, to Wichita.

Michelle was always in the backseat next to her, watching out the window. The Flint Hills were one of the few things, their parents said, that would keep them from punching each other.

Kelsey settled into the rug on her floor, resting her chin in her hands.

Peter leaned back in his chair and closed his eyes.

"So you're on 70," Kelsey began, "heading west, and there's nothing but overcast sky and fence and prairie. Until all of a sudden, you see this wrinkle in the flat lines. It's almost a hallucination. Until you see another wrinkle, and another one, and the land is moving like the ocean. And each hill is spilling into the next. The grass is a color you've never seen before and you'll never see again. It's orange, gold, white, green, brown. . . ."

"Mmm," Peter said, his eyes still closed.

Suddenly, a man's voice filled the speakers. "Let's move, Petey!"

Peter clutched his gun again, turning away from Kelsey toward the man who had just entered. He left the screen for a moment, and she could only hear patches of their sentences. *Raid*, she heard. *Found something.*

Peter returned to the frame, along with a stocky man slightly older than himself, with red hair.

He smiled, tense. "This is Rooster," he said.

"Sam," the guy said, touching his chest.

"Nice to meet you," Kelsey said.

"Pleasure, ma'am."

"I hate to go, but we have to," Peter said.

In the background, Kelsey heard what she could recognize as an Islamic call to prayer.

Another soldier screamed blurry, angry words.

Peter looked at her, and she could see his eyes moving back and forth, memorizing her face. Just in case. His mouth was a thin line.

"Soon?" he said.

"Soon," she replied.

He took a deep breath. He smiled. He held his hand up to his lips and put them to her screen, and the call ended.

Kelsey snapped the laptop shut and flipped to lie on her back, staring at the ceiling.

From the living room, she could hear someone in the support group weeping. Animal, gut-wrenching sounds that echoed the moment of knowing all over again. She knew how the woman felt, whoever she was. There was no reason to bring that sound into the world again. There was no reason to open another wound.

Now that she had conjured Michelle as she spoke to Peter, her own hurt felt smaller. Her sister was back in the room with her, stepping over her as she lay on the floor, digging through her drawers, asking to borrow a scarf.

*Is this okay?* she asked silently as Michelle wove around her.

But memories don't answer back.

As long as Peter saw Michelle, she would not have to be ripped away. As long as Kelsey could keep Michelle's death to herself, Peter would not have to know that kind of pain.

# CHAPTER THIRTEEN

The next morning's winter sun was shining through the red paper pasted on the windows of Lawrence High School, casting everyone in the hallways in an amber glow. Kelsey was in position with her team, waiting for a signal. When they heard the bloodthirsty cries coming from the gymnasium lobby, they started to run. Kelsey filled her lungs with air and expelled it to make the loudest scream she could muster. Her girls did the same. Through the halls, they formed a stampede, belting out the Lions battle cry, dodging bodies and bookshelves.

Soon, they were joined by the cheerleaders and the basketball team, everyone calling the school to war with Topeka High. The posters read GET FIRED UP! and MAUL THE TROJANS! and LION VICTORY! Kelsey zipped past kids who wouldn't even go to the game—the smokers, the gamers, the drama kids—and they all joined in, yelling just for the hell of it. Soon, the whole school was a cacophony, friends and enemies forgotten, mouths wide open and wild, fists banging on lockers and classroom doors.

As tradition mandated, after exactly one minute, the noise stopped.

This was the drill on game day. Faces returned to normal, except for the occasional sly look. Homework was extracted and shuffled. It was time to go to first period.

The Lions Dance Team had made it to the southeast side of the cafeteria, to the other end of the school, panting.

"Good one, dudes," Kelsey told her team, placing loose strands of her hair back into her ponytail as they walked to class.

Ingrid was the color of an eggplant, as usual. She looked worried. "I think I made that kid Frankie pee his pants."

Kelsey and Gillian laughed. "How did you manage that?" Kelsey asked.

"I banged open the door to the boys' bathroom just as he was unbuttoning."

Kelsey closed her eyes and folded her hands with faux wisdom. "A small price to pay in the spirit of victory."

"Poor Frankie," Gillian said. "And poor anyone who has to sit next to him."

Ingrid peeled off to go to Comp Lit. "No one tell him it was me," she called.

As she left, Gillian tucked another loose strand of Kelsey's ponytail behind her ear. "You seem good today."

"I feel good," Kelsey said, putting her arm around her friend.

"What's different?" Gillian asked. "Because I've been trying to cheer you up for three freaking months now, and I'd kind of like to know."

They paused in front of Gillian's AP Euro class. Kelsey did her best to look like she was thinking, but she knew. Last night was the first night in several weeks that she hadn't cried herself to sleep.

"I mean, I know it doesn't happen just like that—" Gillian snapped her fingers. "But if there's anything I can do so that you're like this all the time, I want to do it. You know?"

She couldn't tell Gillian about Peter. She wished she could but she couldn't.

"It's probably just time," Kelsey said, smiling. "Don't read too much into it."

At that, she was alone, on her way to Geography. She was late, but it didn't matter. She took her time, basking in the red, in the quiet of the main staircase. As she sidled down the first two stairs, she felt the air on her back change, a little colder, a little clearer.

Someone must have opened a window. She turned to look.

The air came from the art wing. Kelsey had only been to this section of the school once, for Michelle's junior art show, but she could barely remember it. On impulse, she went back up the stairs.

Four classrooms bordered the small gallery. Inside, two short pedestals holding student sculptures stood in the center: one, a hand made out of clay; the other, a ceramic vase. The walls were lined with portraits in dark pencil, and Kelsey recognized some of the students. Most of them had eraser marks streaked across their faces, noses off-center, hands twisted into too many lines. Michelle had done this assignment, too, back when she had her mermaid hair.

In the corner, Kelsey found it. Unlike the others, it was framed, with a plaque, and it was perfect. Michelle had drawn herself curled up on her side of the porch, sitting on a chair, looking out onto the yard. Sun shone on her face. Tiny hairs, lines that could almost be mistaken for stray pencil, lifted in a light breeze.

A loud creak sounded from across the gallery, and Kelsey jumped.

A teacher, her head full of gray curls, was opening another window.

"Sorry!" she called. "The smell of paint leaks out of Mr. Henry's room and it gives me a headache."

A door labeled MRS. WALLACE was propped open, revealing an empty classroom.

The name was familiar. Mrs. Wallace had been Michelle's AP Art History teacher. *Can't go to the game*, Kelsey could remember her saying. *Have a paper for Wallace.*

"Mrs. Wallace?" Kelsey asked, tearing her eyes from Michelle's portrait.

Mrs. Wallace paused. "Yes." Then she squinted, and walked closer. "Miss Maxfield," she said, a smile of recognition growing on her face.

"The other one," Kelsey said.

"I know," Mrs. Wallace said, glancing down. "I was at Michelle's service."

They were both quiet for a moment, side by side, and their gazes fell on Michelle's drawing.

"How is your family?" Mrs. Wallace asked.

"They're all right."

"Really?"

Silence. Visions of her father, leaking tears as he did the dishes. Her mother in her corner, listening to *Carmen*, the opera, on repeat.

"We've all lost it," Kelsey let out. She looked at Mrs. Wallace and shrugged. "To be honest."

Mrs. Wallace put a hand on her shoulder. "I don't blame you."

Mrs. Wallace hadn't told her to get to class and Kelsey didn't want to leave just yet. "Did you know my sister pretty well?"

"She was one of my favorite students. A wonderful girl. A little manic, at times, but brilliant. She knew who she wanted to be."

"Yes!" Kelsey paused, thinking. "And for me, well—" she continued. "It's like, I had my opposite my whole life." Kelsey gestured at the portrait. "So I knew exactly who I was. I knew who I was because I knew who I wasn't. And now she's gone."

"I can't imagine what you're going through," Mrs. Wallace said. "But I will say, Kelsey, that as for who you are, you've got a whole, long life to figure that out."

That's what Davis had said, too. And Gillian. And everyone else. But the truth was, in some very messed-up way, speaking for Michelle, if only for a few minutes, had made her feel less hollow. The only time she felt like moving forward was last night, with Peter, who needed Michelle as much as she did. *Yes,* she wanted to tell them, *I have plenty of time, but Michelle's time has already run out.*

And that wasn't fair.

Mrs. Wallace looked at her watch. "I better start preparing for next period."

"I want to take your class," Kelsey said suddenly.

Mrs. Wallace's forehead wrinkled. "Which class?"

She couldn't have Michelle, but she could still get to know her better. She could do what she never bothered to do when Michelle was alive. She could find out what made her tick. "Your Art History class."

"That's an Advanced Placement class," Mrs. Wallace said, then gave a pitying laugh. "You missed the first half! We're already on French Impressionism. I don't think you'll be able to catch up, Kelsey. This is for students serious about art history. It won't be fun for you."

"Please." She found her eyes.

Mrs. Wallace sighed, shaking her head. "You'd have to switch your schedule around. . . ."

"Let me try. I can do it. Really, I would like to know more about . . ." Michelle's portrait next to her, in the corner of her eye, hair lifting. The soup can. Ian's directions. The print on the wall. "Warhol. Will we study Andy Warhol, for example?"

"Mmm." Mrs. Wallace narrowed her eyes, thinking. The teacher turned and walked away toward her classroom. Kelsey's heart sank.

Then Mrs. Wallace called behind her, sighing. "All right. Sort it out with the counselors."

"I will!" Kelsey called back, and fought the urge to do a little dance.

"Okay, then," Mrs. Wallace said as she closed the door. "I'll see you at sixth period."

POSTMARK 1/6, RECEIVED 1/13

Dear M— Forgot to send you this postcard from the Brussels Airport, so I'm sending it now. I was about to write something else but a huge rat just scurried through the computer room and scared the shit out of me. And I'm wearing flip-flops. My dad always told me flip-flops were the worst kind of shoes because they leave you unprepared. I always told him to screw off and wondered what on earth I would need to be prepared for but now I have rat residue on my foot. You live and you learn. I'm changing into my boots, though their more accurate name is portable ovens. Oh well. Give yourself an awkward sweaty hug for me. —P

# CHAPTER FOURTEEN

"Berthe Morisot."

Anyone who happened to be passing through the alley behind the Maxfields' backyard would hear an extended list of notable French Impressionists floating through the night in Kelsey's scratchy voice, a little scratchier than usual. Maybe she was coming down with something.

"Auguste Renoir." Kelsey was pacing on her side of the porch, puffy coat unzipped, earbuds blasting. She sniffed. She was definitely coming down with something.

"Mary Cassatt," she called into the darkness.

Mrs. Wallace, as Kelsey had found out over the past couple of weeks, was a pop quiz sorceress. She had a sixth sense for when her class was most comfortable, and at the precise peak of relaxation, BAM! Quizzes up her sleeve.

"Claude Monet."

She had recorded herself stating dates and names of

paintings, and put them on her phone. She would match the artist to their facts out loud, because staring at a book would find her using it as a pillow. She needed her limbs involved somehow. She was walking to stay awake.

"Edgar Degas."

"Kelsey?"

She turned to see her deck door slide open, her father's scraggly, hulking frame dominating the light. She took out her earbuds.

"Hi, Dad."

A smile peeked through his beard. "Whatcha doin' out here?"

"Studying."

"Pardon me, what word just came out of your mouth?"

Kelsey let out a laugh, and said it slower this time. "Stud-y-ing."

He backed into her room. "You have a clown nose. Come in from the cold for a minute."

She followed her dad inside, and he folded his big body slowly to sit in her desk chair, wearing the same old Cambodian cotton white button-down, stained slightly with burger grease. As he looked around with a gruff eye, she kicked some dirty clothes into the closet. For a minute, it was like it used to be.

He crossed his ankle over his knee. "What were all those names? Boyfriends?"

Kelsey let out a sarcastic "Ha! No, I—"

"You switched from Spanish to French, or something?"

"Nope." She flopped on her bed. "I'm taking Art History."

"Art History, huh?"

"AP Art History. What Michelle used to take."

Kelsey was staring at the chipped red paint on her nails, avoiding her father's eyes. "What?" she said finally.

"Nothing," her dad said, a calm smile resting on his face. "Will you be able to handle a class like that?"

"Yes."

She could tell he was waiting for further explanation. He knew her as well as anyone. He knew she had spent most of her high school years driving around Lawrence with Davis, improvising parties in the basements of her friends' houses, avoiding her homework with elaborate excuses. And she was happy that way. But everyone was happier then.

"Have you spoken to your mother about it? I think she'd be very proud you're challenging yourself."

Kelsey hadn't made an effort to speak to her mother since before Christmas, the day of the City Market trip. Her mom left notes for her on the fridge occasionally, and asked Kelsey if she'd missed the deadline for submitting her application to KU. "To your great surprise, I've turned it in already," Kelsey had called to her through the door, and that was it. So, it wasn't as if her mom was busting down the door to speak to Kelsey, either.

"It's none of Mom's business."

"You're her daughter. Everything you do is her business."

"If she wants to know about it, she doesn't have to send you as a messenger."

"Kels," her father said, putting up his hands. "I act alone. I think the Art History class is fantastic." He paused. Kelsey waited. "And that's all I have to say about it."

"Good," Kelsey said, and she felt herself relax. "I'm sorry."

"Don't be sorry." He leaned forward, pinching his nose, just like Michelle used to do when she was thinking. "You've got the biggest burden of us all, Kels." His eyes shone a little, but he blinked, and his smile kept. "You don't remember this, but your mother used to give you and Mitch baths in the sink. You were both very small babies. And even if she set you on either side of the sink, you'd find a way to get next to each other in the water. You two just loved to cuddle."

Kelsey was quiet. Of course she wasn't supposed to remember something like that, but actually, she could.

She could remember the warm water.

Her mother's hands.

She could remember the puzzle-piece feeling of having her sister next to her, which is a feeling that no one in the world could ever know. Not just anyone else with a sister. Not another set of twins. No one but her and Michelle, and the way Michelle could twist her elbow inside out and Kelsey couldn't, and Kelsey's mole on her lower back and Michelle's on her forearm, and how they always knew what the other was thinking.

When they got older, they had stopped wanting to know. Which was the worst part of all.

"Okay?" her father said, smiling.

"Okay," Kelsey said, trying to swallow her tears. She smiled back at him. "I should get back to studying."

"Okay then, strong girl." He stood up, she stood up, and they embraced.

As he closed her bedroom door, Kelsey put back in her earbuds and pressed PLAY, but she could only hear nonsense syllables. The wound had torn again.

From downstairs, she heard her mother call her name.

It was taking Kelsey a bit to return to reality from a rainy day when they were nine, the day she and Michelle invented their own way of walking down the redbrick sidewalks. Every three steps they skipped, always the right leg, knee up, all the way into downtown. They had the same raincoat in different colors.

Kelsey opened her door and yelled down, "What?"

"Guess who I found in the basement?" her mother called. Kelsey stiffened.

"Don't—not right now, Melody," she heard her father say.

"Who did you find?" she asked, glancing at the closed door to her sister's room.

"Billy Bear!"

"Michelle's lizard?" An image of the dirty green stuffed animal surfaced, drooping from Michelle's hand by its tail as she dragged it around.

"Billy Bear the lizard," she heard her father say, laughing sadly. "Where everyone else saw a lizard, Michelle saw a bear. Of course."

"I suppose we'll put it in her room," her mother said, choppy. Kelsey wiped her nose. She felt something thaw inside her, a little, for her mother.

"That sounds good, Mom," she called.

"I can't go into her room right now," her dad said to her mom, quiet. "Put him on the stairs."

"I'll bring him in later," Kelsey said aloud, and softly shut the door. She had just realized something.

She whipped under her bed and brought out Michelle's laptop. In the email sign-in box, she typed Michelle's name. In the password box, she typed another.

"B-i-l-l-y," she whispered. "B-e-a-r."

It worked. Hundreds of unopened emails flooded the screen. The first dozen or so were from Peter. First from his personal account, and then his military account: PFC Peter Farrow. So that was his last name. Peter Farrow. She had to stop herself from clicking open the most recent. This was snooping. This was definitely snooping. And yet . . .

She typed Peter's name into the search function so that only his emails appeared. They were all there, from the very beginning of the summer, from the very first time he and Michelle had met.

The first subject line was "Here is that band I was telling you about." The second was "Saw this on the way to Wichita, thought of you." Another was "Road trip?"

Kelsey paused again.

Peter was the person who knew Michelle most recently. He was, at least, the person who Michelle wanted to know her.

Kelsey's fingertips sat on the warm laptop keys.

It wasn't just about the mysteries behind Michelle anymore.

It was the little things, too. Kelsey craved hearing her voice, the rhythm of her words, her everyday thoughts. A current ran through her, animating her hands.

She clicked the first email open. "Michelle," it read. "Peter here. From the concert. You were a great tour guide. . . ."

"Peter, I like how you said, 'Peter here,' even though your email address has your first name. Of course it's you. Who else would it be? I'm kidding. It was nice to meet you, too. I had no idea the Avett Brothers were originally a punk band. Did you follow them before? Can't say punk is my thing but . . ."

"Michelle, Peter here, again. It's me, Peter. From before? (Haha.) Punk is to me like fantasy novels are to some people. It's like the fantasy of being angry and raw and on drugs. I am none of those things, but when I listen to the Ramones, I can pretend I am while dancing around my room. . . ."

"Peter, this is Michelle, the girl who you have been previously emailing, and met once in person outside the Granada after a concert, when my middle-aged friend Emerald tried to sell you a painting of her spirit animal. I believe it was an egret. Anyway, it's me. . . ."

"Michelle: Kansas, though large, is flat and easily traversed, especially in a car. I would like to see you again and finally visit the Art Museum, preferably without the company of your friend Emerald, but if she wants to come, that's okay, too. . . ."

By the time she got through all of them, it was late. Later than late. It was early. Michelle's words leapt around her mind like exploding kernels of popcorn. She couldn't believe the emails were over. She didn't want them to be over.

The only light in the room came from the computer. Kelsey could feel her eyelids drooping. As she drifted off, a sound like a rock dropping into a pond rang out from the laptop speakers. Kelsey jumped, blinking her eyes open.

**Peter: you there???**

**Me: yep!**

She took her hair down from its bun.

His call popped up in a small window. She pressed ANSWER.

"Hello?" Kelsey said. He hadn't appeared yet, but she could hear him.

"It's late there," Peter said. "What are you doing up?"

Not a second went by. "French Impressionism," she told him, and it was mostly true.

The video loaded. Kelsey's heart stirred in her chest. Peter's grin passed through the screen and lit up the surrounding walls, and suddenly, she was wide-awake.

1/15

Michelle— I might get to talk to you before you receive this, but either way, I needed to write down this dream, so I remember it: You and I were walking in these tunnels made of brick and there were rugs on the floors and candles. It was you but not quite, louder and more loose and happy, leading me by the hand to something great that neither of us could miss. We kept getting lost in the tunnels, but for some reason it didn't matter, even though we were in a hurry. Finally, the walls opened up into a canyon with these ancient faces carved into it and there was a burst of light and color. A sunrise, but it was every-where, with no specific sun. I was overwhelmed by beauty, like, beauty beyond vision, beyond words, beyond sound. It was like my brain was giving me a gift after all the shit we have to sludge through. I didn't want to wake up.

　Yours,

　Peter


1/24

Peter,

　How are you able to remember your dreams like that? I can never remember my dreams. Not the important ones, anyways. Once, I dreamed that I had a pet monkey. I was teaching it to talk. My sister said it meant I was having trouble controlling my impulses—that I'd been having too much fun. No such thing, I told her. I drove to the Flint Hills but I couldn't find the sculpture. Bet a K-State hillbilly thought it was witchcraft and burned it. Just kidding. If I can find the time, I'll try to look for it again. School has been keeping me busy. Art History is kicking my ass to high heaven. Can I write "ass" to a member of the U.S. military? It seems bad for some reason. Anyways we're on Cubism and I got in trouble with Mrs. Wallace for asking her if I could write my essay on plastic surgery instead because they're basically the same thing. Didn't go over well . . .

xo

Michelle

## 2/3

Michelle— "Ass" is nothing. If I had a nickel every time a drill sergeant told me to do something with my ass—get off it, move it, watch it, cover someone else's, cover mine, etc.—I'd have an assload of nickels. The filthy mouths on these men and women rival that of a Scorsese film. A French unit next to us lost three yesterday. We get hit at a lot in this valley. I've gotten used to it. Stopped having such terrible dreams and shaky hands. I'm so tired at night, I pass out until the alarm goes off. Last night, I won a pair of socks and two pieces of nicotine gum in a game of blackjack, so things are looking up. (Haha.) (I had to give back the socks.) A couple of units from New Zealand stationed with us got lost, but we found them. Believe it or not, it can be difficult to understand them when they speak over their radios. It's a good thing I'm not in charge of communicating with them, because I could listen to their accents teeter-totter all day, like music, and forget to focus on what they're trying to say. They're so friendly that one of them offered to sell me a van if ever I were to travel in New Zealand. I was like, no, thank you, and he was like, you'll need a van, trust me, and I said all right, though I don't know why it has to be a van? So if you'd ever like to travel around New Zealand with me—in a van—we've got our man. I didn't mean to rhyme there. (Haha.) I'd like to go somewhere with you.

Yours,

Peter

# CHAPTER FIFTEEN

Three minutes left in the second quarter and the Lawrence Lions girls' basketball team was only up by two. Their undefeated record had them as a shoo-in for regionals, and the final regular season game against Free State High was supposed to be a cakewalk. But senior Marcy Mallman, the Lions' high scorer, sprained her ankle early in the first quarter. As the clock wound down, the Lions and the Firebirds were going point for point.

Kelsey paced by the line of dancers standing just outside the gymnasium doors. "Do you hear that?" she asked her team.

The crowd screamed in protest of a foul called on Lawrence High. When the Firebird point guard missed her free throw, their voices lifted in delight. The bellow didn't stop after the rebound, following the players up the court, goading them to score.

"They're out for blood," Gillian muttered from the front of the line.

"Totally." Kelsey paused to straighten Hannah T.'s strap.

Despite complaints from the younger dancers, Kelsey and the team had been working on this routine for seven days straight. It was darker than usual. It was powerful. It was perfect, in Kelsey's opinion. "Y'all really think they want to hear a pop song at this game?"

"No," they muttered.

"Can't hear you."

"No!"

"Pop is for pep rallies. Pop is for parents." Kelsey pointed at the gym. "We're doing this for them. If we expect the basketball team to kick ass, then we have to kick ass, too. Got it?"

Kelsey's stone face broke into a smile. "Chins up. Knees high. Here we go!"

The buzzer sounded. The players left the court. Kelsey's heart pounded. "And now, ladies and gentlemen," the announcer's voice boomed. "For your halftime entertainment, please welcome the Lions Dance Team and their rendition of 'Dance Yrself Clean.'"

They entered smiling, in step with one another, uniforms red and glistening. Kelsey stood in the center, her head held high.

She scanned the crowd for Davis, who she knew would be late. But not this late. Well, no time for that now.

The beat began, barely audible. As the volume grew louder, the dancers shifted out of their line in robotic steps, their limbs stiff, like moving dolls. The drums began to fall on top of one another, more complex, and the crowd was quiet in their seats. The dancers ended up in a staggered group in the center of the floor, joints bent and jagged, posing awkwardly, a far cry from their usual careful pirouettes and three-point turns.

Then the beat dropped, deep and electronic, slaying the dancers row by row, slack bodies falling to the floor. Seconds of silence between beats. Whispers from the crowd.

On cue, they rose together with the song, triumphant, stomping the floor like tap dancers with a vengeance, kicking, their arms slicing the air.

Kelsey was in it. She was gone. She didn't think about what the rest of her troupe was doing, because these minutes were an extension of her mind, the crowd now clapping along—they were all in a daydream she had, and was now having, in complete control.

Pace. Slide. Pace. Slide. Leap. Land. Up. Hips.

The song ended with the dancers' backs to the home team, pointing painted fingernails straight at the opposing crowd's bleachers, ponytails and buns in wrecked nests, mouths pursed and eyes flashing. Everyone, no matter what team they supported, was on their feet, cheering in approval.

The announcer had to shout to be heard over the clamor. "Wow! What a display!"

Kelsey pulled a whistle out of her uniform. Three blasts, and her team snapped straight and walked off the court.

"The Lions Dance Team, ladies and gentlemen!"

The crowd whooped again as they exited.

"What?! What?!" Ingrid shouted, a happy purple mess.

Outside the doors, next to the locker room, the two basketball teams waited to take the court again.

"That's how we do it," Kelsey said, slapping the hand of every girl on her team, hard.

Over their shoulders, she glanced at the basketball team. Two of the girls nodded, giving her a small bow.

"Badass," one of them said.

Kelsey smiled. *I know*, she resisted saying.

She retrieved her phone. A text from Davis was waiting: *Woulda loved to see you dance tonight baby but my sex appeal would have been too much for the high school basketball moms to handle.*

Kelsey texted back: *Busy with beer pong?*

You know me too well. :)

The Lions basketball team took the court, and then they took the game. The second half was a blowout.

Afterward, both the girls' and the boys' basketball teams

met the Lions Dance Team in the gymnasium lobby, letter jackets on over their jeans.

"Victory party at the Wheel?" Gillian yelled above the happy din.

A few calls of "Yeah!" and "We should call ahead, tell them to make all the pizza they have," and "Nick's house after?"

Kelsey didn't take the time to change out of her uniform. She gave a few more pats on the back and ducked out a side door to the parking lot.

Through the dark, Kelsey heard, "Where are you going, Maxfield?" Under a streetlight, she could see one of the forwards from the boys' team.

"So tired," she called back. "Tell Gil and Ingrid I'm heading home, will you?"

"Have it your way!" he said, and went back inside.

It wasn't that Kelsey didn't want to celebrate. She did, very much.

But it was morning in Afghanistan.

After she had texted Davis, her phone had buzzed again, with a Skype message from Peter. She told him she would be online in an hour.

As the car started up, she hooked up her phone to the Subaru's speakers, and selected the first track of one of Michelle's playlists, where she had found the track her team had danced to tonight. The playlist was mostly filled with bands named "The" and plural nouns. The Breeders, The Strokes, The Turtles. She didn't know if she liked the actual music, or just liked the idea of Michelle listening to it, her hair escaping the windows as she hummed along. Probably both.

At home, she opened Michelle's laptop to three missed calls from Peter, and now a fourth rang out. Kelsey let down her hair and threw a sweater over her dance team uniform before she answered, watching his face fill the screen.

"Good morning," she said.

"Good evening," he replied.

"You look chipper."

He lifted a tin mug. "Thanks to this watery Nescafé we call coffee here."

Kelsey gave him a sympathetic look. "You miss La Prima Tazza, don't you?"

"Ha! Not that chocolaty stuff you drink." That's right. Michelle and her hot chocolate. He continued, "Give me a Styrofoam cup of 7-Eleven drip and I'd be golden."

"Well, if we had one of those machines from *Willy Wonka*, I'd send you a cup."

Peter looked puzzled, his lips turning up into a confused smile. "What machines?"

"You know, the machine that takes the candy bar into the TV, then dissolves it into molecules and transfers it into the other TV?"

Peter put his hands in a prayer position. "I have a confession to make."

"What?"

"I have never seen *Willy Wonka*."

"What?!"

Peter laughed at her disbelief. Kelsey realized her mouth was wide open and she snapped it shut, blushing. "I know you don't watch much TV, but *Willy Wonka* is, like, a classic film."

"It always freaked me out. The little orange men? Come on."

They used to freak Michelle out, too. Kelsey couldn't help but feel a little smug. "They're supposed to freak you out. They scare the characters into doing the right thing."

Peter, who had been sipping his coffee, spit it out all over his lap. Between laughs, he said, "I was going to say that's the wrong way to go about it, but then again, I'm in the army, so that might be hypocritical."

As Kelsey laughed, watching him clean up, she heard a click behind her. "Kels?"

She turned around.

Gillian stood in the doorway, letter jacket over her arm. "You can't say no to pizza. . . ."

Kelsey snapped the laptop shut. But she wasn't fast enough.

"Was that—?" Gillian walked into the room, pointing at the computer. "Who was that?"

"No one," Kelsey said, which was the wrong answer. Any answer felt like the wrong answer.

"That was Michelle's boyfriend," Gillian said, her eyebrows furrowing. "The soldier."

Gillian had seen Peter the night of their party through Michelle's door. But that wasn't the problem. The problem was how guilty she looked by hiding him. Oh no.

"Yeah, but—" Kelsey began. She could feel tears coming on. She blinked them away.

"Kelsey. Calm down." Gillian's head tilted, puzzled. "Why did you end the Skype call?"

"You startled me."

Gillian's lips pursed. She didn't buy it. She was a smart girl.

"So what's up? What were you guys talking about?"

"Just Michelle stuff," Kelsey said. She gave the long sigh she gave her parents when she didn't want to talk, but with Gillian, her breath came out uneven and forced.

"That must be tough," Gillian said.

"Yeah."

"You want to talk about it?" Gillian asked.

"Not right now."

Gillian made a dismissive *hmm*. Kelsey usually told Gillian everything. But where could she start when the beginning was the end of Michelle?

"He's—he's not taking it well," Kelsey continued.

"Well, at least you all were laughing when I came in," Gillian said slowly, not meaning a word. "When did you tell him?"

Kelsey could feel the air get more still, muffling her. "I— soon, I mean, recently . . ."

"He didn't find out from the news?"

"He hasn't read it."

The details dawned on Gillian, now visible in her face, tightening it.

She had figured it out.

"He doesn't know?"

Kelsey tried to breathe through her nose. "Know what?"

"Don't play dumb. You were talking to Michelle's boyfriend."

"It's not a big deal." But Kelsey's jaw, which had started shaking, said otherwise.

Gillian took a step toward her. "Does this soldier guy not know that Michelle is gone?"

Kelsey stared at the carpet. The more she lied, the worse she looked. So she didn't lie. "No. He doesn't know."

"Does he know he's talking to you?"

A pause. "No."

Kelsey finally looked her best friend in the eyes. They were still narrowed, but just as much in question as in anger. "Why the hell would you do something like that?"

When Kelsey opened her mouth to speak, she found her throat was caught again. The tears were back. "I didn't know how to tell him," she got out. "I'm sorry. I know it's bad. But I didn't know what to say. I didn't want to make things harder on him than they already were. He's putting his life on the line, you know? And—"

Gillian shook her head, as if she couldn't bear to hear anymore.

Kelsey wanted to go further, to explain, but she knew the words would make it sound even worse. She had never stated the facts this way, not even to herself: *With Peter, I can pretend it never happened. And I like talking to him. He makes me laugh. We were having fun.*

Gillian's voice brought her back. "I know you miss Michelle, but this is crazy. You have to stop."

Kelsey sat back down at her desk, and looked up. "Of course. Yes. I will."

"Kels. You're playing with fire."

"I'm not doing it to hurt anyone," Kelsey offered.

Gillian scoffed. "Oh, yeah? How does Davis feel about that?"

Kelsey said nothing. A hardness formed inside her. It was the initial shock that ruined it. She had no time to plan for something like this, an interruption like this. "Davis has nothing to do with it. You don't understand."

"No, I really don't," she snapped.

"I'll stop." Then, at her back, Kelsey pleaded, "Please don't tell anyone."

Gillian turned, her eyes roaming around the room, trying

to process. "Yeah." She nodded, but she couldn't look at Kelsey. She didn't want to look at Kelsey. "See you Monday."

With that, Gillian slid on her jacket, and opened the door.

"See you then," Kelsey replied, but by that time, the door was closed between them.

2/10, 1:32 am
From: Maxfield, Kelsey
To: Farrow, Peter W SPC
Subject: (no subject)

Peter,

　　You are such a good person, and you deserve the truth. I'm just not sure that you would ever want to hear this truth, which is why I haven't told you yet. . . . You're probably wondering why I'm emailing you. I'm Kelsey—Michelle's sister, we met in my kitchen. And I need to tell you that

SAVE AS DRAFT?

SAVED

2/10, 1:44 am
From: Maxfield, Michelle
To: Farrow, Peter W SPC
Subject: got cut off

Oompa-Loompa, do-ba-dee-doo / A friend came over to borrow my shoes
Then I remembered we were supposed to eat pizza / Nothing rhymes with pizza
Talk to you next week?

SENDING . . .

SENT

# CHAPTER SIXTEEN

When there was nothing on TV, Kelsey and Davis used to sit on her porch in the summer, drinking AriZona iced tea, going back and forth with "It's so hot . . ." jokes. Most of them were so old-timey they barely made sense. *It's hotter than a two-dollar pistol on the Fourth of July* was a good one. *It's hotter than a pig tart in pig church* was one Davis had said that made her laugh so much that she started laughing at the fact that she was still laughing.

Tonight, Valentine's Day, they met at a table for two at one of the fancier places downtown, Kelsey in her little black dress and heels, Davis in a T-shirt that read THE DUDE ABIDES under his blazer. The waitress at the Eldridge had come around for the third time, but Kelsey still couldn't decide what she wanted. Davis sat across from her, fingers drumming next to his salad fork, or his dessert fork, or whichever fork it was.

"How about the lamb?" he asked.

"Too rich," Kelsey muttered. The smell of garlic from the kitchen was making her stomach turn. Or maybe it was anxiety. Or the fact that Gillian hadn't said one word to her for the last four days. That she'd suggested that Kelsey was being unfaithful to Davis, and even though she technically wasn't, she felt guilty. Or maybe she was guilty.

Davis smiled, clearing his throat. "All the more reason to eat them. These lambs led a good life."

He paused, waiting for laughter. He hadn't noticed she was upset.

"More time?" the waitress asked.

"Looks like it," Davis said, giving the brunette with a bow tie an apologetic wink. Kelsey rolled her eyes.

"Sorry," Kelsey said. "Sorry," she repeated to Davis when the server had left.

"No worries, baby. We've got all night," he said. "How about the gnocchi?"

"What's gnocchi? It sounds like a mythical creature."

"You don't know gnocchi? Little potato things. The turds of the potato, if you will."

"Gross." Tiny, heart-shaped confetti was scattered in gold flecks on the tablecloth. She brushed them off.

Davis stood, bending over to kiss her on the cheek, and signaled the waitress. In his most soothing voice, he declared, "Eat the potato turds. They're delicious."

"If you say so," Kelsey said, surrendering her menu.

"Plus," Davis continued, "I'm getting my degree in psychology, and in my soon-to-be-professional opinion, you are beautiful. And you need to eat some food and enjoy this fake holiday. And now . . ." He bent to kiss her on the other cheek, his scruff brushing her face. "I gotta pee."

Kelsey sat in the wake of his cologne. She was being sensitive, she knew that. But there seemed like no other way to be. Davis didn't want to hear another weepy monologue. He wanted her to relax, to "eat some food and enjoy this fake holiday."

This was Davis's mode of operation, and Kelsey wasn't about to change it now.

When she was in danger of failing all her classes junior year, he had responded to her panic by telling her not to worry, she could always get a job at McDonald's, or as a magician's assistant.

At Michelle's funeral, Davis had suggested getting away, as if grief could be cured by fresh air.

He was perpetually on the bright side. He couldn't help it. Sometimes his optimism was good for Kelsey.

But sometimes, when the dark was so vast, it was impossible to join him.

When Davis returned to his seat, Kelsey nodded along to a story about how he and his fraternity brothers broke into the backyard of the KU basketball coach, and put birdseed in the shape of a Kansas Jayhawk in the grass.

The food arrived.

"Why birdseed?" Kelsey asked, placing her napkin in her lap.

"Good question. To attract birds, of course." Davis picked up his fork and dug into his lamb. With his mouth full, he continued, "So then all these birds feed on it, and it becomes a bird shape made out of several actual birds."

"That's . . ."

"An unconventional, creative way to display school spirit?"

Kelsey took a bite of her gnocchi. The noodles had the texture of large peas.

"Which is why we should have never been arrested," Davis said.

Kelsey coughed. "Excuse me?"

Davis shrugged. "Yes, it was breaking and entering. Yes, the coach has a security system. Yes, I don't know why we didn't think of that. Then again, scouting the surveillance was not my job, that was Smitty's job, fair and square—"

Kelsey banged her fist on the table. Finally, Davis was quiet. "I can't believe you didn't tell me you were arrested!"

Heads turned from the surrounding tables.

Davis lowered his voice, and leaned toward her with a sly smile. "It wasn't a big deal. My dad called the coach, they're not pressing charges, we're all laughing about it."

What was meant to be a whisper came out as a hiss. "Of

course you're laughing about it. You laugh about everything. Why didn't you at least call me?"

Davis set down his fork.

"Would you have answered a call from the Douglas County Jail? *Hello, it's your boyfriend, I need provisions, please smuggle me a jar of peanut butter?*"

Kelsey said nothing.

"Come on. I had to use my one phone call on my lawyer!" A laugh started to escape him. "I'm just kidding. I was only there for two hours. I didn't even need a lawyer."

There he went again, to the bright side. Without her. "I meant after, Davis. After the arrest. You should have told me, like, before now."

Davis signaled the waitress. "Can we get the check?" he called to her, pointing at their table.

"Why are we getting the check?"

"Because I can see you're upset, and you don't like the gnocchi, anyway."

The waitress nodded at Davis and started to lift Kelsey's plate.

Kelsey put a hand on the waitress's wrist. "No," she snapped. "I want to stay." It felt good to snap. To push against his wall of endless charm. The waitress looked at Davis with an awkward smile, as if Kelsey's permission wasn't enough. As if Kelsey wasn't even there. She felt tiny nerves pricking all over her skin.

"All right," Davis said, returning the waitress's smile. They watched her walk away.

"So." Kelsey narrowed her eyes. "What else have you forgotten to tell me?"

Davis stifled a laugh. "What?"

"What else goes on at these frat parties? Girls must be throwing themselves at you, right?" Kelsey knew she should stop, but she couldn't. She was in a pit, alone, and she wanted to drag Davis down with her.

Davis lifted his hands. "Where are you getting this stuff?"

She kept her voice loud. "I'm curious."

"You're picking a fight."

"Tell me, then." Her chest was in knots, and she wished she could press it, smooth it, beat it all out. The liar that she was. The hypocrite. "If you're so sure, then tell me."

"I'm not going to fight with you, Kelsey," Davis said, his eyebrows raised. "Yell at me, fine. I'm sorry I didn't call you about the stupid arrest. But don't accuse me of things I haven't done."

Kelsey's stomach turned when she realized the real reason she was doing this. If Davis could admit he wasn't the perfect boyfriend, maybe she wasn't so bad herself. Her voice came out quieter this time. "You've never cheated on me?"

Davis's face didn't change. Kelsey couldn't tell if he was hiding how he really felt, or if he just didn't feel anything but disbelief to begin with.

"I've never cheated on you," he said, and that was that.

Kelsey couldn't fight anymore. And what's worse, she knew Davis was telling the truth. She was already sorry. But she wasn't going to show it. He didn't seem to need the apology. He wasn't even angry.

Kelsey shrugged and said, "Well, when you do, tell me. People tell each other these things."

They finished their food without a word. Davis reached out for her hand, and Kelsey let him hold it, limp.

When the waitress brought the check, Kelsey stood up, walked through the tables, out the door, and waited, shivering, on the sidewalk.

A few minutes later, Davis emerged from the restaurant and put her coat around her shoulders.

"What do you want to do now?" he asked.

"I think I should just go home."

They got into Davis's SUV and sat as it idled, warming up. After a moment, he asked, "Since when have you been jealous? You've never been jealous before."

"Things change," she answered.

Davis took a deep breath. "I'm sorry, Kels. I'm just not sure what I'm supposed to be sorry for."

On the ride home, she wondered if he would ever bring it up again, or if he'd just try to pretend the fight had never happened, like always. When they were a block away from her house, she looked over, trying to read his expression.

Davis's face was outlined in light from the half-moon. His mouth was straight and resting, his eyes as calm as a stranger's. She didn't know what he was thinking, and wondered if she ever would.

2/19, 12:25 pm
From: Farrow, Peter W SPC
To: Maxfield, Michelle
Subject: Last one in a while

Beautiful Michelle,

We've stopped in Galuch Valley. It is HOT HOT HOT. I live in a big tent that doesn't do much to keep the sand out. I'm like the walking crust man. There appears to be no plumbing, and hardly any food, but we have Internet. The advantages of military intelligence, I guess.

With all this Willy Wonka talk, you're making me miss American candy. As I sit here, that's what I miss most (besides you) (and my family) (and my dog). Nougat. Are you familiar with nougat? It's the cloud of chocolate nonsense that fills a 3 Musketeers bar. It's like solid but not quite. It's almost salty, too. Just the slightest hint of hazelnut. Then the contrast of chocolate shell, hiding it but hinting at its presence little by little as you bite away, peeling the softness. And putting seven sour Skittles in your mouth at once. I used to just sit on my back patio and go through a whole bag of those suckers. Salty-sweet-sour-salty-sweet-sour. I think I'm hungry. Or maybe I'm thirsty. Sorry to waste an email on candy, meant to write more but there are like ten people behind me waiting to use this computer, including Sam so he can email his dogs back home. Just joking, Sam. You can't email a dog. I think I'm hungry and delirious.

Yours,
Peter


2/20, 2:13 pm
From: Maxfield, Michelle
To: Farrow, Peter W SPC
Subject: Sexy pics (3 attachments)

Pictures of nougat attached. What did you think it was?!
Open at your own risk. . . .

xo
Michelle

# CHAPTER SEVENTEEN

Several days later Kelsey was sitting on her side of the porch, trying to keep a pile of Art History notecards from escaping into the March wind as she studied. The smell of grilled burgers hung in the air, as it often did when her father tested recipes for the restaurants' annual menu changes. Kelsey was happy to see him experimenting with portabella mushrooms for the sake of the vegetarians. It was in memory of Mitch, he told her. Meanwhile, her mother had attempted to organize the growing stacks of marked-up papers and books that now nearly hid her wild hair as she sat at her desk. "Organize" apparently meant "buy plastic bins from Target and let them sit near the stacks of papers," but at least she was trying. They were all trying, even Kelsey. Midterms were coming up.

From *Art Through the Ages*, she read, "In Cubist artwork, objects are analyzed, broken up, and reassembled in an abstracted form—instead of depicting objects from one viewpoint, the artist depicts the subject from a multitude of viewpoints to represent the subject in a greater context."

*Like looking at an ice cube that has broken on the floor,* she wrote in the margins. Looking at all angles of something three dimensional all at once.

It was nice to be at home in the afternoon.

Basketball season was over, so dance practice wouldn't resume until after spring break. She and Gillian had been carefully toeing the line between the way they used to be and the way they were, just enough to convince everyone at school that nothing was wrong.

Kelsey and Davis had exchanged conciliatory texts, then emoticons and funny pictures, because that was the way they did things, and her senior year was passing so quickly, and the work was piling on, and it was easy to forget a fight when mint-green leaves were poking through the soggy ground. And today, Peter was supposed to call. When he called, nothing else seemed as important.

Right on time, bright beeps floated from the laptop beside her. Out of habit, Kelsey wiped her eyes, then remembered she wasn't wearing makeup today. Her hair was already down, too, waving just like Michelle's in the cool, wet air.

Peter was in a gray army-issue T-shirt, the too-powerful floodlights casting definition on his chest, the tattoo on his forearm. It was night there. When he saw her, he clapped his hands together, giving her the biggest smile Kelsey had ever seen.

"Guess what?"

"You're not in your uniform," Kelsey observed.

"These are my pajamas," Peter said, dismissing them with a pluck of his sleeve. "So, I've got—"

"When do you get to wear the fancy version of your uniform, the one with the hat?"

"Privates don't get fancy uniforms, and I think you're thinking of the Marines. Anyway, I—"

"You do have a hat, though," Kelsey said, her smile growing as Peter got more and more flustered. She liked to tease him, especially since she could tell whatever news he had was good.

"Hey!" he called out. "Yes, I have a frickin' hat! But, that's not what I want to tell you."

Kelsey waited, folding her hands calmly as if to say, *I'm all ears.*

Peter looked at her, cautious, waiting for another ridiculous question. When it didn't come, he started again. "So, I just found out—"

"What is it that you wanted to tell me?" Kelsey jumped on him again before he could finish, her face innocent.

Peter couldn't help but laugh, and said, "Oh my God, forget it! Check your email."

"No, what is it? I promise I won't interrupt."

Peter made an I-give-up expression, and lifted his hands. "Check your email. That's all I'm saying."

"Okay . . ." Kelsey muttered, and brought up her browser to sign into Michelle's email.

The newest was from Peter, and the subject line read: "Fwd: Your American Airlines Itinerary."

American Airlines? Someone was flying.

Everything in Kelsey's body seemed to speed up as she clicked into the email. It was a plane ticket. For Michelle. The date was next week. The point of origin: MCI, Kansas City International Airport. The destination: CDG, Charles de Gaulle Airport, Paris, France.

She screamed, high and fast, and put a hand over her open mouth. She could hear Peter's laughter, and clicked back over to his image on the screen.

"We were given a three-day leave. Sam and another buddy and me are going to Paris. And you are, too. So, there it is."

Kelsey removed her hand from her mouth, and tried to keep her panic from showing. "How could you afford this?"

"U.S. military flies free on air force planes if we ride up top, with the cargo. Your ticket wasn't so bad, trust me. I had some money saved up."

"Peter, this is amazing, but I have school. My parents won't let me. I don't know where my passport is. I . . ."

Kelsey was shooting off excuses, all except for the most

important one: It hadn't been her dream to go to Paris, it had been Michelle's. Michelle spoke French. Michelle loved art museums. Michelle sang Edith Piaf (out of tune, of course) in the shower.

"It's only for a weekend," Peter said hopefully. Disappointment was beginning to edge in on his open face, but he didn't give up. "Come on," he said quietly.

Kelsey's heart was breaking. She had to look away, to think. Because Michelle's ghost was back again, her outline and coconut smell, made of memories she'd never have, egging her on from the empty side of the porch. *Come on*, she heard Michelle's voice echo in her head. *For me.*

Then she looked back at Peter, who was not pressuring her, just sitting in his pajamas with that faraway look in his blue eyes. "Please," he said, his smile returning as if he already knew her answer.

"Yes," Kelsey said, and the wind picked up, tossing her Art History notecards into a flock of white squares in the air, like a sign from something invisible, though she wasn't sure if it was good or bad.

"Yes!" Peter shouted. He stood up and shouted, "Yes! Yes! Yes!"

Kelsey laughed at his antics and stood to catch the notecards, which were now scattered all over the porch. "Hang on!" she called to him.

"I'm going to bed before you change your mind," she

heard him say from the computer. "Good night." The call dropped.

Kelsey had a lot to do.

Midnight rolled around, and Kelsey took her place at her parents' door. She would tell them she wanted to go on a Prospective Student weekend at KU, where she would have to stay overnight in the dorms. She would ask them at their most vulnerable and sleepy, so they wouldn't ask too many questions. She cleared her throat, so her voice would be soft and unassuming. She was wearing her old bunny slippers. It was all a part of the plan.

"Mom? Dad?" She cracked open the door.

Startled snorts from her father, and a quiet "What?" from her mother.

"Can I come in?"

Five minutes later, it was done, and her parents had gone back to sleep. Kelsey lay in her bed, her mind racing. Michelle's passport, which she'd have to use to match the name on Peter's ticket, was still in her desk drawer. She had Googled the details—the passport wouldn't have been canceled unless her family sent in a request. And as far as Kelsey knew, they hadn't. Even if she were to get questioned at the airport, she would cry and say she had taken it by accident. She would pack dark colors and high-heeled boots. She would let her eyebrows grow out. She could be Michelle— for a little while. For long enough to get there, then do the thing she was dreading. The only thing left to do was waiting for her in Paris, and though the time had finally come, the thought of it made her stomach feel like a nest of coiling snakes.

There, in person, she would tell Peter the truth.

# CHAPTER EIGHTEEN

The plane hummed to a crescendo and air began to close on Kelsey's ears. She watched the cement meadow of Kansas City International speed past her, and wiggled her toes in her boots. They were cleared for takeoff. As the ground fell, her stomach dropped with it. She clutched the armrests tight and let her neck unhook, her head lolling on the hard cushion, hoping to sleep. She wanted time to pass quickly.

"Are you going all the way to Paris, or will you stop in Toronto?" the man next to her asked.

He had a French accent behind the veil of his breath. Kelsey had forgotten the way air could get trapped in airplanes. She hadn't been on a flight since the Maxfield family trip to Costa Rica. Michelle had hated flying, and she hated sitting next to Kelsey. Every word out of her chatty mouth, her sister told her as she had put enormous headphones over her ears, was a new blanket of carbon.

"Paris," she answered the man politely, and turned back to the shrinking scenery, grateful that Peter had booked her a window seat.

Now that they were gaining altitude, the pilot's voice came on the speaker.

"Anywhere else in France?" the man asked, over the announcement, and she turned again. His eyelids drooped over black eyes and, below those, dark crescents in his skin. He had been handsome once.

"No," she said, short.

"Why do you come to Paris?"

"To visit," she replied.

"A boyfriend?"

Kelsey smiled, closemouthed, and said nothing. She tried to hide her face.

"It is a boyfriend, I can tell."

"'Allo, passengers, this is your captain speaking. My name is Rhett du Pont, and your cocaptain is Nisse Greenberg. Sunny skies over the Midwest. We are expecting a clear flight all the way from Kansas City to Toronto, and from there we should land in Paris on schedule."

As the pilot went on, the woman in the aisle seat leaned over and gave Kelsey a wry smile, her face framed in auburn waves.

"He gets loopy on Dramamine," she said. "But he can't fly without it."

"My dad has to take that, too," Kelsey said, thinking of her giant father splayed into the aisle, fast asleep, while Kelsey, Michelle, and her mother giggled at his snoring.

"But I am right," the man said, waving his hand. "She is thinking of a young man when she looks out the window."

"Sorry," the woman muttered again. "He's not usually like this. He typically just mutters to himself about the crossword puzzle."

"Of course I don't do this often! This is a special case. You must tell us about him."

Kelsey picked at the magazines in front of her, wondering how she could ever explain. *He isn't my boyfriend, but I do care about him.* She thought of how Peter had sent her a recording of himself saying something in French before she left, stumbling over the words as he read them from a dictionary, thinking she could understand them. But it hadn't really been meant for her.

"There's nothing to tell." Kelsey shrugged.

The man stage-whispered as he gestured toward the auburn-haired woman. "My wife claims she is not romantic. She pretends she is just a practical Midwestern American woman like you. But she knows, too."

The woman rolled her eyes, but she was smiling.

"Knows what?" Kelsey said, glancing at both of them.

"You're in love."

"No." She snorted. "No. I'm just . . ." She felt her eyes drift.

In love. She tried to shrug it off, but for some reason, all she could think of was Peter on-screen, strumming a chord. "I'm just seeing a friend."

"You've got quite a smile on your face for someone who is just a friend."

"Leave her alone, sweetheart," the woman said.

"It will happen in Paris," she heard the man saying to his wife. "She will have to kiss her friend in Paris, yes?" Kelsey closed her eyes, pretending not to hear.

"She's trying to rest," the woman said lightly. "Let her be."

When Kelsey awoke, the couple was fast asleep. *She will have to kiss her friend in Paris!* She ran her finger over her mouth, and tried to picture Peter's against it. It could happen, couldn't it? They would probably be quite bad at it, considering they had never kissed before. Considering Peter was expecting someone who wasn't her.

She wouldn't let him, of course. She would pull him aside and do what she had set out to do. But as she put a movie on the in-flight screen to pass the time, Kelsey noticed, for some reason, she had goose bumps.

Kelsey wandered in a daze through customs at Charles de Gaulle, her mind still at rest, replaying snatches of dialogue from one of the movies she slept to as she crossed the Atlantic. *You are, and always have been, my dream.*

Soon she was rolling her suitcase through a linoleum

tunnel, a new stamp on Michelle's passport, to the smell of bleach and the buzz of overhead lights.

The tunnel opened into the international arrival gates, and Kelsey gasped. The giant, endless archway looked like the main hall of a castle, each groove composed of infinite windows, dropping fifty feet from ceiling to floor into miles of red carpet. Thousands of people pulling suitcases streamed backward and forward, passing shops she knew but now seemed different, as she caught French and Italian and German requests for Starbucks and sandwiches.

"Michelle!" she heard a man's voice cry out, and Kelsey closed her eyes tight. This was Paris. There could be many Michelles here.

"Michelle!" she heard again, close, and she turned around.

Peter, taller than she remembered, jogged from the center of it all. He wore a tan army-issued T-shirt and fatigue pants. Before she could get out the calm, honest "hello" that she had practiced, he was hugging her so tight her feet left the ground, and he spun her around, her face in the clean scent of the crook of his shoulder, and then, without ceremony, he set her down and kissed her.

He tasted like salt and then nothing; there was only the feeling of his lips on hers. Kelsey couldn't help but start to smile. When he let go, she was speechless, too aware of everything around her to say anything, let alone a rehearsed speech.

"It's so good to see you," Peter said, his blue eyes now hitting her harder than they ever could through a screen.

"You, too," Kelsey replied.

"What is 'welcome' in French?" Peter asked her.

"It's—" Kelsey started, breathless, pretending to fiddle with her suitcase as they walked. *"Bienvenue,"* she said, grateful that she had remembered the pilot's words.

*"Bienvenue,"* he said.

# CHAPTER NINETEEN

Kelsey should have pulled away, but now it was too late. And she was in shock, listening to him talk about their plans for the evening as they strolled through the busy airport. She tried to remove the taste of him from her lips by licking them, but, of course, it just intensified.

Her body seemed to be vibrating with every beat of her heart.

Two more men in fatigues, canvas bags on their backs, greeted them at the entrance to the train into the city. She would have to break the news later, at the hotel. Now wasn't the time.

"You found her, I see," the shorter redhead said, and held out his hand. "Remember me?"

"Rooster?" Kelsey asked.

"Sam, if you don't mind, ma'am," he said, revealing freckles as he got closer.

"No, he likes Rooster better, trust me," said his companion, a lanky, bespectacled guy with caramel-colored skin.

"I do not," Sam said matter-of-factly.

The other guy rolled his eyes. "I'm Phil."

"Hello, Phil," Kelsey said, shaking hands all around.

She took a deep breath as they descended into the metro, and remembered what her parents had told her before she left for the airport, pleased that she was trying to move forward from her grief. Just try to have fun, they had said. They may have been mistaken about where she would be having fun, but Kelsey took it to heart, anyway. She had to.

She gave her biggest Midwestern smile to the severe-looking women in high heels and the old ladies with dark lipstick and the men with sculpted, curly hair who stared at the four Americans as they rode through the underbelly of the city.

She soaked in the yellowed brick and gilded block letters of each platform, just like in the movies, trying to identify the artwork on the rows of posters.

*Even the advertisements are beautiful*, she found herself telling Michelle in her mind.

*That one is Edgar Degas*, she thought, looking at the rough sketch of a woman stepping out of a tub on an ad for a museum called Musée d'Orsay. Next to it, women from a hundred years ago, lifting their dark skirts to reveal petticoats and calves. Next to that, the iconic tulle brushstrokes, her favorite of his before she even knew who he was: *The Pink Dancers, Before the Ballet.*

Peter leaned close to Kelsey, pointing at their stop on a map, and she could feel her skin getting hot under her sweater, from all the excitement, from the pressure of what she had to tell him, or maybe just from having him around, a pair of arms and eyes and boots to go with the face she had grown to know.

They emerged onto the Place de Clichy, at the edge of what Kelsey could only call a roundabout. Motorcycles, old-fashioned taxis, and tiny cars wound around a cement circle to their various branching roads and, in the center of it, a giant copper sculpture.

Even the traffic is influenced by art, she took note for her sister.

Their hotel was nearby.

Soon, everything might fall apart, and Kelsey dreaded it. Especially here. It shouldn't happen here, where it was midday, the sun at the highest point in the sky, bouncing off red awnings and wet stones and linen on tables, beneath the twisting streetlamps, and windows that opened onto narrow streets lined by balconies. . . .

"Coming?" Peter called to her from ahead, holding out his hand.

She nodded and followed the group down one avenue,

then another, then back the other way for a wrong turn, and finally to a building marked only by the number painted above the doorway.

"Okay," Peter said, glancing at the directions he had printed out. "40 Rue Nollet."

He rang the bell.

Inside, they found a steep wooden staircase and a wizened caretaker, whose tiny frame disappeared into her apron.

*"C'est ici,"* she said after four flights, pointing to a thick white wooden door.

She led them inside to find two large beds, and a window from ceiling to floor, opening to a small iron balcony.

*"Merci.* Enjoy," she said, and exited.

Phil and Sam tossed their canvas bags onto one bed and stretched, taking in the view of the city.

"One room?" Kelsey said, turning to Peter.

"Nice and cozy," Peter said, winking. Then he whispered, "Sorry. This city ain't cheap."

"That's okay," she replied.

As she watched Peter peel off his army T-shirt to don civilian clothes, she was also grateful that she wouldn't have to talk her way out of doing whatever it was that Michelle and Peter would do in a bed alone.

She was blushing. Again.

The close quarters would make it difficult to have any private conversation, though, let alone the one they were meant to have. But deep down, Kelsey was grateful to put it off.

Soon, the four of them set out on the metro to find a shop called Shakespeare and Company, at Peter's request.

Sam took some convincing as they hung on to a metal bar for balance, huddled among the passengers. "I'm not shelling out euros to see Shakespeare, no way. Can't understand that crap. Never could. Might as well pay to watch a soap opera in Spanish."

Peter laughed, his hand on Kelsey's back. "It's a book-store, Rooster. Where all the American writers used to hang out in the 1920s. Hemingway's favorite."

The street they searched for, it turned out, was right across the river from Notre Dame Cathedral. When she saw it, she drew in a breath. The cathedral was gigantic, of course, but the late-afternoon light made the small shadows just as important as the enormous towers, emphasizing the structure's tiny curves and faces and leaves. Never before had Kelsey seen a building that asked so much of those who looked at it. Every inch had been carved into something else.

Inside the bookstore, Kelsey found a quiet, hidden corner to collect her thoughts. The wet-wood smell of old books arose from all sides. She knew nothing of the history of this place, but she could feel it in the silence. She was a stranger to everyone except herself, and now that she was alone, she found she didn't care. The boys were just as in awe. The beauty of Paris had made words unnecessary.

Between the shelves, she spotted Peter, absorbed in a large book with bright images.

"Peter," she said quietly.

He looked up, and searched for the sound of her voice. When he saw her, he smiled. "Look what I found," he said.

As she approached, she noticed a leaf bud from one of the trees had gotten caught in Peter's hair. When she removed it, for some reason, she couldn't bear to toss the leaf on the floor. She pocketed it.

"Your book on Andy Warhol, the one you have in your room," he said, pointing at an image of the artist in black and white. "But in French."

Michelle's book. Kelsey had paged through it a few times, when Ian had told her to look him up, and when she was composing her first letter to Peter.

"Tell me what it says," he said, his mouth lifting at the corners hopefully, his eyes washing over her.

Kelsey's mouth went dry, and she looked at the pages full of random syllables, which might as well have been completely blank.

"It says . . ." she said, letting out nervous laughter. Her game was up. The words came out of her, clumsy. "It gives his birth date and says he was a great artist, that his work is not snobby or hard to understand."

"Is that really what it says?" he asked, his eyes narrowing, playful.

Kelsey's hands were in fists in the pockets of her jacket. She met his eyes. Maybe now was the time. She swallowed, trying not to let her voice shake. "No," she said. "I'm bullshitting you."

Peter closed the book, and replaced it on the shelf. "I'm sure it's close enough," he replied. He took her in his arms, her cheek to his chest, and she could feel his voice come through his body and into hers. "Right now, you could tell me the sky was green and I'd believe you."

Kelsey slipped out of his embrace, pretending to browse, trying to resist the look on his face, the look that said he wanted to kiss her again. "But the sky's not green. And that's not what the book says. That's not the truth."

From behind her, Peter said quietly, "I like anything that comes from you. That's truth enough for me."

Kelsey hid a smile, but she wasn't sure who she was hiding it from anymore. She let him take her hand and lead her through the shelves, where Sam and Phil waited for them outside.

They took the train home.

After catching the sandwich shop down the street from their hotel before it closed, they had a dinner of ham and cheese on baguette near the square, in a jet-lagged haze, watching the passersby.

They bought a bottle of wine at a corner store and brought it back to their hotel room, where they drank out of paper cups and played blackjack until the three soldiers on Afghanistan time were exhausted.

Peter and his friends reminded her of long, jokey nights with Davis, watching him and his fraternity brothers shoot guns on the screen of a video game. Unlike the boys with her now, after they turned off the TV, they were done. Every time she thought of Davis, she sighed. Yet another reason why she shouldn't be in Paris, let alone kissing another guy in Paris. She had told him she was having a "phones off" sorry-I'm-such-a-bad-friend weekend with Gillian and Ingrid, which is where she should be, really, all things considered. But it's not like she would have felt better, or less sad, or more like herself if she were at home. She was trying her best just to be there. And, well, being there wasn't hard.

Kelsey was still wide-awake, but she got into her pajamas anyway, suddenly self-conscious enough to wait until Sam was done using the bathroom. Normally, she would have tossed her shirt aside, no matter the company. Kelsey and her body were one, and she wasn't ashamed or scared of revealing it.

But this wasn't Davis, who had seen and touched pretty much everything. This wasn't an audience of hundreds of anonymous faces, watching her writhe around in a costume. This was Peter, who cared so deeply about the little things. Who opened his heart to her.

Judging by how moved he was by a song or a circle in the middle of a Kansas prairie, her bare back might just send him reeling.

When she came out of the bathroom in a T-shirt and shorts, Sam and Phil were already snoring. One lamp, beside the bed, remained lit.

Peter approached her in his boxers, and put his hands on her waist, tucking his fingers under the hem of her shirt. He was so close she could see the blonde hairs on his skin. Maybe he wasn't as prudish as she thought.

Kelsey seized up.

He must have sensed she was feeling shy, so he took a step back.

He kissed her on the cheek, and turned to switch off the lamp. Kelsey took the opportunity to jump into bed, under the covers, her face toward the wall. Her cheek was burning.

"Hey," he whispered as he lay beside her. "Today was crazy."

"It was," she said, swallowing.

"Tomorrow will be great," he said, shifting his weight closer.

"Mm-hmm" was all Kelsey could get out.

"Good night."

"Good night."

She waited for the sound of Peter's deep breathing to breathe herself, silently begging the universe over and over, for what she wasn't sure. For a lot of things. For everything to be okay. For Michelle, wherever she was. And for the kind soldier beside her to be all right.

Above all, for that.

As far away as it seemed right then, the thought of Peter safe and happy granted Kelsey peace, and she fell asleep.

# CHAPTER TWENTY

Iron beam after iron beam fell past Kelsey's eyes, and between the lattice, Paris grew smaller and the sky grew bigger. As the Seine River lengthened, the green of Champ de Mars unrolled in a graceful U shape. Her stomach flopped. They were getting higher. Peter held her hand tight, catching her eyes, laughing at the absurdity of a dozen nations squawking together in one elevator.

"The sound people make when they're traveling up the Eiffel Tower is the same in every language, isn't it?" he whispered.

"You mean, ooh and aah?" she replied.

"Exactly."

"Except not here. Here they say, Ooh la la."

Peter cringed. "Bad. You are good at bad, bad jokes."

"No, here they say: Who gives a merde about the Eiffel Tower, I am so cool, I am from Paris."

"Merde? Is that shit?"

Kelsey was using her limited French to her full advantage. "*Oui*. As in: Western Kansas smells like merde, because of the hog farms."

Peter gave her a shove. "Do not knock my place of origin. And that's Emporia with the hog farms, not El Dorado."

"Why are we talking about hog farms right now, of all times?"

"A valid point. I feel like we should be reciting poetry."

"Roses are red, violets are—"

"Anything but that."

They laughed.

Kelsey hadn't let go of Peter's hand the whole way up.

It was a windy, cool afternoon in early spring, and that morning the four of them had walked down the Champs-Élysées as the sun broke the clouds. Even the Parisians were loose and talkative in the metro, smiling below dark sunglasses.

Everyone seemed to have forgotten their troubles, and Kelsey was powerless against the pull of an entire city. She was distracted. Love this, everything seemed to say, in the haughty way a girl like her might flaunt her own good looks. How can you not love this?

Peter let go of her hand briefly, to point out the pyramid shape of the main entrance of the Louvre in the distance, then took it again, squeezing.

He was lighter than she had ever seen him. He didn't have anything to shove away, to swallow, to pretend wasn't happening. That morning, they had watched Phil and Sam do one hundred push-ups each, but Peter had cheerfully refused. "Unless someone is going to yell in my face about it, I don't feel the need." On their way to the tower, Peter had made dirty jokes about the nude statues that lined the park hedges, including one that made Kelsey spit out her latte on the manicured gravel.

The elevator continued to rise, away from Peter's friends, who were now somewhere near Notre Dame Cathedral.

Kelsey realized how long she and Peter had been alone.

As the city blocks began to blur together into one vast carpet, her resolve crept back.

*Peter, I'm not who you think I am. I am, but I'm not.* Kelsey felt her eyes squint. This was going to be terrible.

At the top, the wind blew stronger and the iron creaked, sending a group of Italian tourists into shrieks.

Kelsey buttoned up her trench coat and Peter pulled her to him, kissing her lightly on the forehead as they stared out across the city, entwined.

*Peter, this may come as a shock. But I am not Michelle. I do care about you, though, which is why I am here.*

No matter what would happen between them, they were the only two people there who knew each other in that particular way, so far from home. She couldn't imagine keeping a secret from him. This should be her chance to make every-thing right. This was her chance.

She stepped back, putting a hand on each of his arms, their solidness now shivering under his cotton sweater.

"Should have brought my jacket," he said, and they were both quiet.

"Peter—" Kelsey started.

Just then, a man—whose red tracksuit mirrored the woman beside him—tapped Peter on the shoulder. "Excuse me." His accent sounded Eastern European. "Photo, please?" He gestured at himself and his wife, then at the sweeping landscape.

Peter looked at Kelsey, raising his eyebrows. "Sure," he said. "Long shot or close-up?"

"Sorry?" the woman responded, flipping her dark lenses up to reveal regular glasses underneath.

"Never mind," Peter said, glancing at Kelsey again, close to laughter. He was having fun. They were both having fun.

This was a terrible thing she had to do.

Kelsey smiled stiffly and folded her arms, trying to keep her courage.

The blonde couple held each other and posed, their cheeks rosy from the chill, hands united at their waists. They had probably been married for decades, pounds and wrinkles away from their youth, further and further from the moment they met but always in love, until the end.

But that had nothing to do with Kelsey.

She bit her lip, trying to wet her cotton mouth, to still her nerves.

Peter snapped a couple of photos and returned to her, the faraway look in his eyes now justified, in sight of the shadowed bottoms of clouds over the rusted railing.

Kelsey took in a breath to begin, but he turned suddenly, to speak first.

"I'm so glad you came, Michelle. I'm glad we're here. . . ." He put his arm around her. "Taking pictures of portly Austrians."

Kelsey tried to keep her voice steady. "Yeah?"

He turned his head close to hers, speaking into her hair, prickling her neck. "I'm serious. You know I'm serious."

She turned her head, still in his arms, and they were facing each other, inches apart.

"Every time I read your letters, I'm going to come back here. I read them and I hear you speaking. Especially now that I can hear you in person. Your voice sounds like it does in my head. Which is a weird thing to say."

Kelsey looked away, overwhelmed.

"Really," Peter continued, shrugging. "These past few months of being apart, it's like, now we know each other better. You've become more real to me through your letters, I think. Or more open or something. I—" He paused, smiled. He was nervous. "I've begun to fall for you pretty hard. I don't know how I could go back without the thought of you waiting for me when I come home."

She had heard Peter say something like this before, but now she saw in his eyes that he meant it, felt it in his arms.

He kissed her on the forehead. "And seeing you now, well, this is just a bonus."

Kelsey put her head on his chest, everything blank. If she told Peter now, his heart would break. He would return ruined. Her mind was static, the scenery as flat as a post-card. Nothing was three-dimensional except for her body, pulsing in her coat, and the boy that held her, both of them wrapped in a lie. A nice, warm lie.

No, now wasn't the time.

It couldn't be the time, because Kelsey couldn't think. She could only feel, and what she felt was—well, lips.

Because he was kissing her again, but the message that she should pull back hadn't traveled from her brain to her hands. She sent it again, but it didn't arrive, or her hands weren't listening.

And he kissed her again.

And again.

# CHAPTER TWENTY-ONE

That evening, Kelsey, Peter, Sam, and Phil found themselves in a tiny bar just a few blocks from their hotel on Rue Nollet. The walls were pasted over with photos and graffiti, fragments of concert posters, and different layers of paint. The ceilings sagged under wooden arches. The only new items in the place were the candles on every table—tall, sleek, red—and the young patrons, as tall and sleek as the candles.

Kelsey watched as Peter and Phil flipped through selections on the old-fashioned jukebox from the other side of the room.

"Parisian women," Sam muttered beside her, taking a seat at their table as he sipped his beer. He shook his head, staring at a lithe blonde in a flowing dress who leaned against the bar, radiating effortless cool.

"It must be something in the water," Kelsey replied.

Sam pointed to the bottle she had ordered. "Or the champagne."

Kelsey poured herself a glass. "If you can't beat 'em, join 'em," she said. She took a large swig and coughed on the carbonation. She was all mixed up.

"So you're an artist," Sam said. He had an intimidating, steady gaze under strawberry-blonde eyebrows. He was wearing a Metallica T-shirt and New Balance tennis shoes, both unapologetically white. Kelsey wondered what he had seen over there. More than Peter, it seemed.

"Sort of," Kelsey said. She was tired. She had walked several miles that day, reveling in the sight of every cobbled street corner, asking art history questions of the tour guide in the echoey corridors of the Musée d'Orsay, trying to speak to an accordion player in the Marais in fake, butchered French.

But the exhaustion was just as sweet as it was bitter. No matter who she was, she had been changed by the city, by the art, by Peter. And already it was their last night.

"What kind of art do you make?" Sam asked.

"All kinds," Kelsey said. *And that's not a full-out lie*, she assured herself, thinking of her conversation with Ian so long ago. *Dancers are artists, too.*

"Peter showed me one of your paintings," Sam said, interrupting her thoughts.

"Oh, yeah?" Kelsey said curtly, in between sips of champagne. "Which one?"

He tilted his head, confused. "The only one. The one you gave him before he left, he said. I'm no art critic, but it's good."

Kelsey had no idea what he was talking about, of course. She didn't know which painting Michelle had given Peter. She looked over Sam's shoulder for Peter and Phil, who appeared to have found a fellow American near the jukebox.

"Thank you," she said, trying to keep her voice low.

Maybe she could turn the conversation away from herself. Away from Michelle.

"What about you? What do you do as a civilian?" she asked him.

"I breed dogs with my brother."

"That's cool." *Must be nice*, Kelsey thought. *Must be nice to be able to answer who you are in one sentence.*

They sipped from their glasses in silence. Across the room, Peter and Phil high-fived each other, laughing.

Something worked behind Sam's gaze that made her uneasy. He didn't have the usual nervous politeness of a stranger.

"I have to be extra careful in my business, buying and selling beagles," he began. "I only buy certain lines of heritage, and I pay a lot for them. People try to pass off common beagles for rare breeds, but there are ways to tell. Markings. Affinity for the hunt." He leaned closer to her. "I can also tell when a person is trying to sell me bullshit. Their body language. Their eyes."

Kelsey said nothing.

"You have any brothers or sisters?" he asked, as innocent as can be.

Kelsey choked on the champagne she was drinking.

When she recovered, she took a minute to answer, staring absently at the crowd. "A sister," she finally said. "My twin."

"What's her name?"

"Kelsey," she answered quietly.

"Kelsey," he repeated.

"Yes," she said, her fist tightening around her glass.

"You know what? I knew that. Peter told me that. I saw a picture of you."

"Of me?"

"Of you and your sister. Or maybe it was just you. Which one was it?"

The snakes were back in Kelsey's stomach, winding their way around. "What do you mean which one?"

"Which picture did you give Peter?" When she didn't answer, her throat frozen tight, he kept going. "Which painting does Peter have?" His voice was louder now, and he picked up the candle sitting beside them. "Peter said you spoke French. What is 'candle' in French?"

Kelsey couldn't move from her position, her eyes wide. He knew. He could tell, somehow. Slowly, she turned her gaze to Peter. Still occupied. Still happy. Out of range.

Sam leaned closer, following her eyes to Peter across the room. "I don't know what game you're playing," he said. "But you should leave him out of it."

Kelsey sighed, looking around to make sure no one could hear. Sam knew she was lying. She might as well explain herself. "Peter is the only reason I'm playing in the first place."

They looked at each other, best friend and alleged girlfriend, and finally, in a trickle to a flow, Kelsey poured it all out. Every detail she had held in for so long. The day Michelle died. Her trip to the Army Recruiter's office. The first Skype call. The letters. She told him the whole myth of Michelle, explaining that if it fell apart, then the only person who still believed in that myth would also be destroyed.

Sam sat quietly with his empty beer glass, absorbing Kelsey's confession. Then he spoke. "Well, first of all, I don't think Peter's the only person who still believes in her. You do, too. That much is clear."

Kelsey nodded, staring at the floor. She felt drained. Dry. She looked up at him. "Please don't tell Peter. Not yet."

"I won't," he said, his brow furrowed. "It's not my crazy, insane, totally nutso secret to tell."

Kelsey smiled, half relieved. "Thank you. Really, thank you."

Sam stood up. "But it is yours to tell." He bobbed his head toward Peter. "And he deserves the truth."

"You're right." There was no doubt about that. That part

was easy, to agree to it, to say it. To do it was the tough thing. And she would. Perhaps after another glass of champagne.

"Now, pardon me, ma'am, but . . ." He began to drift away, squeezing through the tables. "After that, I need another beer."

As Sam left, Peter and Phil made their way over to their corner.

Phil pointed toward the jukebox, tipsy. "That guy's from Kansas! I've never been to Kansas but what are the odds?"

Peter, beside him, pointed in the air, his eyes sparkling. "Listen," he said.

Kelsey recognized the song from Michelle's playlists. It was "Baby" by the Cicadas, the same band Peter had sang for her over Skype the day he received his guitar. The twanging sounded over a slow bossa nova beat, the lyrics in buttery Portuguese.

Peter took her hand. "Will you dance with me?"

Kelsey stood up, and led him to a space near the jukebox, ignoring Sam's pointed looks as he loitered near the bar.

She needed not to care so much, just for a moment. She was also tipsy, and Peter was so handsome, and they didn't have much time left of being a regular guy with a regular girl, dancing in a bar across the ocean. She put one of his hands around her waist as they swayed, and took the other, letting him twirl her.

He laughed in surprise at her assured movements, and

soon he couldn't take his eyes off her. She smiled back at him, letting everything else melt away.

Peter had asked Kelsey the only question she would always have the answer to. Wherever she was, whoever she was, no matter how much she had messed up, the answer was the same. Yes, she would dance. She would always dance.

The next day, the four of them stood in the airport, where they had met just thirty-six hours earlier. Kelsey had never seen time pass so quickly. That morning, at the break of dawn, the three soldiers had changed into their fatigues and taken turns in the bathroom with an electric buzzer, slicing centimeters of hair back down to regulation length.

Their gates were on opposite ends of the terminal, and as they watched the departures screen, the flight to Kansas City via London began to flash. Kelsey's plane had started boarding.

It was time to go.

Phil gave her a quick hug with his gangly arms, then retreated to a bench.

Sam shook Kelsey's hand. Then he leaned closer and said, "I know you don't mean any harm, but you know what you have to do. Bye, now. We'll meet again."

"I know," Kelsey said, trying to put on a firm smile. "Bye, Sam."

Finally, they were alone. Peter had been silent and sullen since they woke up, and now was no different. He gave her a sad smile, glancing anxiously at the screen. If she wanted to tell him in person, it would be now, or never.

She braced herself, and let go of his hands.

"I have something to tell you, but I haven't been able to figure out how to say it."

In response, he put his hands on either side of her face, and tilted her head toward his. Then he kissed her, longer and slower than he had ever kissed her before.

"I have something to tell you, too, but I don't have the time," he said, his mouth next to her neck, sending shivers through her body. "When I get home from Afghanistan, we'll have all the time we want. We'll have a surplus of time. We'll have so much time, we'll forget we were ever apart. I'll drive you around and we'll say everything we want to say. Because—yeah. I have so, so much that I want to say to you."

Kelsey hadn't allowed herself to picture such a fiction, the two of them in Kansas, in the summer, free to do what they wanted. What Peter saw was never going to happen, and for some reason, that part of the truth made her saddest. She couldn't bear to face it. At that moment, it wasn't nerves stopping her, it was the fear of destroying what they had made. The time they had spent together hadn't been completely right, but they had spent it all the same.

She squeezed his hands, kissing them briefly as she brought them down from her face.

"Good-bye," she said, and tried not to look at him as she turned to walk away.

When she gave the flight attendant her boarding pass, she was surprised to find tears had been running down her cheeks, quiet, unhindered, and they didn't stop when she took her seat at the window, gazing out at the horizon, toward where Peter would be, until clouds spilled out from under the plane.

# CHAPTER TWENTY-TWO

Exactly three days had passed since Kelsey had driven home from the airport, walked across her lawn, through her front door, past her parents, and up into her room to shut the door. Except for intermittent trips to the kitchen, the door had remained shut. Her phone remained off. School was on break, therefore Kelsey had no reason to leave her cocoon of blankets, pillows, and disgustingly rich housewives making fools of themselves on national television.

What was the use of bringing herself out into a universe of more confusion? She had been sucking up the air for seventeen years, and in that time, she had managed to lose a sister and a best friend, and she was on the brink of losing the only person who made her feel like all of it would be all right.

No need to change out of her tank top and sweatpants, which were beginning to smell like barbecue potato chips.

No need to expose herself to the outside world. Seventeen years was enough.

She emerged from her room on the lookout for her parents. They were downstairs. She crossed into Michelle's room and opened the closet, reaching to the top shelf, beyond the notebooks and markers and brushes, until her fingers brushed the box.

Michelle's secret stash: Marlboro 27s and a unicorn lighter. Probably stale by now, but Kelsey was glad her mother hadn't found them.

Kelsey rarely had a cigarette, but when Michelle was feeling down after a breakup, Kelsey had accompanied her to their porch to watch her blow out smoke and cry. Most of the time, especially as they got older, she had only come outside to judge her sister. To tell her she was asking for it, falling in and out of love so quickly. That she shouldn't smoke, that she was killing herself.

Now Kelsey was opening the screen door to light one up, Michelle gone.

She had always said it helped her calm down.

*It helps me think.*

The memory of Michelle, diffused in the misty afternoon smoke, joined her.

*I can't do it.*

She had gone halfway across the world to tell Peter that Michelle was dead, but she couldn't do it. She couldn't bear to tear him up, but it was more than that. She could have sat him down at the airport, and let the facts do their job. But she didn't.

*I just don't want it to be true.*

That was it. The myth would be over. Michelle would be over. She stared at the smoke as it curled around her hand, down through the rungs on her sister's porch. She thought of all the conversations they had here, and then she realized: Michelle didn't have to die again.

Kelsey may not have had the courage to tell Peter the truth, but lord knows she had spent enough time on this very porch, listening to Michelle fall out of love. If Kelsey couldn't push Peter away, then Michelle could. She would tell him she had met someone else: a fry cook at Burger Stand. A DJ at the Taproom. She would hang up on him, refuse to write him, whatever it took. She would make him angry, which would force him to do something she could never do: move on.

When she flicked the finished Marlboro over the wooden railing, she returned inside through her side of the porch, spraying herself with Chloe perfume to hide the smell.

She grabbed Michelle's laptop from under the bed, slipped on a jacket, and put her bare feet into her boots.

"Where are you off to?" her mother called as she passed her in the living room.

"Fresh air," Kelsey replied.

She walked the two blocks to Central Park, named haphazardly by the city of Lawrence after the park in New York City, but twenty times less its size. When she arrived, she sat on a bench near the community center, where she could pick up Wi-Fi, and opened the laptop. There she waited, hoping the battery would keep until Peter saw her online. He had told her on their last night in Paris that he was supposed to return from a mission today.

When his Skype icon turned green, Kelsey wasted no time.

"Hi, Peter," she said when he answered her call. His video was still loading. "Are you there?"

"I'm here," he replied, but when his image appeared, he didn't look like the Peter she knew in Paris. Dark circles had returned to his eyes, which were bloodshot, the clear blue clouded over.

"What's wrong?"

"Can't tell you," he said, his voice hoarse.

"You have to tell me," Kelsey said, swallowing. She was finding it difficult to be as numb as she had been determined to be. She was finding it difficult not to cry herself at the sight of his distress. He had become her best friend after all.

Peter looked behind him, making sure no one had followed. Then he grabbed a notebook and pen, scribbled something on the paper, paused, and scribbled more.

*Our company lost 2 men on the way back from a mission,*

the paper read, and when Kelsey saw the name written underneath, she held a hand to her head, pulling her hair until it hurt.

*Sam.*

"No."

Peter nodded. He looked away to compose himself.

"I'm so sorry," she said, but she knew it wasn't enough.

She wished she could tell him she knew how it felt to lose someone so close, and nothing anyone says can change the stripped, punched-in-the-gut feeling. She was stabbed by guilt, knowing Sam had died keeping her secret.

"His truck hit a mine," Peter said, his voice low. "Right in front of ours."

At that, he put his head in his hands, and let out a string of curses. Words she had never heard Peter use before, unintelligible, a broken language.

"Hey," she said gently.

He looked up. "He wasn't my best friend, but he was a good man. A better soldier than me, that's for sure. We were partners, you know? He had my back, I had his." Peter looked around again, twitching at the sound of a door closing. No one interrupted, so he continued, breathing through his nostrils, trying to calm himself. "I met his mother at the airport in Maine. What is she going to do now?"

"Oh, Peter."

Before she realized what she was doing, Kelsey was

touching the screen, brushing her fingers on his shoulders, his hands, as if he could feel her.

She lost all desire to push him away. She wished she was next to him again, as she had wished so many times since she had left him in Paris, and now, he needed a friend more than ever. He needed her. And unless she intended to mope in her room for the foreseeable future, she needed him, too.

Peter looked up, noticed her hand on the screen, and put his fingers where hers might be. After that, he simply stared at her, his shoulders straight again, his mouth hard.

Kelsey grew nervous. She was suddenly aware of her unwashed hair and potato chip–stained shirt.

"I have a lot of . . . feelings for you," Peter said, and he paused, embarrassed. "And I'm sorry it took me this long to tell you. I thought I loved you from the moment I met you, but I wasn't sure. I was worried when I went overseas. But after seeing you in Paris . . . the way you were. The way we were together. Your, you know, your terrible jokes. When we were at Notre Dame, the way you looked at the building, like it was the first time anybody had ever seen it. When we danced at the bar. Sorry, I'm thinking out loud here. But I know. I know now."

He paused.

"I love you."

As she listened, Kelsey realized he was talking about her. He wasn't talking about Michelle, or the combination of the two of them she had made, he was talking about Kelsey. Kelsey dancing, Kelsey telling bad jokes, Kelsey as he knew her, and, for the past five months, as she knew herself.

Peter waited, poised, and the fact that he could have been taken with Sam, taken at any moment, sank into the quiet.

She heard herself say it before she knew the words were out. "I love you, too."

Immediately, she realized it was true.

And she knew she would have to do what she set out to do, but she would have to do it as herself.

She would have to let go of Michelle for good, and she would have to trust that their love could survive it.

# CHAPTER TWENTY-THREE

Kelsey, on her way through the University of Kansas campus, was trying not to skip. She passed students on the narrow sidewalk, grass now erupting on either side of the cement, though she could still see her breath in the air. Kansas weather had a reputation for being a bit schizophrenic. Kelsey fit right in.

She caught the students' eyes, smiling at engineering majors bent under their backpacks, nodding hello to the football players who loitered outside the union, gliding past gaggles of bleached-blonde girls who shivered in short skirts, desperate for the state's first bit of sun.

They all stared back. Maybe they were curious about the spring in Kelsey's step, her unfettered air of joy, or maybe they were just looking at her pajamas. It was the day after she had spoken to Peter, but Kelsey still hadn't changed out of her barbecue dust–streaked tank top and sweatpants.

She didn't care. She was in love.

Kelsey climbed the streets of Mount Oread to Delta Sigma, where Davis was waiting for her on the front porch, comfortably lounging in a wicker chair between the white columns, like an old Southern gentleman.

As she approached him on the green lawn, Kelsey took a moment to appreciate his long, thin legs splayed out, wearing loafers and no socks, eyes behind Ray-Bans. He took a hand from around a bottle of Gatorade to wave.

She would miss him.

"I thought you'd never come," he said, enfolding her in a hug and kissing the top of her head. "I thought you might have gone to Boca Raton by now, dancing on tables with your girlfriends."

Kelsey let out a "ha!" at the ridiculous image. "I wouldn't get on top of a table right now if somebody paid me."

"Oh, you," Davis said as they sat down on the porch steps. "Still on your parents' dime. Fraternity dues are expensive. Baby, I'd grind on a church altar if someone paid me."

Kelsey rolled her eyes. "No one would pay you to grind on anything."

Davis laughed, draining the last of his drink. They sat in familiar silence, except for the distant sound of two of Davis's frat brothers screaming at each other about a video game. On the lawn of a neighboring frat, two guys in pinnies threw a Frisbee back and forth, trying to avoid beer cans scattered everywhere. What a cartoon world.

What a foreign, flat world, even compared to the simplest of exchanges with Peter through a screen. Kelsey smiled to herself. The thought of Peter made her feel strong, free. She took a deep breath, and blew it out, fortifying herself.

"So," Davis said, nudging her shoulder with his. "What's it going to be?"

Kelsey looked at him, taking in the square-jawed face she had been kissing and yelling at and talking to for the past three years. They had barely spoken in several weeks, and now, there was a wall between them. They both knew what was about to happen, but to soften the blow, she said, "What do you mean?"

Davis's jaw clenched. "C'mon, Kels. Your text said, 'We need to talk.'"

"Yeah," she said, looking at her nails. "We do."

"So, talk," Davis said, and for the first time in a while, Kelsey saw hurt cross his face.

Her chest tightened. "I think I've changed. And you've changed."

"I think you're mistaken," Davis said. "I'm still the same person. I'm a pretty simple guy. The guy who loves you and supports you."

"Well, we've changed, then. The way you and I are," Kelsey said, putting a hand on his knee. It stiffened underneath her hand.

"I'm not going to deny that," he said, pushing his sunglasses up his nose.

"We've drifted apart."

Davis shrugged. "A few miles, across the city."

"I'm serious."

"So am I," Davis said, and tipped back the bottle, though it was now empty. He shook it. "You don't think I can be serious, but I can."

Kelsey could feel herself grimace. Someone from inside the frat house had started playing a rap song. The bass bumped, vibrating the wood beneath them.

"You're pushing me away," Davis said. "You've been pushing me away since Michelle died."

Kelsey said nothing, knowing it was true. He rarely spoke so plainly. He had been thinking about the two of them, just as she had.

"I'm sorry it has to be like this," she said.

"But it doesn't!" he said, laughing but angry, incredulous. "We've grown together before. We've gone through stuff. We were kids when we met."

Kelsey almost smiled, the memory swelling inside her. "You had just gotten your braces off," she said quietly. "Everyone thought you were so hot and cool and funny. And I was the one to get you. I was so proud."

He stood up. "I'm still proud."

Kelsey stood with him. "Davis—" she began.

"So it's over?" he said quickly, stretching, trying to be as casual as he could be, though his jaw was still tight.

Kelsey nodded. "It's over."

Davis forced himself to smile down on her. "For now." Then he clapped his hands, rubbing them together, like he did before a game or a night out.

Kelsey couldn't help but smile, shaking her head. Always on the bright side. In her mind, there was no "for now." Their relationship was over for good. But she would be losing a dear friend, too, and hoped she hadn't lost him forever.

Before she got to the street, Kelsey paused, and turned back to Davis.

"Are you going to be okay?" she called from across the lawn.

"Me?" he called, picking up the empty bottle. "I'll be fine. I'm not the one wearing my pajamas."

Kelsey looked down at herself, then back to her ex-boyfriend.

"It's a long story," she said, and before she could reconsider the solemn, handsome figure on the porch, she let a new beginning tug her away.

# CHAPTER TWENTY-FOUR

The next afternoon, the first day back from spring break, Kelsey sat in the far corner of the Lawrence High cafeteria, her tray of spaghetti ignored, unwrapping a 3 Musketeers bar. First she bit into the end, to snap off the chocolate casing. Then a bite from the top, and the bottom. She watched the nougat reveal itself, as Peter had put it. The chocolate nonsense.

"Sugar is bad for you," she heard a voice say. She looked up.

Above her, Ingrid stood, jean jacket unbuttoned over her purple dress, her golden hair curling more than usual in the moist chill.

"But chocolate is good for your emotional well-being," Kelsey said, and held the half-eaten candy bar out to her friend.

Kelsey hadn't had more than a couple minutes alone with Ingrid since the iciness between Gillian and her began.

Ingrid took the candy bar and tore off a big chunk with her teeth. Kelsey smiled.

She handed it back. "Speaking of no sugar, how's rehearsing for Rock Chalk Dancer auditions?"

"Oh, geez. I haven't—I haven't thought about that for a while," Kelsey said, feeling her brow furrow at the reminder. "Want to sit together?"

Kelsey motioned for her to join, but Ingrid jerked her head toward the window, where the three of them used to sit.

Kelsey stood with her tray and followed, cautiously. She had avoided their usual table near the window since she and Gillian had begun to fight. And even before that, right after she had returned to school, she had made excuses to be alone during lunch.

"Just for the heck of it, huh? For old times' sake?" Ingrid said as they plopped down across from each other. They used to have competitions to see who could speak the longest in British accents. Ingrid always lost. Gillian used to teach the two of them Korean swearwords, which they delighted in shouting over the din without getting in trouble.

The spring sun shone warmly on the courtyard, through the glass, and Kelsey couldn't help but burst out laughing as Ingrid, after finishing another mouthful of candy bar, began to chug an entire carton of milk.

"Thatta girl," Kelsey said. "You can have mine, too."

Ingrid finished, swallowed, and let out a small burp. "So," she said. "I heard that you and Davis broke up."

"Yea." Kelsey furrowed her brow. "It was a long time coming, actually."

Ingrid dug into her lunch, still looking at Kelsey with her puppy-dog eyes as she slurped spaghetti. "Why?" she asked.

"Why? Um . . ." Kelsey stalled, poking at her food.

Ingrid always had a way of cutting to the chase. When they were freshmen, she asked the Sex Ed teacher what the difference was between a banana, on which she was putting a condom, and "the real thing." Gillian, who had also been in the class, answered, "Bananas aren't attached to morons." They had been best friends ever since.

Ingrid swallowed a mouthful of noodles. "You seemed happy."

Kelsey felt her throat tighten. She thought of lazy days on the front porch with Davis, bullshitting for hours. "Yeah, we were, weren't we?"

"I liked his T-shirts."

"Me, too," Kelsey replied. But Davis didn't strike her with anything other than friendly nostalgia now. Now her thoughts, her heart, her future: All of it was Peter. "I can't believe we spent three years together," she muttered, almost to herself.

"Do you wish you hadn't?" Ingrid asked.

Kelsey folded her arms. She wasn't ready to think

about all this. She bit into her candy bar and said, "I don't know."

"You were both just kids," Ingrid said, thoughtful. "I mean, I think we'll always look back and wonder what the heck we were thinking. No use trying to justify it."

Kelsey looked in surprise at Ingrid. She was rarely so reflective.

"That's what my mom tells me, anyway," she continued. "She tells me I better get all my stupid out now, because soon I won't be so cute, and no one will forgive me."

"I can't decide if that's really wise, or kind of mean," Kelsey said, trying not to laugh.

Ingrid smiled. "Well, you know best. It's love, you know? If you are, you are. If you aren't, you aren't."

Kelsey uncrossed her arms, leaning forward. Finally, the word she had been looking for. The word that wove through everything and injected her with a good kind of poison, the kind that sent soda through her veins, that made everything else a blur. She was dying to tell someone about Paris, how the simplest things like traffic lights and water fountains reminded her of its beauty. Maybe Ingrid would understand.

"That's the thing, Ingrid, I am in love, but not—"

Suddenly, a bang. Kelsey and Ingrid jumped. Gillian dropped her tray next to Ingrid's, an apple held in her teeth, her eyes cold.

"Oh, um—" Ingrid looked at the two of them in turn,

pasting on a smile, as if she was about to introduce them to each other.

Gillian removed the apple and matched Ingrid's blank smile. "Hello, Kelsey! Where have you been?"

Kelsey's face turned hot. "You mean, in general, or—"

"How was the open house weekend at the University of Kansas?"

Kelsey tried to keep her eyes locked on her best friend, but Gillian's stare was too hard. She looked down. "I didn't end up going."

"What?" Gillian said, her voice lifting in mock surprise. "Did you get *tired* all of a sudden?"

Kelsey's eyes snapped back to Gillian. She wasn't even giving her a chance. She opened her mouth to speak, but Gillian interrupted her again.

"Don't tell me that you lied? I never took you for a liar, Kelsey."

Kelsey tightened her jaw. If Gillian wasn't going to give her a chance to tell the truth, then she would just have to take it. "I told my parents I was going to KU because I had to tell them I was going somewhere. They would never have let me go. . . ." Kelsey gulped, her chest tightening. "They would never have let me go to Paris."

"Paris, France?" Ingrid gasped.

"No. No way." Gillian put a hand on Ingrid's arm. "You went to Paris? Do not tell me this is about that soldier."

"What soldier?" Ingrid asked, excited.

Gillian stared at her in disbelief. "I thought you said you were going to end it."

Kelsey leaned toward her, trying to keep her voice low. "I messed up. I know. But I can't end it because—"

"Yes, you can."

"You're not even giving me a chance to tell you why!"

"I gave you a chance!" Gillian almost shouted. "I went to your friggin' house over spring break! I came to you!"

Kelsey felt as if she had been punched in the gut. "And I wasn't there?"

"You weren't . . ." She could see Gillian's eyes beginning to water, but she resisted. "You're never there anymore."

Kelsey put her head in her hands. "I've had a rough year, Gil."

"Not so rough that you couldn't go to Paris, huh?" Gillian sat up straight and pushed back from the table, refusing to look at Kelsey.

Kelsey jumped on the silence, trying to get it out as fast as possible. "I'm so sorry—I went because he invited me—Well, not me—But I went and while I was there—"

But as she spoke, Gillian stood, leaving her tray, and walked toward the cafeteria exit.

"Ingrid," she called from the door. "I need you."

"She needs me," Ingrid said, avoiding Kelsey's eyes. "We'll talk later, okay?"

"Tell her I'm sorry!" Kelsey called, and watched her walk away.

She fought the urge to bang her fist on the table. It seemed the only people who would listen to her were so far away. The only person, rather. Maybe she wasn't saying the right things. Or maybe she just wasn't saying them to the right people. Should she follow her friends?

No point, she decided. No point in trying to wrangle their anger into understanding.

She unwrapped the bottom of her 3 Musketeers bar and put the rest of it in her mouth in one bite, trying to savor its sticky richness until it was all gone. Michelle loved sweet things, too. Michelle and her hot chocolate. She would never tell her sister that sugar was bad for her. She would never tell her to give up something or someone she loved.

Ingrid had said it herself. *It's love, you know? If you are, you are.*

She was.

# CHAPTER TWENTY-FIVE

Weeks passed, embedded in routine. The sun got higher in the sky, up earlier, out later. As graduation grew closer, the seniors at Lawrence High School were starting to anticipate the leap they were expected to take, equally itching for it and fearing it. They flocked in the cafeteria and the courtyard like inquisitive birds around bodies of water, disseminating at the slightest ripple of responsibility.

Kelsey kept her head down. She cleaned her room. She dragged herself out of bed to practice her routine for the Rock Chalk Dancers audition. And she wrote.

She wrote to Peter as often and as deeply as if she were writing in a journal. Since the company's loss, security had tightened, and he wasn't able to Skype until they moved bases.

4/2

Dear Peter, I was in the locker room and I put my right shoe on my left foot because I was thinking of how the end of one of your eyebrows is somehow a shade blonder than the rest of your hair. Did you know that? Did you get a lemon in your eye at a young age?

xo

Michelle

**4/20**

Michelle— Abstract Expressionism is in fact the vomit of a sea creature. I mean that in a really good way. Think of it as an orca having just ate a school of angelfish, then he gets sick, and the pool of sickness is suspended in water. I'm writing that here because I don't think Mrs. Wallace would appreciate it like you would.

Yours,

Peter

She was still Michelle in his eyes, but besides the name, she was Kelsey in every way. She would tell him the truth when his tour was over. And then, well, she didn't know what would happen then.

Today, Kelsey was returning to the main doors of the high school from lunch, which she now opted to eat downtown. She waved at a car full of classmates and they waved back, their music fading as they squealed out of the parking lot.

She felt the itch and fear as much as anyone else, wishing she could duck out of the gymnasium doors and pile into a car bound for Clinton Lake. But she had said no for too long. There were friendly hellos from the dancers in the hallway, condolences about the breakup, and nods from the fringe of ordinary faces who used to cheer for her team at pep rallies and guzzle beer in her house.

Her phone lit up, and she grabbed for it, hoping to see Peter's name, but it was just a text from Davis: *It's hotter than a billy goat in a pepper patch*, it said. Kelsey smiled. She typed, *It's hotter than two cats fighting in a wool sock*, then deleted it. He was always better than she was at them, comedian that he was.

And she couldn't keep going back and forth. She remembered what Davis had last thought about their breakup: *For now*, he had said. She shouldn't give him any ideas.

At her locker, she could smell Gillian before she saw her. Hair spray. She turned, finding Gillian there, trying to look at anything in the surrounding hallway but Kelsey. Next to her, Ingrid froze.

"Please ask Kelsey if she wants to have the dance team meeting at four or four thirty tomorrow," Gillian said, her eyes locked on Ingrid.

Things between Kelsey and Gillian had turned from bad to worse. Gillian had even requested to move desks in Chemistry, the only class they had together.

Ingrid, meanwhile, was trying to remain neutral, but found herself more on Gillian's side because Gillian was the one who, literally and physically, yanked her there.

Ingrid looked at Kelsey, saying sorry with her eyes. "Did you hear that, Kels?"

"Four," Kelsey said. "And, Gil, please, just talk directly to me. This is so immature."

"Tell Kelsey she doesn't know the definition of mature."

"Forget it," Kelsey said, unable to stop herself from rolling her eyes. "I have to get to Art History."

"Hear that?" Ingrid said, talking to Gillian as they walked away. "Kelsey has to go to class."

As usual, the room was already dark when she got there, and half empty now that the year was winding down. Mrs. Wallace was bathed in the light from a slide featuring a complex orange-and-pink flower shape. Below it were the words "Feminist Visual Culture."

"Good afternoon, Kelsey," Mrs. Wallace said. "You're late, but I'll let it go this time."

"Sorry, Mrs. Wallace," Kelsey said, smiling sheepishly, because she was late most days. But she was always there, and never fell asleep, like she would have had this been any other year, any other time.

"The first slide is of a painting by American artist Georgia O'Keeffe."

Kelsey's eyes followed the lines of the painting slowly,

taking in every detail from top to bottom, as she had been taught.

"But before we get into that," Mrs. Wallace continued, "we have to go back to the beginning. Well, a little after the beginning. We have to go back to 1848. Who can tell me what happened in 1848?"

"Pre-Raphaelites," someone muttered.

"Exactly," Mrs. Wallace said, pointing her remote to the projector with a dramatic wave, moving to the next slide. "The Brotherhood, as they say. Kelsey, read those names."

Kelsey stumbled through the list.

"This is a list of people in Rossetti's salon, one of the most exciting places to be if you were an artist at that time. They were rebelling against flat, conventional composition. People standing still in perfect portraits: boring! They wanted layers, asymmetry, backdrops, romance!" Then Mrs. Wallace smiled, pacing back and forth in her corduroy jumper. "And what do you not see?"

Kelsey's eyes scanned the pale faces in the frame, burning to answer the question, but nothing popped into her head. She was stuck.

"Let me put it this way," Mrs. Wallace said. "What does Rossetti's salon and a boys' locker room have in common?"

Kelsey cried out, "Oh! No women!"

"Bam. Right on the nose. And there's your problem right there. . . ."

The rest of the class, Kelsey was riveted. Mrs. Wallace had a way of talking about the most minute details of what they were seeing so that they expanded into very big, important facts. The facts didn't just relate to whatever time period they were studying, they were facts about the way a person looked at anything: a movie, a billboard, her mother's decorating style. All of these types of seeing influenced one another, and they all found their root in the past.

Today Mrs. Wallace ended the class with a video clip, and as they watched, Kelsey felt something wash over her. The video was supposed to be an example of the way feminist art had evolved, to the point where the artists would use their own bodies as a canvas.

Kelsey didn't know exactly what this meant. She imagined them painting on themselves.

And then, the artist danced. She danced in a way Kelsey had never seen before, but understood all the same. The dance awoke something in her, the same sort of feeling she would have if she had answered one of Mrs. Wallace's questions correctly, but bigger than that. Better than that, because she could imagine herself in the artist's shoes, losing herself to her limbs and torso and the music that played. It was as if the artist were answering a question Kelsey had asked since she was a little girl. The artist's name was Maya. Maya Deren. She reminded Kelsey of her sister. She reminded Kelsey of herself.

When the video was over, Kelsey fought the urge to applaud.

The bell rang, but before she could gather her things, Mrs. Wallace put a hand on her arm.

"Forgetting something?"

Kelsey was still lost in thought. "Huh?"

"I graded the paper you handed in before break." Mrs. Wallace looked at Kelsey, her eyebrows raised. "The paper on Cubism you handed in a day after the deadline? Remember?"

"Oh, yeah," Kelsey said, clearing her throat. Her face burned. She was working harder, but it didn't seem to be good enough. "Thank you. Sorry about that."

Mrs. Wallace tapped the paper in her hands with plain, shorn fingernails. The grade wasn't visible. "Well, you've never been famous among the administration for being on time for class, or present, for that matter. I didn't expect a lot—"

"Yeah." Kelsey sighed.

Mrs. Wallace continued, "When you gave me an A-plus paper, I was very surprised."

She smiled as broadly as Mrs. Wallace could smile, which wasn't very broad, and put the paper in Kelsey's hands.

Kelsey flipped it over, her eyes wide. Sure enough, at the top near her name there was an A+. She could see small notes Mrs. Wallace had made here and here: *Creative observation*, she had written, and, *Well said*.

At first, all Kelsey could do was look back and forth

between Mrs. Wallace and the paper. Breaths replaced words. It was the first A+ she had ever received.

"I can't believe it."

"Believe it," Mrs. Wallace replied, and went back to her desk.

Kelsey left the room with a fire underneath her. She couldn't wait to tell Peter, and to tell her parents. Her mother and father had always told her she could do better. But she often wondered if any of them really thought she could, including herself. She had tried her hand at studying before, and always lost interest. What was different now?

She paused in the hallway, the faces filtering around her, remembering the person who she had done this for in the first place. She had been moved by this subject in the way her sister was probably moved by it every day. Her eyes blurred with happy tears.

*I get it now, what you saw in it all,* she told her sister, wherever she was. *I see what you see.*

4/26, 11:55 pm
From: Farrow, Peter W SPC
To: Maxfield, Michelle
Subject: A short list

The things I would rather do than go on patrol:

- Talk to you

- Take you on a date

- Make out with you

- Play music for you

- Listen to you play music for me (not on a guitar, just on the radio or something, no offense)

- Make out with you

- Read your letters

- Talk to you through a computer screen

- Make out with you

- Sit and stare off into space while thinking about you

- Stand and stare off into space while thinking about you

- Walk and stare off into space while thinking about you

- Sleep and stare off into space while thinking about you

- Bathe and stare off into space while thinking about you (sorry if that's explicit)

Tomorrow we go out for a few days. I'll try to email you again, but I can't guarantee it won't be complete gibberish. I'm having trouble making my hands or brain do anything else but . . . yeah. You get it already. I love you. I'm in love with you!

—P

# CHAPTER TWENTY-SIX

The mutters of fifteen members of Kelsey's dance team echoed throughout the Lawrence High gym, but Kelsey wasn't listening. She went in phases with the real world: Sometimes, she wanted to describe every detail in her head to Peter, just to know that he, too, had once tasted food, seen sun, tripped over a rug. But sometimes, everything in the world felt somehow unnecessary, because she didn't need any of it if it wasn't a part of him. The Lions Dance Team was waiting for Gillian to arrive at the last—and most important—dance practice of the year. Today, they voted on next year's captains.

Kelsey forced herself out of a daze to look at the clock on her phone. 4:18.

"Where is she?" she asked Ingrid.

"Beats me," Ingrid said, rotating her blonde head to look around the gym, as if Gillian were hiding in a corner. "Maybe she forgot?"

"No way," Kelsey said dismissively, and then corrected herself. "I mean, that could be it, but I wouldn't think so."

She reminded herself to be nicer to Ingrid, the only real friend she had left at Lawrence High. "So," she said, giving her an affectionate rub on the back. "How's your mom?"

As Ingrid was about to answer, the gym doors opened with a bang.

Gillian walked, slow and deliberate, to where they were gathered on the bleachers. She stood in front of the group.

"Sorry I'm late," she said. "I must have gotten the time wrong."

Kelsey scoffed and stood, taking a place next to Gillian facing the group. She muttered, "I said four o'clock yesterday. You were right there."

"Anyway," Gillian said, putting on a fake smile as if Kelsey wasn't right next to her. "Let's begin. For the freshmen unfamiliar with nominations and voting, here's how this works. . . ."

As Gillian spoke, Kelsey felt her pocket vibrate. The phone lit up with a notification from Michelle's email, which she had guiltily loaded onto her own phone. From Peter. "Tried calling you," the subject read. He would have to wait. A minute later, however, her phone was lighting up again.

Kelsey glanced down. Another email from Peter, no subject. The content read "Hello?"

"Take these pieces of paper," Gillian was saying, "and

write down the name of the dancer you believe shows the most leadership, strength, and creativ—excuse me." Gillian was looking at her. "Could you not?"

Kelsey apologized, and a minute later, her phone buzzed a third time. "Why is your phone disconnected?" Her phone? Her mind raced. Peter must have been trying to call Michelle's old phone number for some reason. She would have to make something up later.

Her team was now voting and it was her job to collect the ballots. Kelsey went around to each dancer with a happy face, though she was composing a reason for Peter's call in her head.

Then, a fourth email read "I'm in KS. Call me ASAP at my home #." He had included a number with a Kansas area code.

Peter was here? Peter was home. Why was he home? Was he hurt? Kelsey's stomach dropped, and she felt faint.

She backed away from the group, holding up her phone. "This is an emergency; I'm really sorry."

As she left the gym, Kelsey caught a glance of Gillian's face, knotted in concern. She sent a flicker of gratitude to her friend as she exited the school doors, dialed, and then—

"Hello?" The voice sounded like Peter, but it was his home line, so she had to be sure.

"This is K—Michelle Maxfield. May I speak with Peter?"

"Hi! Hi. It's me."

She put a hand to her chest. He was safe, at least safe enough to be at home, on the phone. "What happened?"

Five minutes later, she was in the Subaru on her way to El Dorado.

When he gave her the news, Kelsey tried not to sound too relieved.

Peter's mother had had a stroke, and when his father was able to reach him in Afghanistan, he was given special dispensation to return home temporarily. The stroke turned out to be milder than they initially thought. His mother was now in stable enough condition to wake up on and off, but she was still showing symptoms, so she would be kept at the hospital for observation.

The prairie lining I-70 whipped past her, and now she was deep into the Flint Hills, rising in waves just as she had described to Peter so long ago.

He had asked her to come see him.

"Are you sure?" she had replied, because this was a time for family.

He had told her that aside from his family, she was the only person he wanted to see.

He wanted her there, and she would go to him, and even if she couldn't touch him, even if she couldn't put her hands on his face and her mouth on his like she wanted to, she would be happy enough at the sight of him in the same space as her, the sound of his voice, the mere feeling of him in the next room.

It would be enough that he had the ability to enter the same room, and put his hand in hers, to send warmth throughout her body, to her fingertips, her hair.

That Peter would not be just the idea of Peter, even for a short time; this was enough to press her foot down on the gas until the landscape became a blur.

Physical possibilities. Land moving under her tires. The miracle of physics. She would see him in three hours.

At the hospital, Kelsey followed the attendant in scrubs to the second floor, and there, in the hallway waiting for her, Peter stood in his fatigues.

"Peter," she said.

He turned, and his face lit up. There was the old Peter, the smile that reflected on the walls.

She squeezed him, feeling the chain of his dog tags against her chest. "Did you come here straight from the plane?"

"This morning," he said, still holding her. "I haven't slept in twenty-four hours."

Peter took her hand, leading her into the room. Carnations, daisies, and chrysanthemums bloomed from every corner, covering up the smell of stale bleach.

Peter's mother was pale but sitting up, her hospital gown under a zip-up sweatshirt that read EL DORADO WILDCATS.

She looked at Kelsey with the same blue eyes Peter had. "This is my mom, Cathy."

Kelsey smiled and found another pair of blue eyes in a girl slightly younger and shorter than herself, with sandy hair like Peter's, pulled into a high ponytail. "That's my sister, Meg."

A stocky, brown-haired man with a thick mustache nodded at Kelsey and put an arm around his daughter. "And my dad, Bill."

Peter touched the small of her back. "Everyone," he said, "this is Michelle."

"Hello," Kelsey said, waving to all of them and none of them, trying to unclench her jaw at the sound of Michelle's name. "I'm glad you're all right, Mrs. Farrow. It's so wonderful to meet you."

Peter's mother gave her a small smile in response.

"Nice to meet you in person. Is it one 'l' or two?" his father asked.

People used to ask Michelle how to spell her name all the time. This was Peter's family she was deceiving, the people he trusted most in the world. The lie had sprouted another branch.

"Two 'l's,'" Kelsey said with a forced smile, and looked at the floor.

"Where do you go to school?" his sister asked.

"Lawrence High."

Peter began to tell them about Paris, and occasionally, Kelsey would jump in with a detail.

Every time she spoke, his mother looked at her as if she had popped out of the floor. Which was understandable, because she had kind of done just that.

Peter and his father started talking about how the KU basketball team had performed in the NCAA championship, how much of the season he had missed overseas.

Peter's sister pulled her mother's blanket around her legs, glancing at Kelsey.

Kelsey wished she had been painted white to blend in with the wall.

She was happy Peter wanted her to meet his family, but the smell of flowers and all those blue eyes looking at her, wondering . . .

Even if she hadn't been lying, she didn't quite belong here. Who would want to see an unfamiliar face when they were feeling sick? What good could she do?

"You all must be so tired," she announced. "Can I go down to the cafeteria and get you some coffee?"

Her voice must have been quieter than she thought. No one turned, including Peter.

"Soda?" she said louder.

"What?" Peter's sister said.

Kelsey coughed. "Coffee or soda?"

Peter's father paused what he was saying for a moment to

answer, "That would be great," and continued railing on the Jayhawks' inability to play fundamental defense.

Kelsey stepped out into the empty hall, looking around. Which one? Coffee or soda?

Exit signs hung at either end. She could hear Peter say something. His family laughed.

She didn't even know if there was a cafeteria in the small hospital, let alone where it was. She blew out a breath and decided to go the way she came, toward reception. Maybe she could drop coffees off with one of the nurses and wait for Peter somewhere else. She wondered if she should have come at all.

"Hey!" she heard behind her.

She turned around.

Peter was walking toward her. "Coffee machine's this way," he said, pointing behind him.

"Oh" was all she could manage to get out, and she walked quickly past him with a cursory smile.

"Wait for a second, I'm going to get some change," he said.

"No, no, that's all right," she said, continuing toward the exit.

"Please wait?" he said, a puzzled smile growing on his face. "I want to come with you."

"Okay," Kelsey said.

He must have sensed she was feeling out of place. Those

faces looked at her with Peter's eyes, Peter's nose, his childhood, giving her the wrong name. Her body, her trusted self, mislabeled in a tiny room.

But with him by her side, she was simply someone he had chosen.

When he emerged from the room, putting his arm around her, a grateful feeling spread in her that she was not used to. She could get used to it, though. She wouldn't even have to try.

# CHAPTER TWENTY-SEVEN

When they left the hospital that evening, Peter insisted that Kelsey stay over at their house so she didn't have to make the four-hour drive back in the dark. As he said it, he subtly ran his hand down her back. Kelsey bit her lip, wishing, but politely refused.

Peter's sister said, "You should totally stay," but Kelsey declined again. She was surprised to see Meg's mouth fall in disappointment. When Peter mentioned that Meg was trying out for El Dorado's dance team at the end of the year, the girls had slipped immediately into dancer talk, discussing pirouettes and fouetté turns and high kicks. She had to explain she knew all this through Kelsey, careful not to get too excited.

"Please stay?" Meg said.

"Come on," Peter said, and he had that look again. The look that said, *I've already won.*

"Thank you, but I don't want to impose," Kelsey said, and they entered the parking lot.

Peter's father unlocked their car and said, "Stay, or we'll tell everyone in Lawrence you should be jailed for treason."

Kelsey opened her mouth, aghast. "Why?"

"Anyone who doesn't know the starting lineup of the KU basketball team is committing a gross betrayal of the state."

They laughed, Kelsey shrugged, and Peter muttered, "He's serious, though."

She answered her mother's multiple voice mails with a text that she was staying at Ingrid's, and followed them in her car to pick up ingredients for dinner at the nearest grocery store, a Kroger with the *R* portion of the sign flickering in and out.

"Welcome to the finest twenty-four-hour food store in El Dorado," Peter said as they went through the automatic doors. The store was empty except for two cashiers manning the late shift.

"The *only* twenty-four-hour food store in El Dorado," Meg said, rolling her eyes. Kelsey had to suppress a smile at how much Meg reminded her of herself at that age, right down to the attitude and the high ponytail.

"Carly, Todd," Peter's dad said in greeting to the cashiers.

"Hey, Bill," Carly said. Kelsey noticed that she didn't even have to look up from her manicure to recognize him.

"Welcome home, Pete," called Todd.

"All right, you know the drill," Bill said to his children, looking at a list he had pulled out of his pocket.

Meg sighed. "Do we really have to do this? Even with Mom in the hospital?"

"Wait, what are we doing?" Kelsey asked, looking around the fluorescent, empty store for a clue.

"No excuses," Peter said, bracing himself against the shopping cart as if he was about to run. "Mom would have wanted us to get a good score tonight."

"It's not like she's dead," Meg muttered, but then she posed on the other side of the cart, also ready to run.

Bill cleared his throat. "Peter, you've got spaghetti noodles, garlic bread, romaine lettuce, onions, and mushrooms. You know what kind of mushrooms. Meg, you've got marinara, ground beef, Caesar dressing, Parmesan, and croutons. Stopwatch set," he said, setting off a beep on his watch.

"You're going down, Meg," Peter said, and then he raised his eyebrows at Kelsey.

"I may be small, but I'm fast," Meg said, leaning forward.

"On your marks, get set, GO!" Bill yelled, and Meg and Peter bolted to their respective aisles.

"Go, Peter!" the cashier, Todd, yelled from Lane 3, putting his fists in the air.

"Is this a regular thing?" Kelsey asked Bill.

"If 'regular' means 'every time we get groceries,' then yes," Bill replied.

Peter hurdled out of the pasta aisle, tossing a couple of bags of spaghetti in the cart before he jetted off to produce. "Help me!" he called back to Kelsey.

"Not fair!" Meg yelled, tossing a few jars of red sauce into the cart before running to the meat section.

"Michelle with two 'l's'!" Bill pointed at Kelsey. "Ice cream sandwiches, eggs, bacon, orange juice, and bread. Go!"

"What?" Kelsey was too busy laughing at the sight of Meg putting Peter in a headlock to pay attention. Did Peter's dad actually want her to run around with them?

"Go!" Bill pointed again, the first traces of a smile appearing under his mustache.

"You better go," Peter called from under Meg's arm.

Kelsey walked quickly to the frozen aisle, trying not to slip on the linoleum in her boots.

"No walking allowed!" Bill called to her.

On the edge of embarrassment and mirth, Kelsey broke into a sprint. There was no point in not playing along. And hell, she was kind of fast. She could win this thing.

"Thatta girl," Bill said as she threw ice cream sandwiches into the cart with force.

On her way to get eggs, she ran smack into Peter, and they bumped heads.

"Ow!" He collapsed to the floor, red-faced, with mushrooms in hand, and they cracked up.

"Here, let me help you," Kelsey said between laughs as she keeled over.

When he reached for her hand, she pushed it aside, leapt over him, and pretended to laugh villainously. "Muahahaha!" she cried, and turned the corner to the eggs and dairy.

"Treachery!" Peter called, but when he was on his feet, he followed her, leaping in front of the eggs as if he were a mother hen, protecting them.

Kelsey snatched around his side, but he was too quick, blocking her again.

"Do they really do this every time?" she asked, out of breath.

"Only when I'm home," he said, and while he was distracted, she reached under his legs and got her prize.

"I'm impressed," she said over her shoulder on the way to the cart, eggs under her arm.

Then it hit her: She was having a great time. With Peter's middle-aged father and his kid sister. In a mostly empty supermarket in El Dorado, Kansas.

She set the eggs gently in the cart, feeling a pang of envy. She thought of the day she and her mother and father had tried to go to the market. Since that day, they had not tried again.

It wasn't like the Farrows had it easy. They had a son in Afghanistan and a mother in the hospital. But they were making the best of it. They were quite a family.

Meg ended up victorious, with a time of five minutes and thirty-two seconds, mostly because Peter and Kelsey met in the aisles too often, out of sight, getting distracted by each other.

Back at their cozy, ranch-style home, the four of them sat down to dinner, where Kelsey learned about Cathy's job as an art teacher at El Dorado High School. Bill talked less about his work in insurance and more about his passion—college basketball. Kelsey told him about the game she had seen against Nebraska at Allen Fieldhouse, conveniently forgetting the rest of that night, with Davis.

When Meg expressed how nervous she was about the dance tryout, she offered to "send her twin sister" over to El Dorado sometime, to help her with her moves.

She saw the pride in Bill's eyes when he looked at Peter, and the closed-mouth way he encouraged his dream to study at a good school far away from Kansas, though he didn't quite understand it.

When Kelsey and Peter offered to do the dishes, Bill and Meg said good night, and the two of them were left to wash and dry.

They stood in silence for a while, their forearms occasionally touching as their hands worked, submerged in the soapy water, waiting for the sounds of teeth brushing and doors closing from down the hallway.

"I don't know how else to say this," Peter said, glancing at her out of the corner of his eye. "But the thing is, unless you want to sleep on that polyester couch, there is only one open bed in this house."

Kelsey knew what he was saying, and feeling the way she did about Peter, she would have to choose her words carefully. She turned to him, taking his still-wet hands, and placed them around her waist until they soaked through her shirt.

His palms went lower, to where the straight line of her back curved. She kissed his neck, slowly, many times, until she was right near his ear.

"I have a deep hatred of polyester," she said.

His fingertips found their way under her shirt, and then out again, leaving hot traces. He took her hand.

"We can't have that," he said. "You need your privacy."

"We need our privacy," she replied, and kissed him softly on the mouth.

"Would you like to follow me to my room?" he asked, but before he could finish the question, she was already ahead of him, down the hall.

# CHAPTER TWENTY-EIGHT

The next day, Peter woke Kelsey by kissing her at dawn. She snuck out to the polyester couch.

They drove alone in the overcast morning to the hospital, where they found Cathy so medicated that she didn't wake when Peter shook her and said her name.

The nurse tried to calm Peter's panic, assuring him that his mother was just sleeping. He had only a short time to see her before he had to ship out again, and most of the time she wasn't able to say a word.

They sat as he held Cathy's hand, her breaths steady against the beep of her heart monitor.

After three hours, Cathy emerged out of sleep to say a slurred "hello" to her son, and then sank back into slumber. Peter stood up, brushed his mother's hair aside to kiss her forehead, and told Kelsey it was time to go.

"I want to show you something," he told her.

They drove back to his house, but when Kelsey started to walk to the front door, he motioned her away.

"Back here," he said, and they went around the house.

Peter's backyard extended far past where she thought it would, past the mowed lawn and down a hill covered in wild grasses and weeds, to a clump of trees and bushes lining a small creek that seemed to connect all the houses on their block.

They hopped over the creek and ventured into the woods until all they could see were trees behind them, in front of them, to the right and left.

Then Peter led them farther, until the trees broke.

They stood at the edge of what appeared to be a wheat field, golden stalks reaching to Kelsey's shins, hitting nothing but big gray sky for miles and miles. It was beautiful and still and clear. Everything a person could love about Kansas.

"Is this someone's land?" Kelsey asked.

"Probably," Peter said, looking around. "They don't use it, though. I think it used to be wheat, but now it's just a bunch of dried-up grass. It was like this when I was a kid. Which reminds me . . ." He snapped off a stick from one of the surrounding trees. "You're going to want a stick."

Kelsey found a relatively stiff, skinny branch and snapped it. "Why?" she asked.

Peter looked at her with a sly smile. "You want to know what I call this place?"

"What?"

He whipped his stick through the grass, stirring it. "Snake Country."

Kelsey clenched her stick, trying not to show that she was afraid, and whipped it through the grass around her.

"Don't worry too much," Peter said, feeling the ground for a dry place to sit.

Kelsey let out a "ha!" and sat down next to him, running her stick over the bending blades.

"I played all sorts of games here," he said. "Just a lonely little kid, talking to himself about ninjas and dragons."

Kelsey smiled at the thought, picturing him leaping through the grass, wielding his stick as a sword. "I'm sure you were a great fighter."

"Against all things imaginary, yes." He laughed shortly. "I was undefeated."

They were quiet, listening to the wind rustle the new leaves.

"I'm not a fighter, though," Peter said, looking out. "I wasn't built to be over there."

"I don't think many people are," Kelsey said.

"No, but they can adjust to it. They trained us well. They make everything you ever thought you couldn't do, like—" He swallowed. "Just brutal stuff. They make that stuff into a habit. Into a reaction. And then it becomes necessary, in your mind. My whole world is flipped. Last night, while you were getting the groceries from the car, my sister dropped one of her textbooks on the floor by accident, and it made a banging sound, and do you know what my hands did?"

Kelsey was silent. This was not a question she was supposed to answer.

"They clutched the air for a gun, Michelle. As if I was going to disarm my goddamn sister." He shook his head. "I can't even believe I'm back here, racing with Meg at the supermarket and, you know, kissing you, after I've seen what I saw. After I've done what I did."

When he was finished speaking, Peter shut his mouth quickly, as if he said something he shouldn't, and looked at her, trying to measure her thoughts.

She didn't know what to say. She didn't know what he meant. She would try to understand someday. She put her arm around him, and he sank into her.

She laid his head on her lap and stretched out in the grass, hands folded over his chest.

"I don't want to go back there," he said, hard, quiet, his eyes collecting the gray of the sky. "Not after I've been home."

*I don't want you to go, either,* she almost said, but that wouldn't help him. That wouldn't help anyone. She pushed herself to say what she was supposed to say.

"You have to. Here is here, and over there is over there, and there, you've got an obligation to your country."

"It's not that simple," he replied.

Her fear was now heavy inside her, weighed down by guilt, by sadness at his leaving. *Believe me*, Kelsey thought, *I know how not simple things are.*

She bent her head to kiss him, her hand running across his shorn head, savoring the proximity of his smell, his breath, his warmth in the middle of all this vacant prairie.

"Nothing is simple," she whispered to him. "But for now, we have to pretend it is."

# CHAPTER TWENTY-NINE

Anyone who happened to be driving east on I-70 that evening might have witnessed quite a sight: a Subaru hatchback with four windows down, a seventeen-year-old girl with her head and arm hanging out the driver's side, wind blowing, hands banging the metal door to the beat. Next to her, a young man in army fatigues, his canvas bag in his lap, mirroring her out the passenger side.

It wasn't so much the pairing of the two that they would have noticed, but the rage and sadness with which they sang the songs. Though they were young, they sang them as if they would be the last songs they sang, loud enough to reach a pair of ears miles away.

Kelsey had volunteered to drive Peter to the airport as his father and sister spent the evening with Cathy. She couldn't stand the thought of not having as much time with him as she possibly could.

The two of them spent the four-hour drive drowning out their sorrows with Michelle's playlists.

Kelsey turned the volume all the way up until they couldn't hear their own voices.

They screamed along to the White Stripes' "Seven Nation Army."

They rapped along to Kanye West's "Jesus Walks."

They crooned along to the Cicadas' "Baby," probably out of tune, first the English version and then the one in Portuguese, holding hands across the seats while they remembered the night they danced in Paris.

The airport was two exits away.

"Stop the car," Peter said.

Kelsey scanned the horizon, frantic. "Where?"

"Anywhere," Peter said. She looked at him. "Please."

They found an emergency pull-off between exits, and while traffic surged around them, Peter unbuckled his seat belt. He took Kelsey's face in his hands and brought her close to him, kissing her on the lips, on the cheeks, on the nose, on the chin, wherever he could find.

"It feels like I've only seen you for three seconds," he said between kisses. "This is not fair."

She steadied him, found his lips. "It will be over before you know it," she said, and wished she did not mean it in any other way.

"Seeing you does that to me," Peter said, moving his hand

down her hair, to her shoulders, to her arm, and back up again, lining her, memorizing her. "I forget how time works. I forget we weren't always together and won't always be together."

A passing semi rocked them slightly, but neither noticed. Kelsey took his hand and kissed his fingers.

"Tell me we will, one more time." His eyes moved up and down her face, his lashes wet.

"We will . . ." Kelsey began, and paused. All she could say was what she knew, but she knew enough. Something with wings had spread behind her ribs, pushing against them, too big for her chest. "We are permanent. No matter what happens, everything we have will be there forever."

"We are permanent," he said, and sat back in his seat, his hand in hers. Headlights grazed the side of Peter's face. He was so beautiful. She kissed his smooth cheek.

"I love you, permanently," she said with as much force as she could put behind it, and looked forward, put the car in drive.

"I love you, permanently," he repeated, setting his jaw, and squeezed until her hand hurt.

It was said, and remained said: Time was different when it was just the two of them. But he would be gone again. Permanent doesn't always mean forward. Permanent doesn't always mean with you. Permanent like the Flint Hills, to be thought of, to be passed through. To be seen, but not carried.

When they reached the drop-off area, Kelsey put the car in park. Peter would have to run to his gate. Sobs were starting in her chest and she had to swallow them.

"I wish I had some sort of trinket to give you, some token or something," she said as he strapped on his bag.

Peter gave her a pained smile. "Like a kerchief from the Civil War?"

"Like a lock of my hair?" Kelsey said.

"That's disgusting!" Peter cried, and they both made a sound that was almost a laugh.

He stopped, seeming unable to close the passenger-side door.

"I love you," Kelsey said.

"I love you, too," Peter said.

"Wait!" Kelsey searched her pockets, and glanced frantically around for something, anything, she could give him, but all she had was an old pack of cinnamon gum.

"Here, from me," she laughed, and shoved a stick of gum in his hand.

They kissed their last kiss for a long time, with a tenderness and a torment.

He waved, then he had to run. When he was out of sight, something snapped back into Kelsey like a broken rubber band, rocking her.

She got lost in the maze of exits, forgetting where she had come. On a quiet intersection next to the rental car lots, she turned, and parked again. She wondered if all of it had really just happened.

She couldn't stay in the car, which still smelled like him, like canvas and soap. She folded onto the curb, leaning back against the front tire of the Subaru, and wept.

She could see Peter's face before he turned to go, and the yank of terror in seeing him be taken at any moment. If a truck he rode took the wrong turn. If he was two inches too far to the right in a bullet's path.

If all of her fears came true, Peter would become another apparition alongside Michelle, another blur. Perhaps the two of them belonged in another world. They met first after all.

Why did she fall in love with a face on a screen, a figure leaving, forever getting smaller? Why wasn't the flesh good enough? Why did she have to live on fumes?

A couple with a small child on the way to pick up their car called across the street to ask if she was all right. Kelsey didn't answer because she didn't know. She rested her elbows on her knees and tucked her face into the darkness.

Soon, the tears fell again, dripping from her eyes and rolling down her legs.

Michelle had no choice in the matter. She was dead and she could not speak for herself, and yet she was still alive everywhere Kelsey went. She had always hoped her sister was at peace, wherever she was, whatever that meant, but how could a soul be at rest when someone else was conjuring it constantly?

*I can't help it*, she said, *I miss you*, but no one would ever respond, not really.

*I never even got to say good-bye.* Still nothing. Hope was an awful thing, she decided.

*I miss you and that's it. That's why we're in this mess.*

No sign, no ghost, just the sound of her own heaving, the taste of her own snot.

*That's why* I'm *in this mess*, she corrected. *I'm alone in this.*

For some reason, that thought was the only comfort she found. It meant that all her lies weren't the external webs she imagined them to be. They all came from her, from her collapsed, tearstained body. And it meant she, alone, could fix them.

She had spent so long grasping for certain moments, trying to find the "right" time, when the ability to set things straight had been there from the beginning, from the moment she responded to Michelle's name on Skype.

She just hadn't had the strength to face the consequences.

She wasn't lying when she had told Davis she had changed. She had. And if she could send the man she loved to war without crying in front of him, if she could name all the important artists of the past centuries, if she could leave the last three years on the steps of a fraternity, if she could write an A+ paper, well . . . She could write a letter. She could write what might possibly be the most important letter of her life.

Kelsey drove the half hour home and pulled into her driveway. She ran up the steps to her room, and pulled out the engraved stationery from her drawer—her own stationery, with her own initials.

Once the pen hovered over the paper, she didn't know where to begin.

*Dear Peter,* it read.

*Write how you speak,* she could hear her sister say.

But Kelsey didn't write. It was Michelle who had sent letters to Peter. Peter was lied to through the words Kelsey had crossed out and looked up and stolen from her sister's life. And even when she had acted as herself, he had filtered everything about her through the wrong beginning, the wrong memories, the wrong name.

She would tell him face-to-face, as she had wanted to in Paris, or as close to it as she could get.

She opened her laptop, activated the camera, and waited for the screen to load. A tiny green bulb lit at the top of the monitor. Her own image surprised her.

Normally, when Kelsey Skyped with Peter, she was confined to a small square in the lower right-hand corner of the screen. Now, she faced herself in full, glassy-eyed and paler than she'd ever been, hair unwashed and wavy. She was ready. She pulled the strands back into a neat bun, and pressed RECORD.

"Hi," she started, and something about the way she could see herself as she really was, as Peter had seen her and believed in her, stalled her words. Not this time. She shook her head. "I'm not going to make this pretty so you'll have to deal with a lot of stops and . . . whatever."

She focused on her lips, the tiny pixels that made them, finally forming the words.

"Michelle is dead."

She began with the day of the party, the day she met him. The next day, saying good-bye to them from the top of the stairs. The hours passing. The policeman showing up at her house, dissolving life as she knew it into a giant flood, which she had been drowning in ever since.

"I was weak. But that's no excuse. Or maybe it is an excuse. I don't know. I'm all mixed up. I can't get my life in any kind of order. Then there was you."

When it was finished, she loaded the file onto a flash drive, dropped it into an envelope, and sealed it. She remembered Peter had told her that the wives and children of his friends often sent CDs or flash drives with photos, so they could load them and look at them, even if there was no Internet. She wrote out the address of his base, though she knew he was being moved to an unknown location. It would find him eventually.

"Maybe I am a monster," she had told him. "But I still love you. Remember? Permanently. And I'm so, so sorry. Take how sorry you think I am and multiply it by a million. I promise I will never lie to you again. And trust me, I know what it's like to do things every day, like talk to someone and love someone, and then never do it again, all of a sudden. For things never to be the same. So do you. But if you forgive me, I'll keep my promise forever, no matter if you love me or if you never talk to me again. I love you permanently either way. I know how to do that now."

Dawn was rising over Lawrence in pinks and oranges and blues as she placed the envelope in the Maxfields' mailbox.

She shivered, though it wasn't cold. Summer was coming soon.

Hope and fear were a strange combination, but they were better than before. Maybe he would forgive her, and maybe he wouldn't, but at least whatever he felt would be real.

# CHAPTER THIRTY

Kelsey woke in the bright, bare Chemistry classroom later that morning, her cheek flat against the desk, where drool had collected around her mouth. She sat up and found someone beside her, touching her back.

Gillian.

"Hey," she said. "Class is over."

"Oh, right," Kelsey said, wiping her chin and running her fingers through her hair. "Embarrassing." On her phone, she saw a text from Meg, introducing herself and asking to meet up and practice her moves. She had made sure to leave Peter's little sister "Kelsey's" number. Kelsey was touched, but she couldn't deal with it now, half-awake.

Gillian's mouth lifted in a smirk above her. "As your former lab partner, I can assure you that this isn't the first time you've drifted off in Chem."

Kelsey stood, putting on her backpack. "Yeah, but I didn't have you to kick me under the table this time."

"I don't know if that would have done the trick, honestly," Gillian said. "You were almost snoring."

"Huh, well," Kelsey said, and she flattened her wrinkled dress. She wasn't in the mood for a lecture. She started to shuffle out of the classroom, yawning, wondering how she would make it through the day.

Gillian stopped her with a hand on the shoulder, and looked closer at her face, speculating. "Did you sleep at all last night?"

In answer, Kelsey pointed to the drool on her desk.

"You need coffee," Gillian said. "And sugar."

"I didn't have time to grab any this morning," Kelsey said. "So, I guess—"

"Let's go," Gillian said, pushing her back.

"It's only third period, though. Lunch isn't until—"

"Did I say anything about lunch?" Gillian said, smiling.

Kelsey felt her eyebrows rise without her permission, her mouth turn up at the corners. A thousand pounds lifted off her shoulders. She realized she hadn't smiled, or felt anything, really, that didn't have something to do with Peter for the last few weeks. Gillian was not one of Kelsey's phantoms. She was so solid, so real, next to her, and had evidently decided Kelsey wasn't a lying piece of crap.

"Why—" she started, and Gillian stopped, turning to look at her. "Why are you talking to me again?"

Gillian pursed her lips, thinking, and then kept walking, forcing Kelsey to follow her. "Because you're different today. And I'm different today. I just feel different. Best friends have a way of sensing these things, I think. Which I wish I could explain via science, but I can't—"

"Gil, you're right." Kelsey let out a relieved laugh, trying to keep up. "I told him last night. I mean, I took a video of myself telling him. Because it felt too weird to write a letter. Anyway, I sent it in the mail. He'll get it soon, I hope."

"I don't think it even matters when he hears it, actually."

"What do you mean?"

"You were honest with yourself."

"And you were going to just, like, ignore me until you felt differently? Until you sensed something?"

Gillian thought for a moment. "Remember when I knew you had gotten your period before you did?"

It was true. She had handed Kelsey a tampon one day their sophomore year, seemingly out of the blue. "Still. That's crazy."

Gillian narrowed her eyes, smiling at Kelsey, as if to say, *Look who's talking.*

"Fair enough," Kelsey said, shaking her head.

"We have to swing by Ingrid's Theater class," Gillian said, as familiar as could be. "Then you can show us how to skip school."

Kelsey grinned. "It's easy, really. . . ."

Theater class was held in the echoey auditorium at the opposite end of the school. After the bell rang for fourth period, Kelsey and Gillian ducked into the last row, careful not to draw the attention of the Theater teacher, who sat with his back to them. The houselights stayed low.

When Ingrid walked to the center of the stage, Kelsey and Gillian crawled closer to the front, ducking behind the rows of seats.

"My name is Ingrid Krakowski and I will be performing a monogogue from Neil Simon's classic 1991 play, *Lost in Yonkers.*"

Gillian almost spit to keep from laughing out loud. Kelsey elbowed her.

"I'm sorry," Gillian whispered, "but did she just say monogogue?"

Ingrid furrowed her brow and began, tripping over the words with the worst New York accent Kelsey had ever heard. "'Thirty-five years ago, I could have been fighting' . . ."

Suddenly, Kelsey stood up from her auditorium seat, behind Ingrid's drama teacher, and waved frantically, putting a finger to her lips. Gillian joined her.

Ingrid opened her eyes wide, and cleared her throat, continuing louder. "'Remember this. There's a lot of Germans in this country fighting for America' . . ."

Kelsey had an idea. She held her stomach, pretending to

puke, pointed at Ingrid, and pointed at the exit.

Ingrid looked at her, confused. The drama teacher turned, and Kelsey and Gillian ducked behind the seats.

"Um," Ingrid said onstage, pinching her lips. "I don't feel very good."

"Do you need a moment?" the teacher asked.

"Yeah, my friend is going to be sick. I mean, I'm going to be sick."

She ran off the stage.

The three girls met in the hallway, scuttled through the school, across the gym, only half lit as no one was using it. Kelsey peeked around before pushing open the emergency exit, finding herself blinded by the midmorning sun.

"Won't that set off an alarm?" Ingrid whispered.

"If it does, it's completely silent and no one ever does anything about it," Kelsey replied as they jogged across the back parking lot. "Because I've been using that exit for years."

"Good to know this school is serious about safety," Gillian said.

"Where to?" Kelsey asked at the wheel of the Subaru.

"Tazza?" Ingrid asked.

Downtown, the girls took their iced mochas to the benches outside, squinting against the light. They used to do this every day during the summer, watching the shoppers walk by, rating the boys from one to ten.

"We haven't done this in forever," Kelsey said.

"You haven't come out of your house in forever," Ingrid said. "We've been worried about you."

Gillian, who was sitting on Ingrid's other side, leaned forward, catching Kelsey's eyes. "What happened with . . . I mean . . ." She glanced at Ingrid, not sure if Kelsey was ready to tell her what she had done. "You know what I mean," Gillian finished.

Kelsey sighed. The envelope was probably out of the mailbox by now, on its way to Peter. Though she had just seen him yesterday, he seemed so far gone.

"Kels?"

"I don't know," Kelsey said, her exhaustion catching up with her again. Her voice trembled. "We're in love, Gil."

Gillian reached across Ingrid to touch Kelsey's knee. Kelsey tried to keep her lip from trembling.

"Or at least, I think we are. He doesn't know it's me yet, or maybe he does, or maybe he does and never wants to speak to me again. . . ."

"Stop," she said firmly. "Don't cry."

Kelsey steeled her mouth. Gillian took a motherly tone.

"Take a deep breath."

Kelsey did. It felt good. She took another one.

"Tell us everything."

She did. And she didn't eliminate a single detail. Each time the truth left her, she felt stronger, as if she were bleeding out a poison.

"So you didn't know you liked him at first?" Ingrid asked. "You just missed Michelle."

"And now I'm going crazier than I already am," Kelsey said, rubbing her forehead. "I don't know if he's going to be okay, or if he's going to love me, or hate me, or what."

Gillian and Ingrid stared at her in silence.

"Well?" Kelsey pressed. "What do you guys think?"

Gillian's brow furrowed. Ingrid sucked the rest of her mocha through a straw.

"I'm just glad you told him the truth," Gillian finally said.

Kelsey shook her head, feeling her fists clench. "I had to. I couldn't take it anymore. Ingrid, what do you think?"

"I think I don't really care, because I don't know this guy, and either way, you're going to be just fine."

Gillian punched her in the shoulder. "Ingrid!"

Ingrid shrugged. "Well?"

"Do you know what it's like to be in love?"

"Yeah, probably. I don't know. Probably not."

Kelsey couldn't wrap her mind around Ingrid's indifference. She had forgotten what it was like not to care. She wondered if she would have said the same thing if their places were switched. If Ingrid had disappeared just as Kelsey had over the past year, perhaps she wouldn't care, either.

"What are you going to do now?" Gillian asked.

Kelsey considered for a moment. A terrible, floating

feeling had arisen this morning and stayed, even now. "I don't know. Wait, I guess."

Gillian uncrossed her legs and stood up. "Well, we're not going to let you shut yourself in your room this time. For the sake of society at large. Who knows what you might do?"

Kelsey felt herself smile, about to thank her.

"I mean it," Gillian said, and Kelsey had never appreciated her best friend's bossy tone more than right then. Or Ingrid's easygoing innocence, for that matter, blurting out everything without a second thought. She wished she could be more like them in some ways. She wasn't, though, because that's not how people work. They were different, the three of them, and Kelsey was beyond the point of looking back. Either way, they were behind her.

Even though she didn't quite deserve it.

She stood to embrace her friends, and for just a second, she felt like she was on solid ground.

# CHAPTER THIRTY-ONE

Kelsey entered her house that evening and thought she was dreaming again. No, it was real: the smell of dinner cooking. The sound of her father's favorite music taking over the house. The sight of her mother chopping vegetables on a wooden cutting board, tossing the pieces into a large metal bowl. As Kelsey got closer, she noticed the table was set, napkins and all.

Kelsey hadn't witnessed such a scene in a long time.

Her father had been warming up leftovers from the restaurant in the microwave late at night, and she and her mother were left to their own devices, mostly delivery pizza and macaroni and cheese, in Kelsey's case.

"Is this for the group therapy people?" Kelsey yelled over the music.

"Kelsey!" Her mother jumped at the sound of her voice, too concentrated on the cabbage to notice her come in. "What did you say?"

"I said—" Kelsey began.

"Rob, turn that shit down, will you?" her mother called, and slapped her father on the butt.

Her dad turned around, saw Kelsey, and his bushy eyebrows lifted, his spatula in the air. "Hi, sweetie!"

"What's all this?" Kelsey asked, the folk music at a reasonable volume.

"We're having dinner together," her father said.

"Really?"

"Sit down," her mother said, her glasses tucked in her wild gray hair.

"Stay awhile," her father said, and slid a burger patty onto a large plate, flipping the others.

Kelsey sat, forgetting in her sleeplessness to take off her backpack. Her mother removed it. Kelsey almost recoiled at her mother's touch, but didn't. She and her mother smiled at each other cautiously.

"We need to talk to you about something," her mother said.

Kelsey couldn't imagine what it might be, but those words were rarely a good sign.

"We received something in the mail today," her mother said, standing up and going to her desk.

Alarms flashed behind Kelsey's eyes. She gripped the table. She had checked the mailbox on the way in; sure enough, it had been empty. Did they find the letter to Peter? Did they know?

"Surprise," her mother said from behind her, and dropped an envelope next to her plate, sitting back down beside her.

It was stamped with the University of Kansas seal, and it was thick.

"You're in!"

In the strange whirlwind of the past few months, Kelsey had barely remembered to apply. But she did, at the last minute, and from then on assumed she'd get in, because Ingrid had gotten in a few days ago, and Ingrid was, well, Ingrid.

"Wow" was all Kelsey could say, scanning the official letter.

"Congratulations, darling," her mother said.

When they were all sitting, eating barbecue burgers and slaw, Kelsey couldn't help but take a moment to stare. Her parents had not been her favorite people, even before Michelle died, but now, the two of them sitting across from her, passing the wine bottle from one to the other, put a sweet haze on her sleepy vision.

Her father shook his head, smiling to himself. "I remember your first day of school."

"Ha!" replied her mother. "What an ordeal."

"One wanted morning kindergarten, one wanted afternoon."

Kelsey laughed with her parents. "Then, like, two days in, we wanted to switch to each other's class. I remember."

"Fickle, you two. A couple of Geminis." Their birthday was June twelfth, just one month after graduation.

When the plates were clean, as they always were when her father cooked, her mother looked at her father, then folded her hands under her chin. "We're so proud of you."

"But that's not all—" her dad said, pointing at her mother, taking a sip of wine.

"Rob! Dammit. I wanted to wait until after dessert."

"Oh," he said, shrugging. "Oops."

"I had these made," her mother said, suddenly very formal. "I hope you like them."

Her mom took out a box, and inside, Kelsey found a stack of invitations.

*Please help us celebrate the graduation of Ms. Kelsey Maxfield*, they read in shiny gold lettering, the same that graced her stationery. Then the time and the place: their backyard, an afternoon in May, hours after she would be done with high school forever. The invitation was outlined in crimson and blue, KU colors.

Kelsey put a hand to her mouth, and embraced her mother with the other.

"Invite as many people as you want," her mother said.

From across the table, her father said, "I'll cook whatever you want, too. Doesn't have to be burgers."

Her mother added, "We could even have La Parrilla cater."

As they continued chatting about the plans, Kelsey knew

they were all trying to look forward to the celebration, just as much as they didn't want to look behind it. Michelle's absence hung in the small things, like the fact that her sister had expressly said she didn't want a large, fancy party, or that when Kelsey had suggested a taco bar from La Parrilla last September, Michelle had turned up her nose.

Now Kelsey had no one standing in her way. She could make her graduation exactly how she wanted it to be. Kelsey would have to ignore what lay underneath the decorations and happy crowd and Mexican food: that without Michelle, it could never be exactly what she wanted, anyway.

# CHAPTER THIRTY-TWO

Meg was waiting for Kelsey in a high ponytail, a beater, and baggy basketball shorts, watching from the Farrows' front yard as the Subaru pulled up to the ranch house in El Dorado. Kelsey got out of the car, looking around to the surrounding houses, pretending not to recognize her. She was making good on her promise to help Peter's kid sister with her dance moves, but this time she was Kelsey, the less artistic, less academic party girl who didn't share anything with Michelle but their DNA. Basically, herself eight months ago. She could do this.

This is the last time, she assured herself on the drive over, and she meant it. Her plan was to straighten her hair, avoid the parents, and speak as little as possible.

Meg waved. Kelsey approached her on the yard in her stark white Asics shoes and a Lions Dance Team T-shirt. "Kelsey," she said, holding out her hand with a close-lipped smile.

Meg looked her up and down, and for a terrifying moment, right in the eyes. Her hand felt as if it had been in the air for hours.

Then Meg shook it. "I'm Meg," she said, smiling.

"I've heard a lot about you."

"Same here."

Kelsey lifted her shoulders, gesturing ambiguously. "So . . ." She wondered if Meg could tell she was nervous. "Want to show me your routine?"

They went to the backyard where Meg had set up portable speakers, and Kelsey had to use every ounce of will not to look to the woods, toward Snake Country.

For an hour they worked on Meg's difficulty with pirouettes. She was too hunched over and springy, an athlete more than a dancer, Kelsey observed, but that wouldn't stop her. Her footwork was flawless.

"You just need to loosen up a little bit," Kelsey said, rolling her shoulders. Meg followed suit. "Trust your balance, but don't trust it too much or it will get away from you and you'll fall all over yourself like this—"

Kelsey let her pirouette spin out of control, and she fell over on the grass. Meg laughed.

"Try again," Kelsey said, and as she watched Meg, the back door opened.

Peter's mother stood in the doorway. Cathy's health seemed to have multiplied since a week ago when Kelsey had seen her motionless in her hospital bed. Her eyes were bright, and she maneuvered past the patio furniture with confidence.

"You girls working hard?" she called.

"Yes, ma'am," Kelsey said. "Your daughter just killed a difficult turn."

"Well, I can't thank you enough for coming all the way out here."

"No trouble," Kelsey said, kicking an invisible spot on the ground.

"I met your sister, I'm told, but I haven't met you."

They went through the introductions, and Kelsey wondered how much Cathy remembered, mostly if she recalled the slurred hello in the hospital room, the last time she had seen her son. Her heart broke for the woman, who up close, still had slack on the left side of her face, a reminder of the stroke.

They sat down for lemonade, and Meg gushed about "Michelle" to her mother and to Kelsey, how much fun she was, how Peter was in "serious love."

Kelsey tried to stay more curious than familiar as Cathy delighted in the fact that Michelle had run "the Kroger mile," as she called it, swapping stories with her daughter about one time or another, like when Peter was supposed to get his assigned ingredients for lasagna, but brought back an entire frozen lasagna, instead.

Kelsey wished she could tell them that Peter had told her that story, too, on the way to the airport, and he still felt like he had been cheated out of a record time.

But that wasn't Kelsey's story to tell.

Several times, as the shadows grew longer across the backyard, Kelsey wanted to stand up and shout, beating her chest, I AM HER!

She wanted to run until she couldn't run any longer, buried deep in Snake Country, and there she would find Peter, all of her sins forgiven, and they would walk together through the wheat toward the horizon, toward the rest of their lives.

For now, she had to be content to sip on lemonade until all of it was gone.

"I should probably be heading back," Kelsey said. She turned to Meg. "You feel good about those pirouettes?"

"I feel real good." Meg nodded.

"Thank you so much for doing this," Cathy said, standing, pulling Kelsey in for a hug. "And thank your sister for me, too. Tell her to come by again, so I can meet her properly."

"I will," Kelsey said, and gave Meg a hard high five.

Maybe it was the fading light, but it looked like Peter's sister had a strange sadness in her eyes that she didn't have before. Kelsey must be imagining it. She imagined so much lately.

"Good luck! Let me know how you do!" she called to Meg as she exited the backyard.

They were good people, Kelsey decided, no way around that. Hopefully they were as merciful as they were good, but Kelsey had no control over their reaction. It was all in Peter's hands now.

Godspeed, she said to the invisible fates at work, and hoped she wouldn't be seeing El Dorado for the last time.

# CHAPTER THIRTY-THREE

Mrs. Wallace's sparsely attended class transformed into sil-houettes as Kelsey stood in front of them, facing the projector. Her baby-doll dress and go-go boots, an homage to the art-ist's muse, were bathed in the bright red-and-white light of a Campbell's Soup Can projected on-screen.

It was her last day of school as a senior at Lawrence High, and she had chosen the subject of her final Art History presen-tation the night before, poring through Michelle's old books, selecting the pieces that she liked best. It took her mind off of Peter, or rather, a lack of Peter. He had not emailed, called, or even been online for two weeks. It was torture.

Kelsey gathered herself, trying to concentrate.

"Rather than give you useless biographical facts that you're probably going to forget, anyway," Kelsey read off her notecards to the silent room, "I want to tell you what I find most interesting about Andy Warhol."

She nodded at Mrs. Wallace, who changed the slide on cue. The slide showed a photo of the man, hair bleached white, sunglasses on indoors, sitting next to the girl she was dressed as, whom she had seen in many of his short movies.

"I first learned about Andy Warhol from someone I loved very much, who is now gone. My sister. She used to paint these beautiful scenes, like perfect paintings of our back-yard, or our house, or the KU campus, but she did them in these wacky neon colors. I never understood why. I used to ask her why she didn't paint them as she saw them. I thought she was just trying to be annoying."

There were a few titters from the class.

"Then I saw this."

She nodded at Mrs. Wallace, who changed the slide to show three identical rows of the old movie star Marilyn Monroe, each square a copy of her face, but the hues switched in each one, all displaying different, Technicolor combinations.

"This is called Pop Art, something Andy Warhol is famous for, which takes commercials or brands and turns them into art. Michelle was doing the same thing, sort of. She was tak-ing something that everyone could recognize, like a house, or a porch, and using color to make people think about it differently. To make people realize what they were seeing every day was special. Andy Warhol did it through repeating the famous images over and over, or changing their color, and it made me think, well, anyone can do that.

"And I used to think that was bullshit, but actually, it's exciting." She glanced at Mrs. Wallace, hoping she hadn't offended her. The teacher nodded, urging her to go on.

"As long as you have something that people recognize, just any ordinary thing, like the pop songs and dance moves I do, for example . . ." Kelsey felt herself blush. "You can tweak it a little bit, and suddenly it's very special. Or you can tweak it a lot. The point is, you're making people look at it twice. They latch on to something they know, but they think about it more deeply. They don't have to love it, but it's there."

Kelsey had stopped reading off her notecards now.

"We let so much go by without acknowledging it's there," she said, and realized she was talking about a lot more than Andy Warhol.

"Anyway," Kelsey said, clearing her throat. "People say Warhol was doing it for money and celebrity, and maybe he was, but he didn't stop working after he became rich, so I don't think that was it. He just wanted to make people look twice."

She still couldn't see the faces of her classmates, but she didn't care if they had listened. She had said her piece.

"The end," she said, and right then, Kelsey felt a sense of completion. She was done with high school. She had tried to keep her hopes up, but Peter's silence had numbed her.

She might not get the best grades, but none of her teachers would fail her, and she had gotten into KU. Most important, she was pretty sure she had found what she was supposed to find: that she could be an artist someday, too.

On her way out of the classroom, as the next student made their way to the front, she stopped at Mrs. Wallace's desk. "Thank you," she whispered to the teacher. "I'm going now."

Mrs. Wallace whispered back, "Your presentation was a little short for my taste, but well done. Good luck, Ms. Maxfield."

Kelsey roamed the empty hallways, not bothering to change out of her sixties outfit. At her locker, she took out her phone to text Gillian and Ingrid, but paused, seeing the email that waited there.

She opened it, read it, and read it again to make sure.

Then, slamming her locker closed, she ran.

She ran through the back lot, dodging her fellow seniors, who stared suspiciously at her, running in her fake eyelashes and go-go boots. She found her car and rolled down the windows, stomping on the gas to reverse out of the parking space, and flying into the street, letting her hair-sprayed bun blow out in the May wind.

She parked haphazardly on the street in front of her house and ran up the stairs to open her laptop.

Peter had already called twice. She answered on his third

try, tapping the screen with her cursor over and over, begging it to show the face she had dreamed of every night, every day, every second.

"Hello?" she said, her ears buzzing, her face hot from the rush.

Nothing but scrambled sounds from the other end, and when he finally did appear, he was frozen, a wooden background where a green tent used to be. He must be in a new location, and this one had a bad Internet connection. She cursed the place, wherever he was.

But Peter looked happy to see her. Unless he was denouncing her with a smile on his face, he was happy to see her. His image moved again, but only slightly.

"Did you get my video?" she called, hoping she could hear him.

His sound cut in, only for a second, then out again. "Connection's bad—" she heard, then, "I— Got your video— I knew it."

She waited, barely breathing.

"It's okay—" Peter said, and though the sound dropped out again, goodness grew from her center, outward. His mouth formed words as he rubbed his head, explaining something.

"Try again? I can't hear you!" she called.

Suddenly, she heard the two syllables she had been longing for.

"Kelsey—"

Kelsey. Kelsey. He had said her name. Finally, he knew her for who she was and not who she was pretending to be. *I'm Kelsey, and you love me.*

"I love you, Peter," she said, and he appeared to have finally heard her.

"I love you, too—" he said, and leaned closer to the screen, but at that point, the call dropped.

She jumped out of her desk chair, and then on top of it, yelling until her lungs got tired. "YES! Yes, yes, yes, yes!"

She opened the screen door to her porch and fought the urge to shimmy up the drainpipe to the roof of her house.

Her future was still uncertain, and so was his, but they would be together. First, in Kansas, then, who knows? She closed her eyes, feeling the wind.

The sun had risen over a path, she could see Peter there, ready to take it with her. She was free.

# CHAPTER THIRTY-FOUR

Kelsey, Gillian, and Ingrid surveyed the party from above, their graduation gowns in wrinkled heaps on Kelsey's floor. Kelsey was wearing the dress the three of them had picked out from the Topshop in the Kansas City plaza, a simple, short skater dress in bright crimson, to match the crimson and blue balloons her mother had tied on every available surface, making their house appear like a giant playground ball pit.

"But in a good way," she had assured her mom.

Besides the grief group, they hadn't had guests over since Michelle's funeral, and until yesterday, it had showed. Her mother had rescheduled her students' final so she and Kelsey could spend the morning clearing out the pizza boxes from the recycling, sweeping the floors, putting ailing house plants out of their misery.

They had spoken little, handing each other the dustpan, catching each other's eyes with small, warm smiles.

When they were through, Kelsey reminded her to hide the jade statues.

The pomp and circumstance came next: shaking hands with the principal she barely knew, holding up her diploma for photos from every angle, and her favorite part, tossing her cap in the air among so many others, like a flock of one-flight birds.

"Oh, look," Gillian said, pointing to the yard from the porch. "There's that guy from Chemistry. You invited that guy?"

"Sure," Kelsey said, careful not to muss her lipstick on her straw. "I invited everybody. Why not?"

"Even Davis?"

"What? Where?" Kelsey scanned the crowd, then found him immediately, chatting up her father next to Anna and George, as well as some of his fraternity brothers.

"I didn't invite him, actually." Her mother must have contacted her ex-boyfriend, for the sake of good graces.

He caught her looking at him, and waved. She waved back.

Davis made a long, brushing motion with his hand, from his head, all the way down, and pointed at her. *Beautiful*, he mouthed, and gave a thumbs-up.

*Thank you*, Kelsey mouthed, and smiled.

Everything was beautiful. This afternoon, just as the green of the backyard trees had realized its full potential,

Kelsey's mother had strung the leaves with Lions' red streamers, like Christmas. Even the halfhearted peonies that her father had planted long ago looked fertile and content, thick white petals drooping in droves.

Bees swarmed the sugar-soaked rims of margarita glasses.

Someone had brought their French bulldog to the party, who made his rounds licking sauce off of fingertips.

"The frat boys are going to eat all the tacos," Ingrid complained, examining her manicure.

"Let them eat tacos," Kelsey said with a flourish of her hand like a queen over her subjects. She didn't know most of the people crowding the speakers, which were blasting Beyoncé, or at least she didn't know them anymore. But she had barely known herself until now. Today, she was weightless.

She was a graduate. She was a future Rock Chalk Dancer. She was in love with Peter, who would be home in a matter of months.

Which reminded her.

"Be right back," she told Gillian and Ingrid, and went inside to get her phone.

Meg had texted her earlier, asking her what her plans were today.

*Can't come help you practice*, Kelsey typed, because she couldn't see any other reason why Meg would be asking. *My parents are throwing me a graduation party!*

Before she hit SEND, she paused, remembering. Meg still didn't know about Michelle.

She debated, then edited the text to read *My parents are throwing us a graduation party!* and sent the message. Eventually Meg would understand, once Peter got home to explain it to her.

She returned to her side of the porch, which would always be her side. Even Gillian and Ingrid hadn't spread out to Michelle's section, out of habit, or perhaps out of quiet respect.

"To Mitch," Kelsey said, lifting up her glass.

"To Mitch," they repeated, and Gillian put a hand on her shoulder.

Kelsey was transported to last year at this time, when the four of them were attending Davis's graduation party.

Kelsey and Michelle were just about to turn seventeen. They were standing around an enormous sheet cake. As they gathered, Kelsey's mother, Davis's parents, and his grandparents began to take their photo. Flashes sprayed their vision for a few minutes, the lot of them united, barely touching each other's backs as they stood, imagining it was just another five minutes they had together. Together as they were, seventeen and nothing else.

Michelle had chosen that moment to whisper to Kelsey, "This time next year, I'll be long gone."

"Yeah, right," Kelsey had whispered. "Miss your own graduation? Where will you go?"

"I don't know. The East Coast. Maybe Europe."

Kelsey had looked at her sister and raised her eyebrows, sarcastic. "Fine. Good riddance."

Kelsey was pulled back to the present by the stone in her gut. Gillian and Ingrid stood beside her, soaking up the midafternoon heat.

She wished now she would have said something else. No, asked something. She wished she would have asked Michelle what she wanted to do when she got there, what art she would make, who she wanted to be. Had she asked, her sister wouldn't have been such a mystery to her now, in the present.

Then again, maybe Michelle didn't know, either. She might have been a completely different person by now. So much could change in a year. So much could change in seconds.

*Thank you*, she thought, though she didn't know who or what she was thanking. She was thankful for the memories, at least, that would never leave her, but didn't have to haunt her, either. Not all ghosts are meant to make you sad or scared.

She was grateful for the passage of time.

"I wish Peter were here," Kelsey found herself saying aloud.

Gillian glanced at her, winking. After Peter had called the other day, she had told Gillian and Ingrid straightaway.

They had pestered her with questions: What would she do once he got back? Would he move to Lawrence? Would she follow him out East? Would they live out the summer, and leave it at that?

Kelsey didn't know. Love had a way of dissolving every object and detail and fact of reality that wasn't immediately blooming, offering itself to the feeling. She let herself be carried by it.

All she knew was that in two days, she would attend the official tryout for the Rock Chalk Dancers. She had practiced the assigned routine for hours, until it had become pure muscle memory. Ingrid, while watching her, had told her the only thing missing was her face. Kelsey didn't look like she was enjoying it, Ingrid said.

In two days, Ingrid would start her summer job, lifeguarding at the local pool.

In two days, Gillian would leave town, visiting her older sister in New York.

Two days didn't matter right now, though.

Now they were sipping margaritas, all of them in heels that made them several inches taller than usual.

Beside her, Ingrid hit her arm.

"What?"

"We have to go downstairs," Ingrid said, her voice squealing.

"Please don't tell me it's another picture," Kelsey said,

rolling her eyes as she stared into her empty margarita glass. "My mouth hurts from smiling."

Gillian also gasped, and pulled Kelsey away from the porch railing, toward her room. She licked her thumb, rubbing a dab of taco sauce off of Kelsey's cheek.

"What the hell, Gil?" They must have seen something she didn't see. She made for the porch again, but the two of them yanked her away.

"Downstairs. Now," Gillian said.

She followed them as they stomped quickly down the steps, trying not to trip on their heels. When they reached the kitchen, Ingrid opened the back door, and Gillian ushered Kelsey outside.

Against the fence, he stood, almost unrecognizable in army dress blues. He was holding his beret in one hand, and a bouquet of roses in the other, searching through the faces for hers.

Finally, they found each other's eyes from across the yard. Her mouth fell open.

# CHAPTER THIRTY-FIVE

"Peter."

He pushed past the mingling crowd and was suddenly in her arms, swaying back and forth, her body pressed against the buttons of his coat.

"We got pulled," he whispered in her ear. "My company got pulled early."

"When did you get here?" she said, still muffled in his shoulder.

"Just now. Just landed in Kansas City. I asked Meg where you were. I wanted to surprise you," he said, running his fingers through her hair.

"You did!" she said, laughing.

She had so much to take in about him, she didn't know where to look. His smile, sly and sweet and proud, or his dark blue eyes. She found her favorite part, the white blonde streak in his eyebrow, and brushed her thumb over it.

People were looking. She didn't care.

She pulled him to a corner of the yard, away from the crowd. "Look at you." She held him out in front of her.

Peter looked down at the flowers in his hand. "I didn't know if you like roses, but I figure, who doesn't like—"

"Everyone likes roses," she said, and giggled. She led him inside. Shivers poured through her from her chest down to her feet, washing her calm, almost sleepy with happiness.

They sat in the still house, making room on the couch among the balloons.

"I feel like I'm in outer space or something," he said, looking around.

"This is perfect," she said quietly. "How long will you be back?"

"Until they call me for another tour," Peter said. "Which may be in a couple of months, maybe never."

"Let's say never." Red and blue light cast through the spheres. Then Kelsey pulled his face close to her and kissed him. "I love you so much," she said, and his eyes lit up.

Their foreheads touched.

"I love you, too, Michelle."

A muted thunder in her head, like a bomb going off.

Kelsey drew back. She was unsure of what she just heard. "What?"

"What?" Peter repeated, pulling back to look at her, his

brow coming together over a puzzled smile. He batted a blue balloon away from his shoulder.

Kelsey searched his face, unable to ignore a panicked ringing in her ears. "Was that an accident?"

"Was what an accident?"

"You called me Michelle."

His voice lilted, joking, "That's no accident. It's pretty standard for humans to call one—"

"Peter," she said quietly. "I'm Kelsey. You know that I'm Kelsey. You said you got my video when we talked last week."

"What video?" His eyes narrowed, and his smile disappeared. "What do you mean, 'I'm Kelsey'?" He spoke slowly. "If you're Michelle's sister . . ."

Kelsey's pulse jackhammered. "I sent you a video to explain. You said you got it."

Peter spit air, incredulous. "I never got a video, Kelsey! Is this a joke?" Peter frowned. "I honestly don't know what you mean."

"Okay," she started, and humiliation at its purest seemed to form a force field between them. "This is weird. Try to remember the video. Try to remember telling me about the video."

Her image on-screen, as he was supposed to have watched, came to her, hurting her head.

She had opened her mouth and pointed out her crooked incisor to the camera. *See that?* she had said to Peter. *And this?* She had stood and turned to reveal the mole on her lower back. Those are really the only differences. Were. Were the only differences.

"Video? I never said anything about—Oh. I told Michelle the video was bad on our Skype call. That's the only time I said anything about a video."

"I thought you understood. I—" Kelsey swallowed.

Peter's face got gentler, trying to understand. He put his hands on her arms. "You keep saying that. I have no idea what you're talking about. This is insane. Where is Michelle?" His eyes moved briefly around them, as if she were there, somewhere in the house.

Kelsey's breaths were coming slow and frayed. She was paralyzed.

She had already done this. She had already broken down as far as she could go. She couldn't go back now, right here, in a sea of balloons, people laughing and talking outside.

"Say something!" he burst out. "Please tell me what you're doing!" The beret was crumpled in his fist.

Slowly, the two of them stood.

She couldn't speak. It took everything Kelsey had to will herself to the mantel, where a folded piece of paper sat, as it had remained for eight months. She handed it to Peter and waited, her eyes down, just feet from where she stood that day in October.

It was a program from Michelle's funeral. Kelsey had

memorized and recited the passage written inside, from the Book of 1 Corinthians.

She remembered: *I tell you this, brothers: Flesh and blood cannot inherit the kingdom of God, nor does the perishable inherit the imperishable. Behold! I tell you a mystery. We shall not all sleep, but we shall all be changed, in a moment, in the twinkling of an eye, at the last trumpet.*

She tried to push away the sound of her own voice saying those mechanical words, but her brain wouldn't let her forget that cold day. Now of all times, as if it was taking her there to punish her.

Peter read the program, turned it over, and read it again, the letter she should have sent from the beginning.

"She died?" His voice was surprisingly light, with the accidental innocence of a kid. "She's dead?"

Kelsey tried to choke out a response, but her brain was too busy.

*But someone will ask,* her voice echoing in the microphone, absorbed by somber faces, *"How are the dead raised? With what kind of body do they come?" You foolish person! What you sow does not come to life unless it dies.*

Her mother entered the room, stepping over balloons. "Kelsey, what is going on?"

*But God gives it a body as he has chosen, and to each kind of seed its own body.*

"Shut up!" she said aloud, and her mother looked at her

like she was a wild animal. "I'm so stupid," she muttered. A thin layer of cool sweat coated her skin. "I thought you knew. I thought you had forgiven me."

She could see the muscles of Peter's jaw working. "Forgiven you? How am I supposed to forgive you?"

Kelsey's mother took her shoulders gently, turning Kelsey to face her. "Kels, look at me. What happened?"

But Kelsey couldn't stop looking at Peter. She wished he would look at her for just a second, a millisecond, so he could remember who she was, really. His best friend. His love.

Peter's voice bit into the room.

"I can't believe you did this to me." Peter paused to laugh, but there was nothing good in the sound. Nothing mirthful. "What a—what a strange thing."

Her mother's grip tightened on her arm.

"Peter, please!" Kelsey called, her voice weak and strung.

When he finally met her eyes, there was nothing behind them. "I can't deal with this." He set the program carefully back on the mantel.

Kelsey tried to step around her mother, but she held tight to her shoulders. "How was I supposed to tell you?"

"I need to . . ." Peter put his hand to his forehead, trying to find an exit. "It will be best for everyone if I leave, I think."

"Don't leave!" Kelsey was practically screaming. Her

words left her before she thought them, quick and sloppy. "It's still me. . . . No matter what you called me . . . I'm still the person you talked to and wrote to. . . . I love you in every real way. . . . I tried to stop but I couldn't. . . . I . . ."

Her mother put her mouth close to Kelsey's ear. "It's time to be quiet now. Let him be."

The din of her own words collapsed on her. *For not all flesh is the same, but there is one kind for humans. . . .* She felt a deep pain, but had no idea where it was coming from.

The funeral passage, haunting her, now engraved in Kelsey's eyes:

*Death is swallowed up in victory. O death, where is your victory? O death, where is your sting?*

Peter sidestepped the table, the couch, taking the widest route around her that he could, kicking balloons out of the way.

With a creak and a click of the door, he was gone.

Dear Michelle,

My flashlight ran out of power last night because I was reading your letter over and over. I hadn't planned on it, but once I read it, it seemed like the most natural thing in the world to start at the beginning again. You make me laugh too loud late at night. You get me in trouble.

I've heard it said that comedians are the saddest people, that they resort to humor because their world is so dark and absurd it doesn't make sense, that you have to be in deep pain to be funny, something like that. They say that about artists, too, for that matter. Hell, Vincent van Gogh cut off his own ear. What I'm saying is, you are both funny and an artist, and I hope that sadness is not the case with you.

But I would also understand if it was. I've always had a bit of the blues myself, even before I decided that a free college education would be worth nine months in this hellhole. I hate it when older people say that we have nothing to be sad about, that we're young and we couldn't possibly know real sadness. Or maybe no one has said that to you. But I bet they have. Anyway, if I've learned anything here, it would be from the children who hang out in burnt-out buildings by themselves, with no one to talk to but a dog and a beat-up soccer ball. They have lost their moms and dads and brothers and sisters, and who would say they don't know real sadness? Sadness isn't measured in years. Feelings, I don't think, can be measured in anything. We are just bodies guessing about other bodies. That's why songs and paintings and poems exist. They're the best guesses.

I told you once that the thought of you somewhere happy is what keeps me going, but the thought of you somewhere sad is okay, too. I mean, I don't want you to be sad, and if you aren't that's good, but it's just you, as you are, that I think about. However you are.

Are you sad?

You don't have to tell me. But just like you are there somewhere for me, I am here somewhere for you. If you are sad, I want to make you happy. If you are happy, I want to make you happier. Pen is running out of ink. Must get new pen.

Yours,
Peter

# CHAPTER THIRTY-SIX

A knock on her door woke Kelsey from a dreamless sleep. It was dark outside, but her lights were still on. She had no idea how long she'd been out, but the partygoers were gone. One of Peter's old letters lay next to her on the bed.

Her mother entered, now changed out of her dress clothes into sweatpants, glasses on the tip of her nose.

"All right, get up," her mother said.

"Thanks, Mom, but I really don't feel like talking right now," Kelsey said, burying herself deeper in her pillows.

"Sit up," her mother said.

"What time is it?" Kelsey asked.

"It's time for you to be held accountable for your actions. Sit up."

Her mother's tone made Kelsey feel like she was seven years old again, and she hated it, but she did as she was told.

"Put on a sweater."

She followed her mother to the front door without a word. The night air smelled as if it had just rained and they walked toward the river to the sound of the breeze. Yesterday's events were still with her. Michelle's death was, at least, out of her hands. It was accidental, a freak event.

The shame of losing Peter, of losing him because of her lies, seemed more like an endless sickness no one could cure. She would never forget what she'd done to him.

When they stepped aside for a jogger, Kelsey realized it must almost be dawn.

"I didn't sleep last night," her mother said beside her.

"Why?" Kelsey asked. Her throat felt itchy from crying.

Her mother put her hands in her sweatshirt pockets as she walked, and sighed. "I don't know whether to call this boy's mother or take you to a psychiatrist or what."

Kelsey stopped in her tracks. "What? No."

She put up her hands. "You obviously aren't handling your sister's death well—"

"None of us are handling Mitch's death well!" Her voice was raised. Her fists were clenched. It was all coming out now. The rage, the hurt, the sensation of yelling at her mother from the bottom of a well to HELP ME UP, GODDAMNIT. "You criticize me all the time! You fill my house with strangers that you talk to more than me!"

She paused for air, watching her mother's face fall. But Kelsey wasn't finished.

"You don't even like me!"

Her mother spoke softly. "That couldn't be further from the truth. I love you."

Kelsey wiped her nose. "Then why doesn't it feel like you do?"

She couldn't make out her mother's face anymore in the streetlights, just the outline of her mane of hair and her body, more sure of itself than Kelsey's. "Let's keep walking."

The flush of anger had not left Kelsey's face. "Why?" she asked.

"Because."

There was a deep rhythm to that exchange, an understanding that existed before she could even spell her name: *Do this*, her mother would say. *Why?* she and her sister would ask. *Because*, and that was the end of it. They would follow her anywhere.

But this wasn't any other day. "Because why?" Kelsey countered.

She could sense a smile behind her mother's words. "I'm not taking you to the loony bin, Kels."

They continued on until they reached the river, and turned right down the gravel path on the north bank, deep into the trees as morning broke through the branches. Rocks crunched under their feet, birds conversed. The silence was soothing. Maybe it was the act of walking, setting a pace, putting her body back into a steady cadence. Maybe she had forgotten how well her body could speak to her. Maybe her mother knew what she was doing.

When they reached the large rusted gate that marked the end of public property, her mother leaned on it, and Kelsey followed suit. They looked at each other, two versions of the same eyes, one with makeup streaks, one with crow's-feet. Her mother waited, asking silently, Why?

She could tell the story from the beginning, as she had done for her friends, as she had done on the video, or she could just answer.

"I missed her," Kelsey said finally. "I really didn't mean to pretend to be her. I wasn't even good at it. It was mostly just wanting to be close to her again, you know? Even closer than I was when she was alive."

Her mother was looking at her, contemplating. "And Peter wanted to be close to her, too."

"Yeah, I guess. And I just couldn't tell him. I couldn't be the one to break his heart. I kept going after him because . . ."

She had already said that she had missed Michelle. Her mother knew what it was like to miss Michelle, and she could say that to anyone, any old day. She dug deeper.

"I wanted to do something. I didn't want to think. Whenever I thought too much, I wanted to take a seat and . . ." Kelsey thought of the night with Davis and his parents, sitting on the curb. "And never move again. Just rot.

No, rotting would be too slow." She swallowed. "I wanted to die."

"I know how you feel," her mother replied.

Kelsey looked up, in shock. She couldn't imagine her mother thinking anything like that, anything strange and dark and unexplainable. Her mother made lists. People who make lists didn't have room for those thoughts.

Her mother nodded. "I wanted to do something, too, I suppose. But that was easy for me. I had a career."

"That's the thing," Kelsey jumped in, smacking her hand on the iron railing. "It wasn't enough just to do more of the things I already did when she was alive. I wanted to, like . . ." Opening the letter. Comforting Peter. Going to Paris. "Do things for her. Because she couldn't."

Her mother reached out to stroke her arm. "There are limits to what we can do for people. We can't do everything for everyone. And, honey, you're going to have to be strong when I say this."

Kelsey took a deep breath.

"You picked the wrong thing to do. For Peter, for Michelle, for yourself. No matter what you were feeling, that was not the right thing to do. What did you think would happen? You had to have known you'd break his heart eventually."

She opened her mouth. "But—"

"No more excuses. I want you to repeat after me. *That was not the right thing to do.*"

Kelsey took a moment. She had never really said it, the whole time she was talking to Peter. She had never really told herself it was wrong. Because she didn't want to. She sighed.

"That was not the right thing to do," Kelsey said.

"It was selfish."

Kelsey hung her head.

"Repeat," she could hear her mother say.

"It was selfish."

"It was cruel."

Kelsey put her face in her hands. "It was cruel."

Her mother took her hands down and held them, squeezing. "You are a wonderful young woman who was a little mixed up."

"A little more than a little."

"A lot. But you know who's supposed to be there when young women get mixed up?"

Kelsey looked up.

"Their mothers. And I wasn't," her mother started, and her chin began to tremble.

Kelsey put her fingers under her mother's eyes, catching her tears. "Don't cry, Mom."

"And their fathers, too. And we were so wrapped up in our own grief, we didn't do our job. We had no idea how bad it was for you. You were always such a fighter. Michelle was the sensitive one, feeling everything so deeply, but you were tough."

"I'm still tough," Kelsey offered, but it sounded silly coming from her now, her nose red, her pink cardigan over her graduation dress.

"Oh, Kels." Her mother reached out, and Kelsey nestled against her for the first time in so long, feeling some of the pain ebb away. But most of it was still there. It had been there before she knew Peter, and it would be there forever.

"I'm sorry," she said softly.

"Me, too," her mother said.

"I just miss her so much."

"Me, too," her mother said, and Kelsey could feel her mom's chest begin to tighten against her, tears falling in her hair. Kelsey pulled her closer.

After a while, they began to walk again, in step with each other, moving back east, toward the sunrise.

Kelsey realized that the ache inside her wasn't just grief, it was something else. Something simpler. She broke the silence. "I'm hungry. Can we get ice cream?"

Her mother let out her squawk of a laugh, making Kelsey jump. It was so rare to hear these days.

"It's seven a.m.," her mother replied. Then, after some thought, she asked, "You think the grocery store is open?"

# CHAPTER THIRTY-SEVEN

Kelsey stood at the center of Memorial Stadium in a line of dancers, her curls so stiff with hair spray she could almost hear them clack together as she moved her head. Her eyelashes were heavy with mascara, and her lips sticky with a fresh coat of color. She smiled at the enormous empty egg of seats as if they contained thousands of adoring fans. She hadn't said a word to anyone except for hello and her name. She had made herself into a machine, because that was what it took to compete.

Now it was paying off. She was one out of twelve left in a full-day tryout that began with hundreds. After the first round of basic moves, half of them dropped like flies. After the second round, dozens were unable to pick up a basic two-minute sequence in the time allotted. They let her stay. Not because she stood out, and not because she had a certain way about her. No one can pick up individuality from stadium seats. She was still there because she could execute.

A redhead on the current team paced on the Astroturf in front of the line of girls, her poms behind her back. She was Missy, Kelsey remembered, the girl she met at Davis's party so long ago. She'd given Kelsey a little wave and a wink from the sideline.

"Welcome to the final round of Rock Chalk Dancer try-outs! Congratulate yourselves. You've come this far out of a group of incredible dancers."

Missy gave them a few exaggerated claps with her poms, and the dancers on the sideline did the same.

"You were expected to memorize a hip-hop combo. You will perform it solo. Can we see number seven, please?"

The first girl was also a machine, Kelsey observed. But good mechanics shouldn't necessarily mean the dancer looks like a robot. Each motion was crisp, but the movements looked disconnected from one another. They should flow, as if the dancer was exposing something, as if she was thinking about each movement as she went. Like the video Mrs. Wallace had showed her. That was what dance should be.

"Thank you," the redhead called, and looked at her clipboard. "Fifty-two, please!"

The next girl was perfect, until the very end. The back handspring left her off balance, which caused her jump turn to be poorly timed.

Kelsey swallowed, still smiling, clapping for her competitors, but she knew the back handspring might give her trouble, too. Unless you were a gymnast, a back handspring would give any dancer trouble.

"Thank you. Twelve, please!"

As number 12 performed, Kelsey let her mind drift. She had stopped trying to block her thoughts of Peter. In fact, his anger had pushed her to work harder. She found it was easier to lose herself to dance when there was something to run from.

So she would focus on her back handspring. She would visualize herself completing it over and over, until her body did its job.

Watching the flip in her mind's eye, Kelsey couldn't help but think of the absurdity of her entire future resting on one half-second movement.

If she made the team, she would complete hundreds of handsprings each year, and yet this one was so important because she would do it today on the Astroturf, in front of a bunch of girls who called her by a number.

She watched 12 complete the combo, and in lieu of applause, the dancers clapped twice, following their leader.

The row of faces, made up in Technicolor reds and blues, reminded Kelsey of Andy Warhol's prints of Marilyn Monroe. Except she couldn't see how they made anyone think twice about dancing. In fact, if she deviated from the routine in even the smallest of ways, if she made herself "special," she would be eliminated.

Is this how she wanted to spend hours and hours of the next four years?

"Thank you. Thirty-four, please!"

Too late to decide now, the decision was already made. Kelsey was number 34. She stepped out of the line, toes pointed as she walked to the center of the field, marking her spot on the 50-yard line.

The music began, and she let her doubts fall. She let her body do its job.

As she got down on her knees, she thought of the last time she felt special as she danced: when she had made up the moves herself. When her dancers had fallen to the floor and jumped up to the drop in "Dance Yrself Clean."

She didn't miss a beat. She had been working on this combo for six months.

Then she thought of swinging her hips in Paris as Peter watched her. He loved the way she danced. He was discovering who she really was without even knowing it.

Time for the back handspring.

She wound up, and it was perfect. She almost wanted to laugh. All that worrying for nothing.

She killed the routine.

Kelsey was a great dancer.

But she didn't need them. She wanted to make people

feel special. She wanted to make people think twice. And the first person who she needed to do both with was in El Dorado.

As the girls put their poms together twice, Kelsey tore off the number stuck to her tank top, and walked off the field.

If she hurried, she could catch Peter before he left Kansas again. For where, she didn't know, but she wasn't going to let him go without her.

# CHAPTER THIRTY-EIGHT

Kelsey sped west as if a fire spread behind her. It may have not been the right thing to do. She didn't know if this was the right thing in the eyes of her mother, of all others, but she knew it was right for her.

When she arrived at Peter's doorstep, uncertainty kept her on the lawn. She was conveniently forgetting all the hurt she caused him, she knew that.

But it didn't have to be hurt. Anyone who had been in their shoes would know how certain she was that she loved him, and that he loved her.

She knocked.

Cathy answered, dressed in an oversized Kansas Jayhawks T-shirt and Garfield pajama pants. At first, she didn't register Kelsey's face, in all her dance makeup and her Lycra outfit. Then her blue eyes narrowed.

Peter must have told her everything.

"You," she said, in disbelief that Kelsey was right there, in front of her. "What are you doing here?"

Kelsey kept her chin up. She would not be ashamed. She would not be afraid anymore. "I came to say sorry, and to explain."

"Apology not accepted," Cathy said. "Get out of here!"

"Please let me in. I need to talk to Peter."

"You are the last person he wants to talk to."

That hit hard. She had fallen so far. Kelsey said nothing, but she didn't move.

"Listen, I'm telling it to you like it is. He never wants to see you again. Get the picture?"

Kelsey tried to glance beyond Cathy's arm, hoping for any trace of Peter. But she only saw a dark house.

"Please," Kelsey said, her voice smaller now. "I didn't mean for it to get so out of hand. I love him."

Cathy said nothing. She only made an exaggerated pointing motion, whirling her finger, as if she were telling a dog, *Go*.

Her skin glowing with shame and anger, Kelsey walked off the stoop.

"Just stay away from my son," Cathy said to her back. "That's easy enough."

Kelsey whipped back around to say something, she didn't know what, but the door had closed.

She got into the Subaru and started the ignition, staring at her steering wheel.

Suddenly, there was a tap on the window. Her heart jumped.

Meg stood outside the car, with her same high ponytail, this time wearing a T-shirt that said WILDCATS DANCE TEAM.

Kelsey rolled down the driver's-side window.

"Hey," Meg said.

"Hey."

"How ya doin'?" Meg said, and Kelsey could tell she had silently cursed herself for asking a pretty obvious question.

"Can I ask you something?"

Meg nodded.

"Is he in there?" Kelsey pointed to the house.

Meg looked back, and nodded again. He must have seen her, or at least heard her. The house wasn't that big. Maybe his mother was right: He must really, truly hate her.

Kelsey looked at Meg. She was surprised she'd even talk to her. "What do you think of all this?"

Meg frowned, thinking. "Well," she said, hesitant. "I've known for a while, actually."

"How?"

In answer, Meg held up an envelope. Kelsey's video.

"It got redirected here when they switched bases," Meg explained. "I opened it because . . . Well, I don't know why I opened it. I was curious about you, I guess. And then I met you, and I liked you, and then I met you again, and I liked you again. I didn't know what to do! I didn't want to mess with what you had, you know, going on. You and my brother, you're good together."

Kelsey felt her mouth twisting, her teeth clenched. They may have been good together, but it was too late now. He hated her. As he should.

Meg continued, "So, I think . . . you should have it. Right?" She dropped the envelope in Kelsey's lap through the open window.

Kelsey picked it up, and tossed it right back out. "Burn it," she told Meg.

She didn't want another reminder of her stupid mistake. She would cut herself off from this family, from these memories, from this house. She revved her engine.

Meg picked the envelope off the ground and hit herself on the head with the palm of her hand. "I ruined everything, didn't I?"

"Nope," Kelsey said with a sarcastic smile. "I ruined everything." Then she noticed Meg's shirt. "Congratulations on making the team, by the way," she said, and rolled up her window before she drove away.

# CHAPTER THIRTY-NINE

Packing for Paris was much more pleasant this time around. More peaceful, at least. Kelsey folded—well, more like stuffed; she wasn't a big fan of wasting time for the sake of creases—pair of skinny jeans after pair of skinny jeans, cardigans on top of cardigans, never having to worry about anyone's taste in clothing but her own. She left room for all her dance stuff, which was still in the wash. She wasn't sure what kind of apparel she'd need for an intensive modern dance program, but assumed she'd have most of the basics already. If not, she'd wing it. There were worse problems in life.

A week ago, after she had returned from El Dorado, Kelsey had walked with her graduation cash to the bank downtown, created herself an account, and found she had enough money for airfare to pretty much anywhere.

She had considered South America, but her Spanish was as rudimentary as her French, and she was never one to romanticize grand chains of mountains or the rain forest. The prairie did her fine, as far as nature went. She was a Kansas girl.

Paris, however, still called to her as it had the first time she saw it, and after all, she hadn't even gotten to see half the places she had seen on the subway posters.

Her parents had agreed to use her first semester's tuition at KU to fund a month-long dance program in Paris over the summer. Kelsey had deferred her acceptance to college. She would get there eventually.

But first: This evening she'd be gone. She'd have two months to herself in the city until the dance program started, and though it sounded lonely, it was probably just what she needed: time to gather a semblance of Kelsey as she was now, no Michelle, no Peter, no Davis, no University of Kansas dance team.

Her father called up to her from downstairs, "You ready, sweetie?"

"Coming!" she called.

Before she left, the Maxfields had one more thing to do.

As they exited the front door, her mother picked up the simple silver urn they had finally taken from the funeral home. It wouldn't stay in their house. They had agreed there were already enough memories of Michelle there.

With it, they walked down the street, along the jagged brick sidewalks, under the canopy of thick oaks and cotton-woods, all the way to the old railroad tracks.

The three of them passed over the tracks and down the path to the dam, where they found a makeshift trail of rocks through the low water. They climbed the limestone ramp to the top of the dam, where they stood in its center, watching the Kansas River wind all the way west, through the landscape.

Kelsey took the silver urn out of its bag, and handed it to her mother.

Her mother held it to her lips briefly, whispering something Kelsey could not hear. She handed it to her husband.

"Good-bye, my sweet baby," her father said, cradling the urn in his arms for a moment.

Then he handed it to Kelsey, a small smile on his face. It was heavy and warm from the sun.

Kelsey knew she didn't have to say anything out loud. She and Michelle would always be speaking back and forth, whether she wanted to or not. That was the way they worked, and would always work; tied, taking from, pushing, completing the other.

*Have fun*, she said silently to Michelle, and lifted the lid.

The unknowable ache inside her dimmed, and the ashes fell into the breeze, flowered into the water, and traveled on their way.

When they were a block from home, they could see a figure sitting on their porch swing. She recognized him in a second, and her chest burned. Kelsey's mother and father passed him on their way inside, without a word, but Kelsey stayed.

"Hi, Peter," she said.

He was wearing jeans and a faded blue Kansas Jayhawks T-shirt. Where she stood, a few feet away, she could see his eyes capture the color.

"Meg gave me this," he said, standing, and in his hands was the envelope holding her flash drive, now frayed at the edges from its journey to Afghanistan and back.

Kelsey remained quiet. She hadn't had the faintest hope he would have seen it, and now that he had, she prepared for another wound to open. If he hated her then, he would hate her more for her delusion. And yet, nothing could keep her from wanting to pour out gratitude that he was even here, so unexpected. When you love someone that much, you don't get to choose when or how or whether or not to stop. She had tried, but she had given up quickly.

"Did you mean all of it?" he asked.

She sighed. "Every word."

Why was he here?

"In that case," he said, stepping down off the porch, "I'm sorry for the way I treated you. And my mother, I'm sure she's sorry, too."

"Well," Kelsey said, putting her hands on her hips, recovering from a blow that never came. "I forgive you. Of course I forgive you. I'd be crazy not to forgive you."

Peter held up the envelope, with a half smile. "You'd be crazy either way."

"You're crazy, too," she said, shrugging, remembering the way she watched him lie in her lap in Snake Country, fighting battles real and unreal.

"We're both a little nuts, aren't we?"

Kelsey nodded, smiling, staring at the brick sidewalk below her. He touched her arm, and she lifted her head.

Peter's face had shifted. "But we'd be worse off if we didn't have each other. I know I'd have been worse off if I didn't have you, no matter who you were, or were pretending to be. You made me feel brave." His mouth twitched. "Like I could get through it."

"And you did," Kelsey said.

"I kept your letters," he said, speaking quickly, nervously.

A tight smile grew on Kelsey's face. "I dug yours out of the trash."

"Well, thank you," he said. "For doing that."

"They smell like mustard now," she let out.

He laughed loudly, surprising both of them. His eyes met hers, and then their gazes couldn't unstick.

They didn't speak for a while, considering each other. Music began to play from inside the house, some sort of piano. A warm gust blew around them.

"What do you think?" he asked. "Want to start over?"

Kelsey's eyes stung for some reason, though all she felt

was relief. Everything was clear, even the tears through which she saw him.

"Sure," she said, as casual as could be.

"Hi, I'm Peter." And he smiled his smile, holding out his hand.

"Hi, Peter," she said, and she took it. "I'm Kelsey."

# ACKNOWLEDGMENTS

Thank you to my mother and father, and to all of my family and friends in the Sunflower State—Elise, Jamie, wherever you are, for making my memories of Lawrence bright and rich. To my older brother, Wyatt, for his service to our country, and for his consultation on the experience of being deployed to Afghanistan. Ian, for cheering me on as you went to bed, and again when you saw me in the same spot in the morning. Mandy and Emma, I would not be who I am if you were not who you are. A toast to the Revolver crew, who lights a fire in me whenever I see them. Thank you, Katie McGee, for being my editor and champion at Alloy, and for being the inceptor of this incredible story. Thank you to Pam Garfinkel and the entire team at Little, Brown for making all of this happen. We writers would be nothing without you.

TURN THE PAGE FOR A SNEAK PEEK AT
LARA AVERY'S *THE MEMORY BOOK*.

THEY SAY I'LL FORGET. I'M WRITING TO REMEMBER.

the memory book

LARA AVERY

"Things you will probably experience while reading this
wonderful book: gut-wrenching hope, ugly-crying, the joy of
finding beautiful moments in the midst of difficult times. Enjoy."
—ADI ALSAID, author of *Let's Get Lost* and *Never Always Sometimes*

# THE MEMORY BOOK

If you're reading this, you're probably wondering who you are. I'll give you three clues.

Clue 1: You just stayed up all night to finish an AP Lit paper on *The Poisonwood Bible.* You fell asleep briefly while you were writing and dreamed you were making out with James Monroe, the fifth president and arbiter of the Monroe Doctrine.

Clue 2: I am writing this to you from the attic at the little circular window, you know the one, at the east end of the house, where the ceiling almost meets the floor. The Green Mountains have just recently turned green again after a freakish late-spring dump of wet, sloppy snow, and you can just barely see Puppy in the early dark, doing his morning laps up and down the side of our slope in his pointless, happy Puppy way. Sounds like the chickens need to be fed.

I guess I should do that. Stupid chickens.

Clue 3: You are still alive.

Do you know who you are yet?

You are me, Samantha Agatha McCoy, in the not-so-distant future. I'm writing this for you. They say my memory will never be the same, that I'll start forgetting things. At first just a little, and then a lot. So I'm writing to remember.

This won't be a journal, or a diary, or anything like that. First of all, it's a .doc file on the tiny little laptop I carry with me everywhere, so let's not get too romantic about this. Second, I predict that by the time I'm done with it (perhaps never) it will exceed the length and breadth of your typical journal. It's a book. I have a natural ability to overwrite. For one, the paper on *The Poisonwood Bible* was supposed to be five pages and turned out to be ten. For another, I answered every possible essay question on NYU's application so the admissions committee could have options. (It worked—I'm in.) For another, I wrote and continually edit Hanover High's Wikipedia page, probably the longest and most comprehensive high school Wikipedia page in the country, which is funny because technically I'm not even supposed to go to Hanover High because as you know (I hope), I don't live in New Hampshire, I live in Vermont, but as you also know (I hope), South Strafford is a town of five hundred and I can't go to the freaking general store for high school. So I bought Dad's old pickup on an installment plan and found some loopholes in the district policy.

I'm writing this book for you. How can you forget a thing with this handy document for reference? Consider this your encyclopedia entry. No, consider this your dictionary.

Samantha (proper noun, name): The name Samantha is an American name, and a Hebrew name. In English, the meaning of the name is "listener." In Hebrew, the meaning of the name is "Listen, name of God."

Listen, name of God, this isn't supposed to be a feelingsy thing, but it might have to be. We tried emotions in middle school and we didn't care for them, but they have snuck back into our life.

The feelings came back yesterday in Mrs. Townsend's office.

Mrs. Townsend (proper noun, person): A guidance counselor who has allowed you to test into all of the advanced classes you wanted to take even if they didn't fit your schedule, and has made you aware of every scholarship known to woman so that you don't have to bankrupt your parents. She looks like a more tired version of Oprah, and with the exception of Senator Elizabeth Warren, she is your hero.

Anyway, I was sitting in Mrs. Townsend's office, making sure that I hadn't missed any deadlines because Mom and I had to go to the geneticist in Minnesota two times in the past month. I didn't even get a real spring break. (I type that as if I've ever had a spring break, but I was hoping to get some major prep in with Maddie, Debate Nationals being just a month away.)

I will try to reconstruct the scene:

White walls covered in old MILK: IT DOES A BODY GOOD posters, left over from the last guidance counselor because Mrs. Townsend has been so busy since she started five years ago, she hasn't had the chance to replace them. Me, on a carpeted block that was supposed to be a cool, modern version of a chair but is really just a block. Across from me, Mrs. Townsend, in a yellow sweater, her hair jetting out in thick black curls.

I was asking her to get me a twenty-four-hour extension on the *Poisonwood Bible* paper.

Mrs. T: Why do you need an extension?

Me: I've got a thing.

Mrs. T (*staring at her computer screen, clicking*): What thing?

Me: Google "Niemann-Pick Type C."

Mrs. Townsend types, and begins to read.

Mrs. T (*muttering*): What?

I watched her eyes move. Right, left, right, left, across the screen. I remember that.

Me: It's very rare.

Mrs. T: What is it, Neeber Pickens? Is this a joke?

I had to laugh in spite of her face scrunching up, still reading.

Me: Niemann-Pick Type C. Basically, it's dementia.

Mrs. Townsend takes her eyes off the computer, her mouth hanging open.

Mrs. T: When were you diagnosed with this?

Me: Two months ago, initially. It's been a back-and-forth process to confirm. But yeah, I have it for sure.

Mrs. T: You're going to have memory loss? And hallucinations? What happened?

Me: Genetics. My great-aunt died of it when she was much younger than I am now.

Mrs. T: Died?

Me: It's common among French Canadians, and my mom's originally French Canadian, so . . .

Mrs. T: Excuse me, died?

Me: I'm not going to die.

I don't think she heard the part about me not dying, which is probably for the best, because at this point it is a statement I can neither confirm nor deny. What I do know, which I forgot to tell Mrs. Townsend (sorry, Mrs. T), is that people my age who exhibit symptoms (without having it when they were younger) are extremely rare. Usually kids get it very young, and their bodies can't handle the strain. So we're looking at a "different timeline," the doctor said. I asked if this was good or bad. "At the moment, I believe it's good."

Mrs. T (*hand on forehead*): Sammie, Sammie.

Me: I'm okay right now.

Mrs. T: Oh my god. Yes, but . . . are you seeing someone? How are your parents handling this? Do you need to go home?

Me: Yes. Fine. No.

Mrs. T: Tell them to call me.

Me: Okay.

Mrs. T (*throwing up her hands*): And you told me this by asking for an extension on your AP Lit paper? You don't have to write it, for god's sake. You don't have to do anything. I can call Ms. Cigler right now.

Me: No, it's okay. I'll write it tonight.

Mrs. T: I'm happy to do it, Sammie. This is serious.

Yes, I guess it is serious. Niemann-Pick (there are three types—A, B, and C—and I have C, commonly called NPC, the only C I've ever gotten, ha ha ha) happens when the wrong kind of cholesterol builds up in the liver and spleen, and as a result, blockage collects in the brain. The buildup gets in the way of cognition, motor function, memory, metabolism—the works. I don't have any of that yet, but I have been exhibiting symptoms for almost a year now, apparently. It's interesting the names they put on stuff I thought were just weird tics. Sometimes I get this sleepy sensation after I laugh: That's cataplexy. Sometimes when I reach for the saltshaker, I miss it: That's ataxia.

But all of that is nothing compared to losing my memory. As you know (ever hopeful!), I'm a debater. Memory's kind of my thing. I wasn't always a debater, but if I hadn't become one four years ago, no joke, I would probably be addicted to weed. Or erotic fan fiction. Or something like that. Let me tell you the story:

Once upon a time, Future Sam, you were fourteen, and you were tremendously unpopular (still true) and felt alienated and like there was not a place for you in high school. Your parents wouldn't buy you cool clothes, you were the first one out in dodgeball, you didn't know you were supposed to say "Excuse me" after you burped, and you had become a human encyclopedia of mythical beasts and scientifically impossible space vehicles. Stated simply: You cared more for the fate of Middle Earth than actual Earth.

Then your mom forced you to join a club, and debate team was the first table at the club fair. (I wish it were more epic than that.) Anyway, everything changed. The brain you used to employ memorizing species of aliens you used instead to memorize human thought, events, ways of thinking that connected your tiny house tucked in the mountains to a huge timeline, one just as full of injustice and triumph and greed as the stories you craved, but one that was real.

Plus, you were good at it. After all those years of devouring books, you could glance at a passage and repeat it verbatim ten minutes later. Your lack of politeness was to your advantage, because politeness isn't necessary in getting your point across. Debate made you realize you didn't have to lose yourself in invented worlds to experience life outside the Upper Valley. It gave you hope that you could be yourself and still be part of the real world. It made you feel cool (despite still being unpopular). It made you want to do better in school, so that once you reached the real world, you'd be able to actually work on all the issues you debated.

So yeah, ever since then, I have counted myself proudly among the people who roam the halls of high schools on a weekend, talking to themselves at a million miles an hour about social justice issues. Yes, the weirdos who decide it might be a fun idea to read an entire Internet search yielding thousands of articles on Roe v. Wade and recite them in intervals at a podium across from another person in a battle to the rhetorical death. The ones who think they are teenage lawyers, the ones who wear business suits. I love it.

Which is why I haven't quit, even though I'm now kind of stuttery at practice, and I make excuses when I miss research sessions for doctor's appointments, and I have to, you know, psych myself up in the mirror at tournaments. Before this happened, my memory was my golden ticket. My ability to memorize things got me scholarships. My memory won me the Grafton County Spelling Bee when I was eleven. And now it's gonna be gone. This is, like, inconceivable to me.

ANYWAY.

*Back to the office, where I can hear people in the hallway, yelling at one another about stupid shit.*

Me (*over the noise*): It's fine. Anyway, can you give me the name of that NYU pre-law mentorship thing again? I know only college juniors are eligible, but I think I could—

*Mrs. T makes a choked sound.*

Me: Mrs. T?

*Mrs. Townsend pulls Kleenexes from her drawer and starts wiping her eyes.*

Me: Are you okay?

Mrs. T: I just can't believe this.

Me: Yeah. I have to go to ceramics now.

Mrs. T: I'm sorry. This is shocking. (*clearing her throat*) Will you have to miss more school?

Me: Not until May, right around finals. But it will be a quick trip to the specialist. Probably just a checkup.

Mrs. T: You're very strong.

Me (*starts packing up stuff, in anticipation of leaving*): I try.

Mrs. T: I've known you since you were a little fourteen-year-old with your (*puts fingers in a circle around eyes*) little glasses.

Me: I still have glasses.

Mrs. T: But they're different glasses. More sophisticated. You look like a young woman now.

Me: Thanks.

Mrs. T: Sammie. Wait.

Me: Okay.

Mrs. T: You are very strong, but . . . But considering everything . . . (*begins to choke up again*)

At this point, I began to feel an uncomfortable tightness in the back of my throat, which at the time I attributed to a side effect of my pain medicine. Mrs. T really had been there for me since I was a freshman. She was the only adult that actually listened to me.

Sure, my parents tried, but it was only for five minutes, between their jobs and feeding my younger siblings and fixing some hole in our crap house on the side of a mountain. They don't care about anything I do as long as I don't let my siblings perish and I get my chores done. When I told Mrs. Townsend I was going to win the National Debate Tournament, get into NYU, and be a human rights lawyer, the first thing she said was, "Let's make it happen." She was the only one who believed me.

So for what she said next, at the risk of being melodramatic, she might as well have stuck her hand down my esophagus and clutched my heart in her hands.

Mrs. T: Do you think you can even handle college?
*Explosions in head.*
Me: What?
Mrs. T (*pointing at computer screen*): This—I mean, I will read up on it more, but—it seems like it affects everything. It could do serious damage.
Me: I know.

And here's the thing. The health stuff I could take, but don't take away my future. My future I had worked so hard to set up so nicely. I have worked for years to get into NYU, and now I was in the homestretch. The very idea that Mrs. Townsend would even consider that I would give it up filled me with rage.

Mrs. T: And on top of that, your memory is going to suffer. How are you going to go to class with all of this? You might—
Me: No!

Mrs. T jumped back. Then it was my turn to begin weeping. My body wasn't used to crying, so the tears did not come out in clean, clear supermodel drops like I thought they would. I shook a lot and the saltwater pooled up in my glasses. I was surprised by the strange whine that came out of the back of my throat.

Mrs. T: Oh, no. No, no. I'm sorry.

I should have accepted her apology and moved on, but I couldn't. I yelled at her.

Me: I am NOT not going to college.
Mrs. T: Of course.
Me (*sniffling*): I am NOT going to stick around Strafford, riding around on four-wheelers, working at a ski resort and smoking pot and going to church and having tons of children and goats.
Mrs. T: I didn't say that . . .

Me (*through snot*): I pushed my way into Hanover, didn't I? I got into NYU, didn't I? I am the valedictorian!

Mrs. T: Yes, yes. But—

Me: Then I can handle college.

Mrs. T: Of course! Of course.

Me (*wiping snot on my sleeve*): Jesus, Mrs. Townsend.

Mrs. T: Use a Kleenex, hon.

Me: I'll use whatever surface I want!

Mrs. T: Sure you will.

Me: I haven't cried since I was a baby.

Mrs. T: That can't be true.

Me: I haven't cried in a long time.

Mrs. T: Well, it's okay to cry.

Me: Yeah.

Mrs. T: If you ever need to talk to me again, you can. I'm not just an academic resource.

Me (*exiting*): Yeah, cool. Bye, Mrs. T.

I walked out of Mrs. Townsend's office (perfectly normally, thank you) and skipped ceramics and went straight home to work on my paper until the feelings went away. Or at least until the feelings and me got some miles between us.

I cried because I have never been more scared in my life. I fear that Mrs. Townsend has a point. I envision a vague gray shape that is supposed to be my brain inside my head, but instead it's this blob outside of me, empty, that I won't be able to use.

And I'm tired.

It's like, take my body, fine, I wasn't really using it anyway. I've got this enormous butt on ostrich legs, the hair of a "before" picture, and weird milky brown eyes like a Frappuccino. But not my brain. My true connection to the world.

Why couldn't I wither slowly and roam around on an automatic chair, spouting my brilliance through a voice box machine like Stephen Hawking?

Uggggghhh. Just thinking about it makes me—

g;sodfigs;ozierjgserg

I don't know how else to say it right now. And I don't like not knowing. Anything. I don't like not knowing in general. I should always be able to know.

And that's where you come in, Future Sam.

I need you to be the manifestation of the person I know I will be. I can beat this, I know I can, because the more I record for you, the less I will forget. The more I write to you, the more real you will become.

So: I've got a lot to do today. It's Wednesday morning. I've got to read seven articles on living wage conditions. I've got to call Maddie and remind her to read these articles, too, because in her three-year tenure as my debate partner, she has had a terrible habit of "winging it" because she thinks she's God's gift to affirmative speeches. (She is, sometimes.) The dumb chickens still need to be fed. The window is cracked open. I smell dew and cool air coming off the Green Mountains. No one else in my house is up yet, but they will be soon. And look, the sun is rising. At least I know that.

## FUTURE SAM

- goes by "Sam" or "Samantha"
- eats only nuts and berries
- wears fashionable glasses (or maybe contacts?)
- wears tailored outfits, only in solid neutrals, blue, or black
- laughs only on occasion and always in a low register
- gets cocktails every week with group of witty, professionally competent women
- reads the *New York Times* in bed in a soft white robe
- is recognized by people on the street and told that her op-ed on international development changed their life

## CURRENT SAMMIE

- goes by "Sammie" because no one in house/school will adjust to address her as Sam—except for Davy, but with lisp it sounds like "Tham"

- eats anything put in front of her, including fake fruit by accident at a church function
- glasses are okay, just way too "gold" and "huge" and possibly disco
- wears whatever free school-function T-shirts haven't been visibly slobbered on by one of the smaller organisms in the house
- laughs at SpongeBob and fart jokes even when stupid people make them (I can't help it, it's actually so funny)
- closest female friend is Maddie, but I'm not sure if we're really friends or just that she and I spend so much time in the government classroom that we are friends by proxy, and between you and me, her ego is way too off the charts
- reads the *New York Times* at Lou's when other people throw it out because Mom and Dad refuse to pay for it
- gets high fives from debate team, so at least that's a start

Jeremiah Satterthwaite

# LARA AVERY

is an editor at *Revolver* and the author of
*The Memory Book*, *A Million Miles Away*,
and *Anything But Ordinary*, which *Booklist*
praised for its "tender and lyrical prose."
Raised in Kansas, where *A Million Miles
Away* is set, she now lives in Minneapolis,
Minnesota. You can follow her on Twitter
@laraavery or find her on Facebook at
facebook.com/laraaverybooks.